About the Author

Robert Shearman has worked as writer for television, radio, and the stage. He was appointed resident dramatist at the Northcott Theatre in Exeter, the youngest playwright ever recognised by the Arts Council in this way, and has received several international awards for his theatrical work, including the *Sunday Times* Playwriting Award, the World Drama Trust Award, and the Guinness Award for Ingenuity in association with the Royal National Theatre. His plays have been regularly produced by Alan Ayckbourn, and on BBC Radio by Martin Jarvis. However he is probably best known as a writer for *Doctor Who*, reintroducing the Daleks for its BAFTA winning first series, in an episode nominated for a Hugo award. He lives in London, and this is his first book.

First published in Great Britain in 2007 by Comma Press
3rd Floor, 24 Lever Street, Manchester M1 1DW
www.commapress.co.uk

'Mortal Coil' was first published in *Phobic: Modern Horror Stories* (edited by Andy Murray, Comma 2007). 'Meanwhile, in a Small Room, a Small Boy...' was first published in a different form in *Life During Wartime* (edited by Paul Cornell, Big Finish, 2003) and is reprinted by kind permission.

Copyright © Robert Shearman 2007

All rights reserved.

The moral right of the author has been asserted.

This collection is entirely a work of fiction. The names, characters and incidents portrayed in it are the work of the author's imagination. Any resemblance to actual persons, living or dead, events or localities, is entirely coincidental.

A CIP catalogue record of this book is available from the British Library

ISBN 1-905583-14-1
EAN 978-1-905583-14-0

The publishers gratefully acknowledge assistance from Arts Council England North West, as well as the support of Literature Northwest.

literaturenorthwest

www.literaturenorthwest.co.uk

Set in Bembo by XL Publishing Services, Tiverton
Printed and bound in England by SRP Ltd, Exeter.

Cover image: 'Black Holes' by Rachel Goodyear, courtesy of P. Scott and Alexandra Cunningham. Thanks to MARCdePUECHREDON Gallery.

tiny deaths

Robert Shearman

ACKNOWLEDGEMENTS

For this book, and everything, my thanks to:

Alan Ayckbourn, Rosalind Ayres, Lisa Bowerman, Nicholas Briggs, Martin Bruce, Owen Bywater, Patrick Carpmael, Cathy Collings, Kate Copeland, Paul Cornell, Russell T Davies, Karen Davison, Mike Dow, John Durnin, Barnaby Edwards, Karen Edwards, David Farnsworth, Nev Fountain, Mark Gatiss, Vikki Godwin, Jason Haigh-Ellery, Clayton Hickman, Hannah Houghton-Berry, Fiona James, Martin Jarvis, Rob Lines, Dan McGrath, Steven Moffat, Ian Mond, Simon Murgatroyd, Andy Murray, Heather Murray, Connal Orton, Tara O'Shea, Rachel Paterson, Nicholas Pegg, Helen Raynor, Gary Russell, Will Shindler, Gill Spaul, Tom Spilsbury, Heather Stoney, Gabrielle Trio, Beryl Vertue, Sue Vertue, Peter & Jo Ware, Fiona Williams, Clive & Pat Wolfe, Philip Wolff.

And especially to my family - Mum (Joyce), Dad (Dennis), and Kid Sister (Vicky). Who always encouraged me to be a writer. Or, at least, never discouraged me forcefully. Or, at least, never discouraged me forcefully enough that I actually paid them any attention.

But mostly to my wife, Jane Goddard - who read all of these stories in every single tortured draft, and whose support has been unfailing, even at three in the morning when I want to discuss with her a new plot point I've thought up when she'd really much rather sleep. (Sorry about that.)

Contents

Mortal Coil	1
Perfect	21
Grappa	35
Ashes to Ash	49
Extra Ordinary	57
Stuff We Leave Behind	69
Damned if You Don't	79
Favourite	103
Static	119
No Looking Back	139
So Proud	147
The Storyteller	157
Tiny Deaths	175
Meanwhile, in a Small Room, a Small Boy...	211

Mortal Coil

On first impression, it looked like an apology. But the more you reread it – and it was reread a *lot* that day, it was pored over and analysed, governments around the world made statements about it, dismissing it first as a hoax, then taking it more seriously as the afternoon wore on, until by evening you could have sworn they had been in on the whole thing from the start, television programmes were rescheduled to make way for phone-in discussion shows and cobbled-together news reports that had very little actual news to report... The more you reread it, you couldn't help but feel there was a note of disappointment to it. It was almost patronising.

This is what the message said:

'You've got it all wrong. And we're sorry, because it's our mistake. If we'd made things clearer to you right from the start, none of this would have happened.

'We gave you a knowledge of death. We thought it would make you rise above the other animals, give you a greater perspective on how to live your lives fruitfully, in peace and in happiness. But it's all gone horribly wrong, hasn't it?

'You obsess *about death. Right from childhood, it seems to exercise your imagination in an entirely unhealthy way. You count all the calories on every single tin in the supermarket, you go to the gym twice a week, just so you feel you can ward it off that bit longer. You pump Botox into your cheeks and stick plastic sacks into your*

breasts so you can kid yourselves you look younger, that death isn't on the cards yet. And then, when death finally does happen, to someone you know, you go to long boring funerals and sit on hard benches in sullen silence, dressed in smart clothes that make you itch, with only flat wine and sausage rolls to look forward to. And the growing certainty that soon it'll be your turn, the sausage rolls will be eaten for you.

'You're frightened and you're miserable. We can't blame you. Looking down at you, it makes us pretty miserable too!

'Houseflies and worms and llamas have the right idea. They understand that death is just part of the system. As much as birth and procreation. A thing to avoid when it isn't necessary, and to accept when it is. And so houseflies and worms and llamas have a better grip on what's expected of them, to be as good houseflies, worms and llamas as they can be, and not let all that death baggage get in the way.

'As we say, sorry. We made the mistake of giving you a little knowledge, when either none or more would have been more sensible. There was some hope we didn't need to spell it all out for you, but don't you worry, that's our fault, not yours. And so we're going to put an end to it.

'We did consider that taking away the knowledge of death would be the best thing. But there was a general feeling that it'd be a shame to go backwards – and that we've enough houseflies and worms and llamas as it is. They're coming out of our ears! So, starting tomorrow, expect things to be different. It'll be a new chapter. For you and for us!

'And in the mean time, please accept our apologies for any distress we may have caused you.'

You see, that patronising disappointment was hard to ignore. Especially after multiple readings of the message. Some very well-known intellectuals appeared on the phone-in discussion programmes that evening to complain that they'd been so obviously talked down to. 'After all,' grumbled one, 'what do they expect? If they're going to turn the secrets of life and death into a crossword puzzle, they can hardly object when we all sit around trying to solve it.'

The first message had naturally taken everyone by surprise. In every country around the world, on every television set, on every radio and in every newspaper, the words appeared. All in the language of the country in question, of course. Many people studied the different translations, just to see whether they could glean any hidden meanings, but all they could conclude was that (a) German words can be irritatingly long and never use one syllable when six will do, and that (b) French is very romantic. So no-one was any the wiser.

The next morning everyone was glued to their television screens. Even the sceptics, who stubbornly insisted the whole thing was some elaborate conjuring act, waited with bated breath to see what trickery was lined up next. And in countries where casual murder had become a part of everyone's daily lives, the perpetrators surprised themselves by holding back for once, and tuning in to see whether the killings they executed so nonchalantly had any deeper meaning. In Britain, the BBC didn't even bother to prepare their scheduled programmes. And so, when a second message resolutely *failed* to appear and explain life and death and matters besides, the BBC were caught on the hop and forced to transmit a series of Norman Wisdom films. Worldwide, the excitement gave way to disappointment, then to anger. It's quite certain there would have been riots in the streets, causing more bloodshed and more death, had Something Not Happened.

So it's just as well Something Did.

Of course, it took some people a while to realise anything had. They were so intent on the TV screen that they ignored the sound of the letterbox, of the daily post falling onto the mat. Had they stopped to consider that all the postmen were at home, the same as them, they might have shown more interest.

The envelopes were light brown, soft to the touch, and seemed almost to be made of vellum, like medieval manuscripts. There were no stamps on them – and the names weren't handwritten, but typed. And there was one for each member of the household, however young or old. Inside, each recipient found a card, stamped with his or her full name. And underneath that, as plain and unapologetic as you like, was a short account of when and how the recipient was going to die. Some poor unfortunates, either elderly or obese, found the news so startling that they died right there on the spot – and the card in their dead hands had predicted that exactly. Sometimes the explanation would be moderately chatty, and full of information. Arthur James Cripps learned that he was to die in fourteen years and six days, by 'drowning, after being knocked off a bridge by a Nissan Micra; frankly, if the water hadn't finished you off, you'd have died minutes later from the ruptured kidneys caused by the collision in question'. A lot of people learned that they were just going to die of 'cancer'. No fripperies, no more detail, no context – the word 'cancer' on the card saying it all, as if the typist had got so bored of hammering out the word so often that he could barely wait to move on to more interesting deaths elsewhere.

The Norman Wisdom films were interrupted, and news updates directed people to their letterboxes. The anticipation was terrible – worse than checking your exam results, or your credit card statement after a particularly expensive holiday. Parents with large families had to be put through the torture again and again, forced to confront what would happen not only to them but to their offspring. And if, inevitably, some were appalled by the bad news – a twelve year old child to die of meningitis, a three year old girl whose ultimate fate was to be abducted after school some seven years later, raped and strangled and her body never recovered – most went to bed that night somewhat reassured. At least they *knew* now. They might only have one month – one year – fifty years – but at least they *knew*. In fact, sales of cigarettes trebled almost overnight, as smokers and non-smokers alike realised that all the agonising over the health risks was now redundant. If it wasn't going to kill you, why not take it up? And if it was, well – it's a *fait accompli*, isn't it? Might as well enjoy it whilst your lungs last.

Just about the only person who wasn't reassured was Henry Peter Clifford.

Harry would never have thought he was an especially special person. Even in his moments of hubris or overweening arrogance – which, for him, were few and far between – he'd have been hard pushed to have described himself as anything better than distinctly average. He naturally assumed, on that fateful morning, that his envelope simply hadn't arrived yet. This was nothing new to Harry – his birthday cards were always late, he only received postcards after everybody else had had theirs. His wife Mary read her fate with shaking hands, and all he could think was that he'd probably have to wait until tomorrow to go through the same thing. But the next day there was still no envelope for him, nor the day after. The world had subtly changed, but for Harry it all looked pretty much the same.

The Government had quickly set up a number of help centres to deal with the crisis, and so, on the fourth day that Harry *still* hadn't found out when he was due to die, he caught the bus down to the citizens' advice bureau. The streets were that much more dangerous now; cars sped along roads knowing full well they *weren't* about to be involved in some tragic accident, and pedestrians ran the traffic with similar impunity. The bus driver catapulted his eight ton vehicle of red metal down the hill with the certain knowledge that his number wasn't up, and as Harry gripped the seat to prevent himself from being flung bodily down the aisle, he only wished he could be as sure.

There was a surprisingly long queue at the help centre, which cheered Harry somewhat – in spite of the long wait he'd have to put up with, it reassured him to think others were having complications too. But it turned out these people in line were just wanting grief counselling for deaths that hadn't even happened yet. Indeed, the rather bland blonde behind the desk suggested that Harry was the only person who *hadn't* received a death envelope.

'Well, what can I do about it?' asked Harry lamely, and she shrugged as if the oversight was in some way his fault. 'Is there anybody I can write to?' The woman told him that since no-one knew where the envelopes had come from there wasn't much she could do. 'But if you don't know anything about this whole thing, why have you set up a help centre?' The woman shrugged again, and called the next person in the queue forward.

'Maybe you just lost it somewhere?' said his secretary brightly. 'It fell behind the sofa cushions or something. I'm always doing that.' The secretary had been saying *everything* brightly after finding out that her death, in sixty-seven years' time, would be a painless little thing, her heart giving out in the throes of sexual congress with a South American toyboy. 'I should check under the cushions again,' she said, not a little unhelpfully.

The trouble was that everyone seemed to share his secretary's scepticism, and expressed it much less complacently. They were perplexed at first by Harry's outrageous claims he'd had no envelope, that he had been left out of a global miracle that had changed them all – as if he were the one man still claiming that the world was flat when everybody else had accepted it was a bloody sphere now, thank you very much. Then they'd get angry with the idea that he was trying to get attention. 'Why *wouldn't* you get an envelope? What makes you so special?' Typically, Harry hadn't thought of it in this way at all; on the contrary, he had wondered why the universe had deemed him so insignificant that he was the only one to be ignored. He vaguely mused whether he preferred the idea of being singled out because he was the most important person in the world, or because he was the *least* important. And decided he wasn't fond of either much, frankly.

'I'm afraid I'm going to have to let you go,' said his boss. 'You know, it's not my decision. But I have bosses, and they have bosses, and, you know...' He gave a smile. 'You know how it is.'

There had been some controversy about just how much employers had the right to know about their employees' life expectancy. Companies would argue that it was surely relevant whether or not they could expect their staff to go on providing good service, or whether they had to accommodate for the fact they might be dropping dead left, right and centre. At job interviews prospective employees lost out to candidates who could demonstrate they had longevity on their side, and those already in work found their bosses would rather ditch them quickly before they were subject to expensive health plans. The government said something non-committal about the data protection act and employee confidentiality, but also that any organisation had the right to expect full productivity from its staff. None of which helped anybody very much. When Harry was first asked to show his death envelope at work, his inability to do so was taken to mean he had something terrible and contagious and doubtlessly fatal to hide.

His boss gave him another one of those smiles. 'Really, you're lucky,' he said. 'Getting out of work is the best thing that can happen to you. Enjoy yourself. Enjoy the rest of your life. I wish I could,' he said with apparent regret, 'but it seems this old ticker of mine has another forty-seven years to go. Bloody thing!' He held out his hand to wish Harry goodbye, and in spite of himself, Harry shook it.

And later that night his wife told him she was leaving.

'I can get another job,' said Harry. 'Nothing fancy, I know. But there's lots of casual labour, they don't care whether you snuff it or not. We can make it work, Mary.'

'No, we can't,' said Mary. And she told him how when she'd held that death envelope in her hand, scared to open it and find out how long she'd got, she'd made herself a vow. If I've only got a couple of years, she thought, if that's all I've got, then I'm out of here. I'm not going to waste any more of my life. Because we only go around once, and I'm letting it slip by. I should be climbing mountains and exploring deserts and scuba diving and sleeping with people who'd do it with the lights on. That'll be the present to myself. If I've got two years or less, I'm leaving Harry.

'But,' Harry pointed out gently, 'you haven't got two years. You've got thirty-eight. The cancer doesn't get you for thirty-eight.'

'I know,' said Mary. 'And I was so disappointed. And then it dawned on me. If I'm *that* disappointed, that I'd rather be dead than living with you, then I shouldn't be living with you. Goodbye, Harry.'

He couldn't argue with that.

Mary wasn't a cruel woman. She recognised that Harry wouldn't easily be able to earn money, whilst in her robust and not-yet-carcinogenic state the world was her oyster. She left him the house and a lot of the money. She also left him the cat, which Harry thought rather a shame as he'd never much liked it – he'd simply never got round to telling Mary that. And Mary said she wanted to start the rest of her life as soon as possible, and was gone by morning.

And, of course, a lot of people out there were following Mary's example. Those who realised that the end was in sight decided that this was their last chance to see the world. Thousands of elderly English people flew to America, and thousands of elderly Americans flew to England – until, at the end of the day, roughly the same number of the diseased and the dying were roaming the streets in both countries, just sporting different accents. With typical brilliance, Disney decided to exploit this new trend in end-of-life tourism. They used a motto – 'Make the Last of Your Life be the Time of Your Life', which had a certain catchiness. If you could show proof you had three months or less, you were entitled to discounts to *all* the theme parks, and V.I.P. treatment once you were through the turnstiles. There was a special queue for the nearly dead, and a soberly dressed man-size Mickey Mouse or Goofy would respectfully show them to their rides. As it turns out the venture was so wildly successful that the Nearly Dead queue was often longer than the regular one, but that didn't matter – the ticket holders still felt they were being given special treatment. And attendance went up all the more when the elderly, who had always sworn that being spun through the air on a rollercoaster would be the death of them, now had concrete evidence that, in fact, it wouldn't.

Harry wouldn't have much wanted to visit Disneyland, but if his time were soon to be up, he'd certainly have wanted to have gone *somewhere*. But he couldn't afford a holiday. Unemployment benefits hadn't exactly been *abolished*, but it was hard to justify why you should be given a free hand-out when your death envelope demonstrated you had another fifty years of health in front of you and weren't just about to die in penury. And any attempt Harry made to get some money was thwarted by the absence of that envelope. So when, one morning, it came through the letterbox, Harry was delighted.

At first he couldn't believe it was really there. He'd given up hoping it'd ever turn up. But there was no mistaking it – that off-brown colour that you just didn't find anywhere else, the softness to the touch.

He opened it hastily. He didn't care *when* he died, or *how* he died. Just so long as he had proof he did, in fact, *eventually* die.

'**HENRY PETER CLIFFORD**', said the stamp.

And then, typed:

'Awaiting Further Information'.

Harry stared at it. Unable to believe his eyes. He turned over the card, hoping for something else. Something telling him it was a joke, not to worry, he was due to be impaled on a wooden stake that afternoon, anything. But instead, in ballpoint pen, someone had written, 'Sorry for the Inconveniance.'

As the day went by, as he did what he normally did – had breakfast, fed the cat, watched afternoon TV – Harry wondered whether the scrawled apology might even be God's very own handwriting. Still, probably not. He'd probably use one of his underlings, some saint or angel or vicar or someone. He'd always imagined the handwriting of a Divine Being would be a bit more ornate. And that he'd be able to spell 'inconvenience'.

The next morning he thought there might be another envelope, a follow-up to the last. There wasn't. But there was a knock at the door.

At first Harry saw the envelope rather than the man who was holding it. 'I think you should read this,' he said, and he held it out to Harry nervously.

Eagerly Harry read the name on the top, was immediately disappointed. 'Jeffrey Allan White. That isn't me.'

'No, it's me,' said Jeffrey Allan White.

'I don't understand,' said Harry. He held out the card for Mr White to take back. 'This isn't me,' he repeated uselessly.

'Please,' said Jeffrey. 'Read the rest of it.'

And Harry did. Then he read it again. He stared at Jeffrey for a few moments, and saw a man in his late fifties, a bit unkempt, shorter than average, plump, and just as scared as he was.

'Can I come in?' said Jeffrey. Harry nodded, and got out of his way.

Harry didn't know what to do with his strange visitor. He led him into the kitchen, wordlessly indicated he should sit down. Jeffrey smiled a thanks awkwardly. The cat was excited that someone new was in the house, and jumped up on to Jeffrey's lap. 'Sorry,' said Harry. 'Do you like cats...?'

'I'm a bit allergic,' replied Jeffrey. 'But it doesn't really matter any more.'

'Can I get you a drink?'

'I'm fine, thanks.'

'A coffee or a tea...?'

'A coffee then, thanks.'

'All I've got is decaf...'

'Decaf is fine.'

'Milk?'

'Yes. Thanks.' And there was silence from them both as Harry busied himself with the kettle. It wasn't until the water was nearly boiled that Harry thought he should say something.

'But I don't even know you.'

'No, I know.'

'But I don't. So why...?'

Jeffrey smiled, but it was a nervous smile that had no answer. 'Thanks,' he said as he took the coffee. 'Thanks, this is fine,' he said again.

'Why did you come here?' asked Harry. 'I mean, I'd have run away.'

'But really. Where would I go?'

Harry shrugged. 'Well. Anywhere.'

'I almost didn't come,' said Jeffrey quietly. 'When I first found out how I was going to die... I almost laughed, it was so specific. My wife, she's one of the cancer ones, how can she avoid that? But if you know you're going to die at the hands of Henry Clifford at 23 Sycamore Gardens on 16th September, it seems such an easy thing to prevent. If you'd asked me last week,' he said, as he took a gulp of his still too hot coffee, 'I'd have said this was the last place in the world I'd have visited.'

Harry waited patiently for Jeffrey to go on. Jeffrey couldn't meet his eyes, looked at the floor.

'But if it isn't *true*... if I *could* prevent it... then it's all meaningless, isn't it? Isn't it? I'm not sure I could go on like that. I'm not sure I could cope with tomorrow, when I'm not supposed to see tomorrow in the first place. What would it all be for? My son,' he added. 'My son and I never much got on, we hadn't spoken in years. Once he found out I was going to die, he got back in touch. We've been going to the pub. Chatting. Like friends. Not as family, but *friends*.' He looked up at Harry imploringly. 'You've got to help me. You've got to do this. It says...' and he fluttered the envelope at Harry weakly, 'it says you do here.'

'I don't know how to stab someone. I'm not sure I could go through with it.' Silence. 'I mean, it's the actual sticking it in... I think I could do it if I had to shoot you, you know, from a distance...'

'It says stabbing.'

'Yes, I know.'

They both finished their coffee.

'Maybe,' suggested Jeffrey at last, 'you could just hold the knife. And I could run on to it.'

'Okay,' said Harry. 'We could try that.'

Both Harry and Jeffrey were shaking as Harry pulled open the kitchen drawer and looked at the knives. 'Do you have a preference, or...?'

'Best get one that's sharp,' said Jeffrey.

The first time Jeffrey ran at Harry's knife, Jeffrey kept his eyes closed. The problem was that Harry did the same. And so they didn't collide correctly, and the worst Jeffrey sustained was a cut on the arm.

'Ouch,' said Jeffrey.

'Sorry,' said Harry.

'There's no way that's fatal,' said Jeffrey. 'We should try again.'

This time Jeffrey, at least, kept his eyes open. Harry *tried* to, but at the moment of impact he couldn't help but flinch. So all he felt was Jeffrey's body groan against his, and a strange sucking as the knife was pulled out. When Harry dared to look, he was horrified to see there was blood everywhere, on his hands, on the floor, and on Jeffrey's stomach, of course, which was the point at which the knife had obviously entered.

'I'm sorry,' said Harry. 'I'm sorry. Does it hurt?'

Jeffrey laid on the floor, sobbing, clutching at his wound. 'Again,' he said. 'Again.'

Harry looked at all the blood, at Jeffrey's agonised face, and baulked. He left quickly, closing the kitchen door behind him.

An hour or so later he pushed the door open gently, as if trying not to wake his guest. 'Jeffrey,' he whispered. 'Are you still alive?'

'Please,' said Jeffrey, his voice now guttural. 'Finish me off.'

Harry stared. And then – 'No!' he said to the cat, as it poked its way into the kitchen, and began to lick at the blood with curiosity. 'Out of here, come on! Shoo! I'll close the door,' Harry said to Jeffrey gently. 'Leave you to it.'

Harry tried to watch the television, but it was hard to concentrate. Later that evening he went back to see how Jeffrey was holding up. Jeffrey couldn't speak, but looked at him with big desperate eyes. Harry hesitated. Then picked up a heavy rolling pin, stood over his victim, took aim at his head.

'No,' croaked Jeffrey. 'Stabbing. Says it's a stabbing.' And Harry left once more, determined to watch whatever was on the telly, and *make* himself concentrate on it.

Some time before midnight Harry braved the kitchen again. He was relieved to see that Jeffrey was, at last, dead. And had indeed died on the 16th September, even if the actual process had taken rather longer than either of them had anticipated. Harry looked at Jeffrey's eyes, as if trying to find some truth in his death, but all he saw was a glassy stare. He thought about moving the body, but realised that with all the worry he'd put into the actual killing, he'd not given a moment's thought to what he should do afterwards. And so he decided to go to bed, face that problem in the morning. After all, it wasn't as if Jeffrey Allan White was going anywhere.

That night Harry slept rather better than he thought any murderer had a right to – so soundly, in fact, that he was only woken up by frantic hammering at the door. He opened it in his pyjamas, so bleary that for the moment he forgot about the corpse on the kitchen floor.

Outside there were five people, each of them holding death envelopes.

'No,' he said. 'No, no, no.' And he closed the door on them.

But they didn't go away. They were staring death in the face, they were frightened – but each of them knew that their lives had to end somehow, and destiny had chosen them to be at the hands of Harry Clifford. The cat was very excited when he showed them all, one by one, into the sitting room, and with heavy heart read the grisly instructions within their soft little brown envelopes. There were two drownings, which Harry conducted in the bath one after the other – only realising as he lugged the swollen corpses into Mary's bedroom afterwards how heavy bodies became when full of water. Another one had his head caved in with an electric iron, and since Mary had been the one to take charge of all the practical details in their marriage, it took Harry a full half hour to find the right cupboard in which she'd kept it. There was another stabbing to be performed, but this one was quicker than the day before's; Harry had learned to keep his eyes open this time. And there was a hanging, which caused both Harry and his victim no end of problems.

'Did you bring a rope?' asked Harry.

'I didn't know I needed one,' said the rather shy teenager, blushing through a wall of spots.

'I don't just have a rope lying about,' said Harry. 'If you

want me to hang you, the least you could do is bring your own equipment.'

In the end they decided that the shower curtains could be taken down, wrapped tightly around the youth's neck, and with some care he could be suspended over the upstairs banisters until he expired. Then Harry cut the body down, dragged it to Mary's bedroom, and laid it alongside the five people he had already killed. Mary's room seemed the best place for all these strangers; it was a place he'd had little cause to visit over the last two years of his marriage, not since Mary had asked if he could move into the spare room. He surveyed his handiwork for a moment, all six bodies lying higgledy-piggledy across Mary's bed and by the dressing table at which she used to do her make-up and hair. Then, without hesitation, he closed the door tight, went to his own room, packed a rucksack, and left the house.

The next day he was on the Cornwall coast, walking along the cliffs, watching as the sea crashed into the rocks. He began to feel normal, human. He waved politely at the passers-by, managed a smile, as if he too was simply out for a gentle stroll without a care in the world. One kindly looking old man, walking his Jack Russell, said good morning.

'Good morning,' said Harry.

'Here on holiday?' asked the old man.

'Yes,' said Harry. 'I think so. I don't know. Maybe,' he said decisively, 'I'll live here. Yes.'

'Well, it's a beautiful part of the country. I've always loved it, man and boy. I say,' said the old man confidentially, 'I do believe you're supposed to push me off the cliff.' And he produced the telltale envelope. 'I'm sorry,' he said, with genuine sympathy. 'I can quite see how that would disturb your walk.'

Harry pushed him over the side, and his body spun all the way down, glancing off the odd rock. Neither of them had been quite sure what to do with the little dog, so the old man had kicked him off the edge before he took his own fall. 'He loved me, I know it,' he'd said with tears in his eyes. 'It's what he would have wanted.'

If these death envelopes were going to follow Harry wherever he went, he supposed he might as well go back home and live in comfort. The cat was pleased – he hadn't been fed for nearly a day, and was starving. And the people *did* keep coming. Sometimes as many as twenty could be found in the morning, sick with fear, clutching their little death sentences. 'It's all right,' he said to them, soothing, calm. 'We'll make it okay. There's nothing to be afraid of.' And, as the weeks went by, and the corpses began mounting in his ex-wife's bedroom, he realised that he meant it. All this death, there really *was* nothing to be afraid of. If he'd found a purpose in life, at long last, after so many years of not even bothering to look, then this was it – he could make sure that these poor souls shuffled off this mortal coil in as humane and tender a way as possible.

He decided to charge his victims a small fee. They were all too eager to pay, he discovered – it wasn't as if they could take their money with them. And with the cash he bought lots of painkillers, the strongest that could be purchased over the counter. When all's said and done, if your way out of this world is by having a hammer turn your skull to splinters, then a preparatory swig of a couple of aspirin is unlikely to do much good. But Harry realised it was a *psychological* help, that his patients felt it was altogether a far more professional operation. 'Thank you, doctor,' said one gratefully, just before Harry bludgeoned him with a saucepan, and Harry felt an indescribable swell of pride.

He even hired a secretary to take care of them all, to ensure that he disposed of them in order and in good time. He chose the secretary he'd once worked with, the one who so brightly had realised her death was at the thrust of a toyboy.

She was no longer so bright or cheery. 'I've not even had a sniff of sex in ages,' she complained. 'What if this toyboy in sixty-seven years' time is the next bit of sex I get? It's a mistake,' she concluded, with a wisdom that Harry had never expected of her, 'to see in the way you die an explanation of how you live. The fact I'm going to die bonking a Brazilian does not mean I'm a great lover. Death is just another bit of stuff that happens.'

And then, one day, just suddenly, it all stopped.

'A quiet day today,' the secretary told Harry, when, by noon, no-one had knocked at the door. But it was a quiet week as well. At the end of the month, with no patients calling, Harry paid her off. She said she was sorry the job was over. 'I felt we were doing some good.' Harry told her he was sorry too.

But, surprisingly, sorrier still was the cat. The ginger little tabby had been a great favourite with all Harry's victims, taking their minds off the operations ahead of them. It'd enjoyed parading around the waiting room of a morning, checking out all the newcomers, and allowing itself to be stroked and petted and made a fuss of. Now the cat would stare out of the window, eyeing anyone who walked up the street – and visibly sagging with disappointment when the passer-by wouldn't stop at the house. The cat's fur grew matted and coarse, it no longer washed itself. It had no interest in eating, it had no interest in anything. It was beginning to pine away.

Harry could see his cat was dying. And it seemed to him an extraordinary piece of cruelty that he should never know exactly when the cat was to die, when its suffering was to stop. The cat would lie, listless, looking at him with pleading eyes. Harry recognised the look; it was the same expression he'd seen in Jeffrey White's when he'd bled to death in the kitchen all those months ago.

Harry cradled the cat in his arms, and stroked its fur. He'd never liked the cat, and the cat had never much liked him – but it purred for Harry now, and Harry was touched. The cat heaved with a huge sigh that seemed to echo down its thinning body, and then gave the gentlest of mews. And Harry knew there was no person more humane than him to end the poor cat's life, and that the cat knew it too, he'd seen the fact of it countless times in this very house. Because Harry was the greatest killer of all, and he *was* special, and that's why he'd been singled out, that's why he couldn't die, why they wouldn't let him die, he had a job to do. He wrung the cat's neck, so quickly the cat would never have known. And he carried its frail little body up to Mary's room, and left it with all the other corpses.

And then he sat down and cried. He hadn't cried for any of these deaths, he hadn't found the time. But he cried now, and he cried himself asleep.

The next morning he started when he heard something at the door. Still dozing in the armchair, he sprang to his feet. Ready to welcome another client, to practise his expertise with gentle care.

But instead, lying on the doormat, was an off-brown envelope.

Numbly he picked it up. And opened it. And read it.

'**HENRY PETER CLIFFORD**' said the stamp.

And, underneath, just the one word:

'Cancer'.

And that was it. Not even a date. Not even the recognition that there should have been a date. Just this one word, this ordinary death, this trivial death, laughing at him.

He turned over the card. And, in the same handwriting he'd seen before, in ballpoint pen: 'Sorry. We lost this behind the sofa cushion.'

Harry sighed. He put the card back in the envelope for safe keeping, laid it gently down upon the hall table. He wondered what he should do with the rest of the day, the rest of his life. He couldn't think of anything.

So he went upstairs to bed. Drew the curtains. And, lying in the darkness, explored his body for a lump.

Perfect

Tanya didn't often look surprised. It wasn't that she didn't react to the things around her. She was very good at reactions, actually, and she would show interest, concern, and – and only if it were appropriate – a real delight that could melt your heart. But rarely surprise. And so when her parents told her they were going to the seaside that day, and that it was going to be *her* day, her special day, a treat for *her*, and her eyes opened wide and her jaw dropped in astonishment... Well, her parents couldn't help but be surprised right back.

'But it isn't as if it's my birthday,' said Tanya. 'That's not for another six weeks yet.'

'No, we know,' said her Daddy.

'And even when it *is* my birthday, I'll only be nine,' said Tanya. 'It's not as if that's a particularly significant milestone.' She tilted her head at her doting parents, and continued thoughtfully, 'It's very generous of you, but are you quite sure you don't want to rethink this?'

And Mummy and Daddy both smiled and said there was no need for rethinking. Tanya was dubious – most things she felt, in her admitted childhood but nonetheless well-considered experience, benefited from a *little* rethink. And Daddy said if it made her feel any better, he and her mother had given the matter rather a lot of rethinking, privately, before they broached the matter with Tanya, but they were absolutely confident that a day out by the sea was what they wanted to give their darling daughter. And Tanya laughed, gave them both a hug, and told them that in that case she was more than happy to accept.

'How are we going to get there?' she asked.

'I could drive,' said Daddy. 'Or we could take the train.'

'Oh, I think the train,' said Mummy. 'That way Daddy won't have to work either, it'll be a fun day out for all of us.' And Daddy laughed and said he hardly regarded driving as *work*, he was happy to do it, but he supposed a trip on the train would make a nice change, but it was all up to Tanya, it was *her* day, *her* decision. And Tanya said that the train would be lovely, she always enjoyed riding in trains; she always enjoyed riding in cars as well, but trains were really just as good.

That said, even the little drive to the railway station wasn't straightforward. It was a Saturday, and the town was full of shoppers. When they finally negotiated the ring road to the station, they found the car park was full. 'Look at that,' said Daddy. 'Look at that car. He's parked over two spaces. Bloody idiot, bloody selfish bastard.' Tanya didn't say anything, because she didn't like it when her Daddy swore. And Daddy fumed for ten whole minutes until a space was freed. It was a tight squeeze, but they could all get out of the car so long as they breathed in deep. Daddy cheered up instantly. 'Margate, here we come!' he said.

The man at the ticket office told them they'd just missed the train.

'Well, how long until the next one?' asked Daddy.

'Another hour,' said the man. 'Sorry.' He didn't look very sorry. 'You want the tickets or not?' And Daddy bought them anyway, with bad grace.

Mummy was upset. 'Oh, for God's sake,' she said. 'If we'd just left a little earlier...'

'I wasn't to know the roads would be so busy,' said Daddy.

'The roads are always busy on Saturdays,' said Mummy.

'That's why I never go out on Saturdays,' said Daddy

tersely. 'So I wouldn't have known, would I?'

'It doesn't matter,' said Tanya.

'But it's a whole hour in Margate lost,' said Mummy.

'It doesn't matter. We can have fun anyway. So long as we're all together. Let's play I Spy. You like I Spy, don't you? I'll start.' And so they sat on the hard benches and played. And Tanya was right, it *was* fun. Because Tanya was very good at it – she'd start out with easy words like 'Platform' and 'Rail', but soon she was really challenging her parents with 'Coupling' and 'Shunter'. Before too long they were all in good humour again, and the wait just flew by. And before they knew it, they were on the train to the seaside.

'Margate, here we come!' said Daddy.

Tanya suggested they carry on with their I Spy – especially as there were so many fresh things to spy now – but Daddy smiled a little weakly and asked if Tanya wouldn't mind him taking a nap instead. And Tanya said, of course, it was only to make *him* happy, whatever he wanted. Mummy decided to go to the buffet car and see if she could get herself a coffee. She returned a few minutes later and said that it was closed. A few minutes after *that*, she said she was going back to the buffet car anyway. And she returned a lot later, and Tanya could smell cigarettes on her clothes. She didn't say anything, because she didn't like it when her Mummy smoked. For her part, Tanya was more than happy looking out of the window and watching the world fly past. There was so *much* to look at, so much to take in, and Tanya knew she would never tire of it, not ever. She wondered why her Mummy and Daddy showed so little interest in all the novelty that was whizzing by, and she decided it was a consequence of growing up. She decided then and there she'd never grow up.

At long last Mummy settled down, Daddy woke up, and the family listened as the train guard announced they'd reached their destination. 'Margate, here we are!' said Daddy.

'Now, remember,' said Daddy, 'this is Tanya's day, and

we'll do *whatever* Tanya wants. Do you want to go to the beach, Tanya?' Tanya said she did. 'Great!' said Daddy. 'Let's go to the beach!' It wasn't really beach weather – the wind was cold and there was a light drizzle in the air. 'Great!' said Daddy. 'This is perfect! Look, we've the whole beach to ourselves!' In the distance Tanya spied an elderly man peeing unapologetically against a changing hut. 'Pretty much, anyway. Oh, look! There's an ice cream van! Who wants an ice cream?'

'It's too cold,' said Mummy.

'Rubbish!' said Daddy. 'You can't go to the seaside without having an ice cream.' He left Tanya with her Mummy as he walked to the van. 'Three cones, please.'

'Not a cone. It's a Whippy.'

'Three Whippies then.'

'You want flakes in them?'

'Yes,' said Daddy. 'No,' he said. 'I've got a little daughter over there, and it's her special day. So I want a special ice cream, just for her. So a couple of flakes in hers. And hundreds and thousands. And some of those sprinkle things.'

Daddy walked back to his family, ice cream already running down his fingers, almost bouncing with pride. 'Guess which one's for my special girl!'

'Oh, Daddy,' protested Tanya. 'I'll never manage all that!'

'Rubbish,' said Daddy with a smile. But Tanya was right. The cone was top heavy, and the slightest exertion of even a little girl's tongue was enough to overbalance the whole sugary edifice on to the sand.

'Oh no!' cried out Daddy.

'It doesn't matter,' said Tanya. 'Thank you, Daddy, what I had was delicious.'

'Mummy, give her your cone,' said Daddy.

'That's fine, I didn't want one in the first place,' muttered Mummy.

PERFECT

'And after you've had Mummy's cone, you can have mine,' Daddy promised.

Tanya said it was really all right, but Daddy was having none of it – only the best for his little girl, and if parents couldn't make sacrifices for their children, what sort of parents were they? Really, what sort of parents were they, really? And Tanya dutifully ate up both ice creams, and thanked them.

'What shall we do now, Tanya? Shall we walk along the front?'

Tanya said that was a good idea. So that's what they did. Mummy found that it didn't matter what direction they took, somehow she was still walking *into* the wind. The waves rolled on to the sand ever so feebly, as if they too were on holiday in Margate, and hadn't the energy to do anything very much.

'This was a bad idea,' said Mummy quietly.

'The weather's all right,' said Daddy.

'Not just the seaside, the whole thing.' But Daddy gave her a quick warning glare, and said brightly, 'I know! Let's paddle! Would you like to paddle, Tanya?'

'Yes, all right,' said Tanya.

'It's far too cold,' said Mummy. 'You'll catch your death.'

'It'll be fine,' Daddy was sure.

'I'm sure it'll be all right,' said Tanya. 'If that's what you'd like.'

'No,' said Mummy, with a surprising firmness. 'Tanya, you do *not* want to paddle in the cold. Do you?'

'No,' admitted Tanya. 'No, not in this cold. We'll catch our deaths, Daddy.'

Daddy looked for a moment as if he were going to sulk, and then said cheerily, 'It's up to you, Tanya! It's your day! How about another ice cream? Look, there's another van.'

'I don't think so, Daddy,' said Tanya. 'I think I'd be sick.'

'For God's sake,' said Mummy. 'Leave the poor girl alone. She doesn't want to paddle. She doesn't want an ice cream.'

'I'm just doing my best!' Daddy cried. 'At least I'm putting in a bit of bloody effort!'

'Please,' said Tanya. 'You're both right. I *did* want a paddle, and I *did* want an ice cream. And now I don't. So there's no need to argue. You're both right, and both lovely parents, really. All right?'

'Yes,' said Mummy. 'I don't know if he is, though.'

'I'm all right,' Daddy reassured Tanya. 'If you are.'

'That's good, then, that's lovely,' said Tanya. 'And we're all having a lovely day out. Aren't we?'

They all agreed they were. And with her left hand Tanya took hold of her Mummy, and with her right she took hold of her Daddy. 'Come on,' she said, and on they walked. The little girl leading the way, flanked by the two grown-ups either side.

Nobody spoke for minutes. And, at last, there was a certain degree of peace. 'It's nice, all this quiet,' said Daddy at one point, unnecessarily, but everybody ignored it – even *Daddy* ignored it – and the calm remained unbroken.

Tanya said eventually, ever so quietly, 'I spy with my little eye something beginning with F.' And it wasn't until they were nearly on top of it that Daddy worked it out.

'It's a ferris wheel!' he said.

It stood at the centre of a small amusement park. To the right a coconut shy was boarded up. At the left, a dodgem car track, with one lone dodgem on it with nothing to dodge.

'How would you like to go on a ferris wheel, Tanya?' asked Daddy.

'I doubt it's open,' said Tanya.

'I'd like to go on a ferris wheel,' piped up Mummy unexpectedly.

'But you don't like heights,' said Daddy.

'I want to go on a ride, all alone, with my daughter,' Mummy insisted.

Daddy shrugged. 'Well, Tanya says it isn't open.'

PERFECT

'Oh, I expect I could be wrong,' said Tanya. 'Look, there's the man in charge now.' And so he was, in uniform, waving brightly but contractually at his only customers.

Mummy paid the man, Tanya clambered into the seat beside her, and as soon as the wheel jolted into life and she was pulled backwards and upwards into the air, Mummy began to feel frightened. 'I shouldn't have done this,' she said.

'It'll be all right, Mummy,' said Tanya. 'Look, I'm holding on to you. See? And I won't let anything happen to you.'

'Promise?'

'Promise.'

The wheel carried them into the damp wind. 'I wanted to talk to you, Tanya,' said Mummy, shutting her eyes against the weather and the long look down. 'I just want you to know... I want you to realise... Oh God. That although I agree with Daddy, and I do... It wasn't an easy thing to decide. Particularly for me.'

'You're missing the view, Mummy.'

'And I love you very much. Do you understand? ...I hope you understand.'

The wheel stopped. Mummy opened her eyes, and beneath her Margate lay sprawled out, cold and grey and unfriendly. The wind buffeted the car, made it rock from side to side.

'Why have we stopped?'

'They always stop the car at the top. It's all right.'

'Well, I don't like it.' She let go of her daughter's hand and reached inside her handbag for her cigarettes. Tanya looked, and then pretended she hadn't noticed. Mummy tried the lighter, but the wind was too strong, it wouldn't catch.

'Let me,' said Tanya softly. She took the lighter, and it sparked first time. Mummy cupped her hands around it to protect the flame, but she really didn't need to. She inhaled gratefully.

'I'm sorry,' said Mummy.

'I know,' said Tanya.

'Not about this,' said Mummy, indicating the cigarette. 'Well, this too, but everything, you know. I'm sorry I'm not the mummy I'd like to be.'

'I know,' said Tanya again. And smiled. She reached for her Mummy's hand, but with a slight impatience Mummy waved it away – no, I've got a cigarette, that gesture said, I'll stick with the cigarette.

'Why won't they get this bloody wheel moving?' said Mummy. And 'Damn!', as the rain began in earnest. The drizzle turned into big fat heavy drops, and every one of them seemed to make for the two of them stupidly rocking above the south coast. 'Get this bloody wheel moving!' said Mummy, and it was supposed to come out softly, as a joke, with a little laugh at the end, to show she didn't mean it and wasn't scared at all, but she realised it had come out screaming.

'Ssh,' said Tanya, 'it's all right.' And then she stood up.

'No! Tanya, what are you doing?'

'Hold on to me, and don't let go.'

'I won't let you go,' said Mummy, grasping hold of her legs. 'I won't ever...' And she shut up, held her tightly, looked up at her daughter.

And, by God, she was beautiful. Standing there, swaying a bit in the wind. The rain spattering into her face, but Tanya not caring, smiling, *beaming* through it all. And sticking out her arms, tall, up to the heavens. And in that moment her Mummy loved her more than she ever had before.

And she knew too that in a way that'd make it all easier. This moment was the best it would ever get. It'd all be downhill from now on. She'd forgotten she was still holding the cigarette between her fingers, the filter was jammed against Tanya's leg, and she dropped it before it could burn her.

The rain stopped. Tanya laughed, looked down at her

PERFECT

Mummy. 'It's all right now,' she said. 'See? I told you it'd be all right. And look, the wheel's moving again. It'll always,' she said, sitting back down and taking her Mummy's hand, decisively this time, not prepared to brook any refusal, '*always* be all right.'

'Well,' said Daddy, when they reached ground. 'That looked like fun! Did you two enjoy yourselves?'

Mummy marched away. 'I want an end to this,' she said. 'Let's find somewhere to sit down. I can't do this any more.'

There was a café open. The waiter showed them to a table near the back. There was no reason why they couldn't have had a table with a sea view — but nobody bothered to suggest it; it was getting dark, and they'd seen as much of the sea as they could want. Daddy didn't even look at the menu. 'Three fish and chips, please. You've got to have fish and chips at the seaside. And mushy peas,' he added. 'You've got to have mushy peas.' Mummy said she wasn't hungry, and so Tanya said she could share her meal, and Mummy promptly changed her mind and said she'd have a plate to herself after all.

The suppers were put before them. The fish looked as if it had seen better days, but on the whole it still looked considerably more lively than Mummy or Daddy.

'Are you going to tell her,' asked Mummy, 'or...?'

'Let her eat her fish first, can't you?' Daddy snapped.

They watched as Tanya ate a few mouthfuls. She smiled apologetically. 'That's all I can manage.'

'Not even a little bit more?'

'Sorry,' said Tanya. 'I think it may have been the ice cream.' She pushed the plate away from her. 'It's okay,' she said. 'Why not just tell me?'

'Right,' said Daddy. 'Right. Right.'

'It's okay,' she said again.

'I'm pregnant,' Mummy said.

There was a pause. 'So that's good news. That means I'm going to have a little brother or sister.'

'Yes,' said Mummy.

'No,' said Daddy.

'Sort of,' said Mummy.

'No, not sort of,' said Daddy. He looked back at Tanya, and sighed. 'We didn't think we'd be able to,' he said. 'You know. Tests and things. We'd all but given up! But it's real, it's true. I only hope it's mine!' he added with a laugh.

'Of course it's yours. Who else's would it be?'

'Sorry, I was only joking.'

'It was a bloody stupid joke to make in front of Tanya.'

'Yes,' said Daddy. 'You're right.' He leaned forward, took hold of Tanya's hand. Changed his mind, let go, played with a salt shaker instead. 'The thing is,' he said. 'Whoever this child is. You know. In your Mummy now. It won't be as good as you.'

'Oh,' said Tanya. 'It might be.'

'No, it won't,' said Daddy. 'It won't be as clever. Or as kind. As patient. Someone who looks after *us*, who we can talk to when we're down. It'll probably shout and scream, break its toys. And it won't stay aged eight either, it'll grow up, most likely. Play loud music, get its tongue pierced, smoke behind the school bike sheds. God, it'll probably *hate* us.'

Mummy cried, and Daddy turned to hold her.

'I don't want it,' she said. 'I don't want it.'

'Of course you do,' Daddy told her gently. 'You know you do.'

'I want Tanya. Tanya's better.'

'Yeah, Tanya's better. But she's not real. Sorry,' he said to his little girl, 'sorry, but you're not. And sorry, we love you ever so much, we do, sorry. But we have to go with what's real. We have to go with reality. At the end of the day. Don't we?' And Tanya wasn't sure he was asking her, or Mummy, or the fish — which was the one he now seemed to be paying the most attention — and not a single one felt they could answer, the fish was dead, Mummy was sobbing, and Tanya just waited, she felt she should wait. 'At the end of the day. We do. We do. We'll miss you, and it'll be hard for us to... It'll be hard. You know. For us.'

He began to play with the salt shaker again.

'You don't want me any more,' said Tanya.

Even now, her Daddy noticed she didn't look surprised. It was so hard to surprise Tanya.

'Yes, we do,' said Mummy. 'Can't we keep her? We could have them both...'

'No,' said Daddy. 'You know we can't. You know we mustn't.' And he kissed her. Right on the lips, which Tanya had never seen them do before. And they sank into each other, Mummy still sobbing, and Daddy fighting back the tears too. 'We'll be all right. We'll be all right.' And Tanya thought for a moment they'd forgotten she was there. They probably had. She wondered if she should clear her throat or something. But they looked so happy, kissing like that – no, not happy, but *relieved*, as if they'd found out they could still do it even without the practice, and she thought she should give them their moment. *Then* cleared her throat. A little guiltily, both turned back to face her.

'Have you thought of a name yet?' she asked. She didn't know what to say, but that seemed as good as anything. And she had to be strong for them – Mummy's face all puffy, Daddy looking so sad and awkward. She felt so sorry she was putting them through this.

'Tanya,' said Mummy shyly. 'If that's all right with you.'

'Tanya's a lovely name,' said Tanya.

'If that's all right with you.'

'No, I'm flattered. Really. And what if it's a boy?'

'Oh,' said Mummy. 'We hadn't thought,' said Daddy. 'We're rather hoping it won't be,' said Mummy.

'I see,' said Tanya.

'So,' said Daddy. 'There it is.' And they smiled at their daughter, the one they'd dreamed up all by themselves, the one they couldn't keep any longer.

'You'll make a great Mummy and Daddy,' said Tanya.

'We will, won't we?' said Daddy, hopefully.

'When do you want me to...?' began Tanya. She couldn't finish the question before Mummy started crying all over again – oh, don't, Mummy, please, she thought, with just a trace of impatience. 'No, Mummy, it's all right,' she said. 'Really, it's all right.'

'We don't want to rush you. Or inconvenience you. I mean, there's no rush,' said Daddy.

'I think I'm going to the toilet,' said Tanya. 'I need to use the toilet for a minute.'

'Yes,' said Daddy.

'Of course,' said Mummy.

'And I think it'd be easier if you weren't here when I got back.' And she smiled to let them know she wasn't angry with them, not at all. 'Now, come on,' she said, as even Daddy began to cry, 'it's all for the best. You know it is. Mummy, you've got to stop the smoking. Not even the secret ones when you think we're not looking. Daddy, you don't need to try so hard. You can't squeeze love out of people like that. And you'll be all right. You will. You'll see.'

She reached out, brushed her Daddy's hand. Then her Mummy's. 'Let go, Mummy,' she said. And Mummy did, because it was Tanya's day, and she got whatever she wanted.

She washed her eyes in the bathroom. She'd supposed she really ought to cry or something too, but the urge frankly wasn't in her. But she washed her eyes anyway, and then washed all over again just to give her former parents a little extra time to leave. And by the time she stepped back into the dining area, they had indeed gone.

The waiter was clearing the table. He didn't like kids, and didn't know how to speak to them. 'They left, sweetheart,' he said gruffly.

PERFECT

'It's okay. I don't really know them.'

'Oh. Okay.' And he got back to clearing the table.

Tanya wished she'd thought to ask if they'd had any money she could borrow – practical matters like that. She presumed they'd paid for the fish dinners at least, that was something. 'Excuse me,' she said to the waiter. 'Silly question, but... I don't suppose you have any jobs going, have you?'

The waiter had never wanted children. He'd not even wanted a wife, not really, but he'd found one of those anyway – briefly, mind, and years ago. But as he looked at the girl some of the frost around his heart melted. He could actually *feel* it – melting. He pointed out that she didn't know him – didn't she want to rethink this a moment? And Tanya paused, and thought, and said afterwards she'd done her rethinking, the rethinking was all over and done, and she'd still like a job.

'How old are you, sweetheart? I couldn't take you on unless you were at least sixteen.'

'That's all right,' said Tanya. 'I'm seventeen.' And she was.

'Then you'd best take those plates, wash them up,' said the waiter with a gentleness he'd not really felt before. 'And I'll make us a mug of tea.'

Tanya emptied away the bits of fish and the mushy peas, and looked around the kitchen, her new home. There was so much to take in of her new life, and Tanya knew that she would never tire of it, not ever.

Grappa

We'd married on the fifteenth of November. There was nothing particularly significant about the date – we'd both checked our diaries, and found that was when we were both free.

And on every fourteenth of November I would say to my wife, would you like to go for a meal tomorrow night and celebrate? And she would always say yes. We hadn't bothered discussing for years what sort of meal it would be; we'd been married long enough now to have ourselves a nice little Favourite Restaurant. It was a lovely Italian called Mario's. We liked it because the food was good and the lighting was gentle and the music wasn't too loud, and every time we went in the owner recognised us and treated us with a familiarity that was warm but respectful. And, it has to be said, we also liked it because there were rarely many customers there, and when there were they tended to talk in whispers that seemed respectful as well. It wasn't far from our house: walking distance if it wasn't raining, a couple of minutes in the car if it was.

It hadn't always been our Favourite Restaurant. There'd been Casanova's, which we'd discovered first because it had been a hundred yards closer. The food wasn't great but the lighting was subdued enough you couldn't tell, and the waiter used to sing in Italian under his breath – how he made us laugh. Then one day the restaurant declared itself to be under new management. Gone was the subtle lighting, gone the subtle music, and our waiter vanished altogether. We were most put out by what was a disagreeable evening. But I suppose if it hadn't happened then we wouldn't have been forced to seek out our pasta elsewhere and discovered Mario's. So it was all for the best. It's funny how life works out sometimes.

My wife always ordered the same starter – an avocado pear drenched in Marie Rose sauce, which Mario called a Mona Lisa. And I always ordered the same main course – a generous bowl of penne with chunks of chicken and spicy sausage. Sometimes before we went to the restaurant we would tease ourselves with the idea we might order something new this time. But at the end of the day, it would somehow have felt *wrong* if we had. If nothing else, it was our way of demonstrating to our Favourite Restaurant just what it was that made it so favourite. It would have seemed disloyal otherwise, that we'd been eating there under false pretences. It's hard to explain. Let me see if I can find an example – yes –

Before we'd got married, my wife sat me down and spoke to me very seriously. She was a smoker, and I wasn't. It was all very well my saying I loved her and I wanted to spend the rest of my life with her, she said, but I had to accept I was taking her as she was, cigarettes and all. She didn't want us to go through the whole laborious process of getting hitched, only to find out later in the day I wanted *changes*. I lied and told her I didn't mind her smoking, in no way found the smell of it repellent, that the scent of it clinging to her clothes, to her hands, to her lips, never in the slightest made me baulk. And so we married, and ever since I've never felt the right to criticise her for it. Although sometimes I'll waft the smoke away with my hand when she isn't looking – and sometimes I'll do it when I know she *is* looking, just out of the corner of her eye, but always so that I can claim I didn't know she was should she ask. But she won't ask. That would break the terms of this unspoken contract by which, smoker and non-smoker, we lived together.

In the same way, I felt, ordering something other than the pear and the penne would be breaking the contract with the restaurant. And, on this particular visit, once our order was taken, Mario himself came out of the kitchen with a beaming smile. 'My friends!' he said. 'I knew it must be you! From the Mona Lisa and the Penne Della Casa!'

We told him it was our wedding anniversary, and he looked delighted.

'I shall make it special for you, very special!' he promised.

Mario was a wiry little man, always full of enthusiasm, always greeting us with a conspiratorial wink. As if all this eating of the food, all this being customers, was part of a joke – we were good friends, and were just *pretending* there was a business contract going on here, that he was charging us money for our dinners, that I was paying for it with a Mastercard. He never called us by name, although I'm sure that at some point we must have told him who we were. And although my wife called him Mario, I could never bring myself to do so. I was never sure whether it was his first name or his surname. If I called him Mr Mario and it was his first name, I would look like an idiot. And if I called him Mario and it was his surname, it would seem as if I were ordering him about, that he was some sort of *servant* or something, a menial, a lackey, that I was saying I was better than he was. And on his own premises! It would have been too embarrassing to bear. So I just kept quiet and winced inwardly whenever my wife talked to him.

She told him that her avocado pear was excellent. When he brought me the penne he gave me one of his winks, and said he'd made a special sauce just for me. Because I was a valued customer, and because it was my anniversary. There was some dolcelatte in there, some spinach, different herbs. He knew I was going to love it.

I did love it, and told him so. But I didn't *adore* it, which, to be frank, I had the regular sauce he'd always served with my penne. I didn't want to seem ungrateful, though.

As usual, after the dishes were cleared away, my wife smoked a cigarette and I paid by Mastercard. And then, as we were preparing to put on our coats, the waitress came to us and said, 'What would you like to drink?' She spoke with such a thick Italian accent we couldn't understand her at first, so just gawped at her in surprise. 'My boss, he says you should have a drink. Whatever you would like to drink.' And before we could politely decline the generous offer, or even choose a drink, she poured us two small glasses of a pale liquid.

That's very kind, we said. You shouldn't, really.

And we meant it. Neither of us had ever much liked spirits. Yes, our sitting room had a drinks cabinet in it, but that was just a matter of form, the shelving *came* with a drinks cabinet. And so we keep scotch and vodka and gin and the like, just in case we ever receive visitors. Not that we get visitors very often, mind you.

But the drink was quite nice. Obviously very alcoholic, but not so much that it made me gasp for air. And there was a pleasing aftertaste that was somehow a little like liquorice, and somehow very very really wasn't. My wife enjoyed it too, and looked as surprised as I was. I think it's grappa, she said. I said I thought it was too, although I had no idea. I'd just heard the word 'grappa' before, and although I'd never had reason to put a picture to it, this pale not quite liquoricey liquid was the picture I would have come up with.

'So,' said Mario, all smiles, appearing from nowhere – the waitress efficiently vanishing into the background as he approached – 'so, it's your anniversary today?'

We concurred. And thanked him for our grappas. Although we didn't call them grappas, just in case we were as confused about the name of his drinks as we were about his own name. 'Time flies,' he said, 'eh?' We agreed it did.

'Doesn't seem that long since you were here for your last anniversary.'

In fact, that may have been our fault. We did rather enjoy celebrating at Mario's, and the anniversary didn't have to be that significant. Not only was there our wedding anniversary, we remembered the anniversary of when we first met (April 7th), the anniversary of when I plucked up the courage to ask my wife out (May 30th), and the anniversary of when she actually said yes (January 5th – a bit of a gap, I know, but a complication in that she was dating a friend of mine when I fell for her, and it took her several months to come to her senses and realise she'd be far happier with me). Naturally, I didn't bother to explain any of this to Mario – besides, by this time he was offering us another drink.

'Oh, please,' he said, when we said no. 'I'm going to have one, you see? And it's good stuff.' He fetched down another bottle, unmarked, and poured himself a glassful. 'Please,' he said, gave his wink, and taking our silence as permission, poured for us as well. Well, I say poured – the liquid was black and thick, and it oozed slowly into our glasses. I idly wondered whether this new drink might be grappa instead. And if so, what the last drink had been called.

'Here's to you,' he said. 'Here's to love. Here's to marriage.' And he drained his glass, smacked his lips in appreciation. 'Hey,' he called to the waitress, waiting at the kitchen door, watching unsmiling. 'Do you want a drink too?' She shook her head. 'Come on, it's good,' but even before he'd finished speaking, she'd turned her back and disappeared into the kitchen. He turned back to us, shrugged, smiled. 'I'll have hers,' he said. 'It *is* good, isn't it?'

Neither of us had touched ours yet, but we assured him that yes, it was very good indeed.

'Marriage,' he said, 'is a blessing. You're blessed. We're all blessed.'

My wife asked if he was married, then. She said it was

odd, in all this time he'd never mentioned he had a wife. I didn't think it was especially odd – I couldn't see any reason he would have furnished us with details of his domestic history – but Mario agreed with my wife, it was odd, yes, it was odd, here we were, all friends, and he had never told us, how odd. My wife asked if she were English or Italian. For a moment he looked confused. Your wife, she prompted. Oh, Italian, he said. Really, said my wife with a laugh, you come all this way to England, and yet you won't marry one of us! What's her name? she asked. But Mario didn't answer immediately. Then:

'There's a funny story, how my wife and I got together. It's funny. Because, yes, here I am, I come to England, and yet I end up marrying Italian! It's funny. It's odd. You want me to tell? Please, please, another drink.' But we hadn't swallowed our last ones yet, and so we both swigged the black liquid down as he stood over us to replenish our glasses. In both taste and consistency it wasn't unlike cough medicine.

'I came to England,' said Mario, sitting back down, 'twenty-seven years ago. Exactly. My brother was here, and I stayed with him.'

Why did you come, asked my wife.

'My brother was here,' said Mario, as if this were an answer. I frowned at my wife. Let him get on with the story. Then we could go home.

'I loved this city. It was beautiful back then. It's beautiful now, of course. But it was *beautiful* back then. I loved it. I found a job, it was nothing grand, I washed dishes. I washed dishes from seven in the morning until seven at night, Monday to Saturday. Not Sundays, back then we had Sundays off, people didn't work Sundays. I never thought,' he said, and looked around him with pride, 'that one day I should *own* a restaurant. Yes,' he said, and the pride seemed to droop somewhat. 'Yes.

'And I learned English. I learned it very well, I wanted

to stay. Evening classes, three times a week, seven o'clock to nine o'clock, I would rush there from the kitchens, from the washing-up. I had to learn the language, you learn the language, you can stay, you fit in, right? Of course, right.

'So I was working hard. And I was playing hard too! There were discos, there were clubs. Friday night I was out, Saturday night. Saturday at the restaurant, washing-up in the morning, I was very tired, I had to keep myself awake, but Sundays were good, Sundays I could sleep.' And he smiled. 'And there were the girls.'

My wife laughed, and he looked at her appreciatively.

'They taught me English,' he said. 'They taught me lots of things! I was just this young foreigner. But they took the time, they liked me, they taught me everything they knew.' My wife laughed again. 'And I fell in love.'

My wife stopped laughing. I hadn't started, but cleared my throat solemnly to demonstrate I had no intention of doing so. Once the word 'love' was mentioned, we both knew things were getting serious. Mario seemed to acknowledge the gravity with which we took the introduction of this concept, he bowed his head to us both very slightly, first to my wife, then to me. As if thanking us for understanding just how complex things had got for this Italian kid far from home. And then he continued.

'I didn't mean to love,' he said, and there was a slight pleading tone to his voice now. 'But it creeps up. It doesn't let you know, and then, poof, it's just there. I think she may have told me first, she said she loved me, and at first I wondered whether my English... whether 'love' meant the same, had such a *strong* meaning as... but it did, it *did*, and I... I realised, yes, I loved her back. Yes, please. Yes, very much. Her name was Beryl.'

It wasn't a romantic name, and I very nearly smirked. But I supposed that had I come from a foreign country there might be something exotic in the word 'Beryl' that would have affected me too. Certainly the way Mario said 'Beryl', as if it were something treasured, as if this were a name he couldn't use easily, gave it a little bit of poetry I could never have lent it myself. I quickly wondered whether there were girls' names in Italian that were as plain and unflattering as 'Beryl' sounded to me – but I couldn't think of any, Antonia, Sophia, Lucetta, they all sounded like starlets. Black and white foreign films, late night on Saturday, the wife's gone to bed but you can't sleep, these Italian girls on the screen, all legs and subtitles, starlets every one.

'We became steady. Is that it, steady? I'd work washing the dishes, and then I wouldn't go to the discos or clubs any more, I'd just want to be with Beryl. I wouldn't do the English classes either, it was just Beryl. Beryl... I can't remember her name. Beryl Evans? Beryl Edwards? I can't remember her name.'

He looked at us in agony, just for a moment, as if hoping that one of us could prompt him. But then his face sagged back to its usual shape, and he even managed one of those winks. 'It's all the same now, isn't it?' he said. 'It's all the same.' And he drained his glass.

'Would you turn the music off?' he called suddenly to the kitchen. Italian folk songs had been playing on a loop all evening, discreet in the background. I'd already heard O Sole Mio three times – I couldn't begin to imagine how many times Mario had heard it. 'There are no more customers,' he called. 'Music off now, music gone please.' For a few seconds the music actually got *louder*, and Mario grimaced at us – you see what I have to put up with? – before the song snapped off.

He was right, too – we were the only customers left. I made a gesture to my wife, suggesting we should – what? – get up and go? Just like that? And she shook her head at me, a little angrily, turned back to Mario.

Gently she asked what happened next.

'My family weren't happy. I didn't see my brother for

weeks, for months even. And I'd get phone calls. He'd tell my parents, back in Italy, and they'd phone me up, they'd complain. Which wasn't cheap back then. They would ask me what I was doing with my time, why I'd turned my back on my family, why I was with this English girl. Which back then wasn't cheap.

'I think Beryl's family... I think they were worried too. But they did a good thing. They asked me to stay. With them for Christmas, big family time, they asked me. They loved Beryl. Very much, I could see. They didn't love me. Because who was I? But I was Beryl's boyfriend, for her sake they asked me. Christmas,' he shrugged dramatically, 'Christmas means nothing to me. Just another day. Another Sunday, but not on Sunday. I worked Christmas Eve, but we finished early because it was a holiday. I went back to my flat. I was tired. I was so tired, and I had to go see this family tomorrow, Beryl's parents, all for her sake. It wouldn't be easy, I didn't want to, Beryl knew I didn't. We argued about it. A lot, I think, but still I was going.

'But when I got back to my flat, my brother was there.

'He said he missed me. That he was worried. That he hadn't seen me for ages, and that it was Christmas. I told him Christmas was nothing to me, I didn't care. But he got upset. He cried. How do you cope with a man like that? A man who cries? He told me to come to the house. For Christmas Eve. For family. And I did. We drank, we ate, we smoked. And the next morning I phoned Beryl to say I wasn't coming.'

My wife actually gave a little gasp. He turned to her. From now on the story was only for her. He didn't take his eyes off her until it was over.

'She was... Beryl was... She... ...I can still see her in my mind's eye. Well, not see, I wasn't there, it was a phone call, but I can still... She was devastated. She cried. She begged. But I'd had enough of crying and begging. And she put the phone down on me. She put the phone down,' he added, almost as if it were a new concept that had only just occurred to him, so many years later, 'on me.'

There was silence for a while. It probably wasn't very long, but it was enough to make me feel awkward. The light in the kitchen had gone out, and the waitress was standing in the doorway, watching coolly. My wife lit a cigarette. Almost as a reflex, Mario waved the smoke away. And without a word she put it out.

'After that,' said Mario, 'things changed. Beryl didn't call. If I called, she'd not answer. Or she'd answer, and then not talk, it's all the same. And I don't know why. I don't know why I hadn't gone to her family, I just knew I wasn't going to. That this wasn't going to be how it was. Do you see? You see, don't you? Sometimes... It's funny how life works out sometimes.'

My wife didn't answer. But he saw something in her face that encouraged him to go on.

'A few weeks later my brother came. I'd seen more of my brother, he would wait for me after work. He said, Mario, I met this great girl. She's special, I really like her, I met her at the disco. And he showed me her photograph.'

Beryl, said my wife.

Mario nodded.

It all seemed a bit unlikely to me.

'I called Beryl. I tried to see her. I had to tell her. My brother, he wouldn't be good for her. He only wanted one thing, fucking...' and he immediately clasped his fist to his mouth, like a little boy – my wife waved him on impatiently, it didn't matter – 'Fucking, sorry, but that's what it was. And she wouldn't listen. No, Mario, I'm with him now, I don't want to see you again. But she'd still park outside my flat, the two of them kissing in the car, doing all sorts of things, when they knew I was in, when they knew I could see them. In the fucking car, kissing and groping and fucking in the fucking car.

'I'm sorry,' he said to my wife, 'I'm sorry.' And I didn't

know whether he was apologising for the swearing, or the rush of emotion, or the fact he'd rejected and humiliated his girlfriend so many years ago and caused this whole problem in the first place. She didn't accept the apology, just asked him what happened next.

'She came to see me at work. Beryl did. This was months later. She asked if we could talk. I said, yes, we can talk, I work until seven o'clock, you know this, every day from seven until seven. If we must talk, we talk at seven. At seven she was waiting for me outside the restaurant.

'She told me I was right. Of course I was right. My brother is a bastard, don't I know my own brother? He was only after the fuck. She didn't love him, she'd never loved him. She didn't know why she was with him, sometimes things just happened, did I always know why I did things? And I told her it was too late. It's too late, Beryl. It's all gone now. She told me she loved me. And I said, all that love, it's all gone now.'

He paused.

'And she went.'

Did you ever see her again, I asked. I was surprised at my own voice. I think we all were. But he still didn't look at me in reply.

'No.'

But you were going to tell us how you met your wife. This was the story of how you met your wife. And *my* wife looked expectant as she said it. Come on, she said.

He looked at her, perplexed. He had no idea what she was talking about.

That's the way things work out sometimes, she said, trying to be cheerful. If you and Beryl hadn't split up... you'd never have married your wife, would you? You wouldn't have the life you have now. This restaurant of yours. Our favourite restaurant. It's all for the best, maybe. It's funny how life works out sometimes.

'Yes,' he said, after considering this, 'it's funny how life works out sometimes.'

'It's time we closed now,' said the waitress, in that thick accent of hers. 'I want to go home.'

'I'm talking to my customers,' said Mario.

'No. No customers. No more music, no more customers, you said.'

'I'm talking to my friends,' and then he jabbered at her in Italian angrily. She answered back, angrier. He smiled at my wife in apology, and got up. 'I'll be back,' he assured us. And he followed the waitress into the darkened kitchen.

My wife and I sat there for a few moments.

We should leave a tip, I said. How much should I leave?

It's ten per cent, isn't it? said my wife.

You don't think I should leave more...?

Ten per cent is fine.

I left three pound coins and a fifty pence piece. We were moving to the door when Mario hurried back.

'I'm sorry,' he said, 'sorry.'

There's nothing to be sorry about, my wife said. Thank you for the meal, I said.

'All these things. I keep them inside. And they never come out. And then, when they come...'

It's all right, said my wife.

Of course it's all right, I said. We're friends, aren't we? (But I thought, suddenly, what's your *name*? Is it Mario Something or Something Mario?)

'Next time you come,' he promised me, gratefully, 'I'll do you penne again. In that special sauce you like. Just for you. No-one else gets that, just *you*.' Bloody wonderful.

Good night, said my wife. We'll see you soon. Christmas, if not before.

'Yes,' he said. 'We're open Christmas. Come at Christmas. Christmas is special, we have special menu. Just for you.'

GRAPPA

★

My wife had brought the car. She'd thought it looked like rain. She'd been wrong. She sat in the driver's seat, put the keys in the ignition, but did nothing. I sat next to her.

'I wonder if that drink was grappa,' I said at last. 'I'll look it up when we get home.'

'Which drink?' she said quietly.

'Well. Either one.'

'I think she must have been very hurt.'

'Who?'

'That girl. Beryl. When he threw her over like that.'

'I suppose so.' I wished she'd drive home.

'I wanted to say to him. You know what she was doing, don't you? With your brother? She was trying to make you jealous. She was trying to get you back. She thought you didn't love her, and she wanted you to realise how hurt that made her, because she loved you, she loved you. And she'd have you back, at almost any price, even sleeping with another man, just to get you to react. I'd have done it. I *have* done it.'

My wife's voice had risen as she said this. Then she fell silent. 'Do you think so?' I said at last.

I didn't think she would answer me. And then she said, very quietly, 'But men never realise. They never realise. And look what we end up with.' And at last she turned the engine, and we drove home. I wanted to take her hand, I felt an impulse to. But I didn't want to surprise her. Not wise, not if she'd been drinking – I didn't know how much the grappa and the non-grappa had affected her.

When we got in, we took off our coats and our shoes. We pulled the curtains and double-locked the doors.

'Thank you for a lovely meal,' she told me.

'Thank you for the company,' I said.

'Happy anniversary.'

'Happy anniversary.'
And we kissed each other on the cheek and went to bed.

Ashes to Ash

Natalie's mother didn't smoke, Natalie had never seen her smoke, but she knew she had smoked once. One day she was looking through an old photo album, and there she was, in a cocktail dress, wine glass in one hand, cigarette in the other. It was some sort of party, there were a lot of strangers looking very smart; Natalie couldn't see her dad anywhere, and her mum was smiling at something a man in a tuxedo was saying, smoking a cigarette of his very own. The picture was black and white, and made her mother look impossibly glamorous.

'I didn't really smoke, not really,' said her mum. 'Besides, everybody back then smoked a little bit.'

'What's it like?' asked Natalie, and her mum frowned, and told her that she never wanted her to smoke, not ever, she might think she'd look cool but actually she'd just look stupid, it was very bad for you and made your hair smell. Natalie must promise her she'd never *ever* start, never even an experimental puff, and Natalie promised, so her mother told her she was a good girl and took the photo album from her, closed it, and shut it away.

It wasn't a hard promise to keep. Julie's mum smoked, and although Julie's mum was very nice, and always welcomed Natalie when she went over and gave the girls chocolate digestives and everything, Natalie thought her house stank. She always wanted Julie to play outside and, as a result, was only really Julie's friend during the summer months. She'd watch Julie's mum, and she'd watch the girls who used to hide behind the bike sheds during break, she even watched Julie herself after she'd turned twelve and got hold of her mum's lighter — and she always remembered what her mum had told her, stupid, you look *stupid*. She was never even remotely tempted, and so when the bus cannoned into her at forty miles an hour, and spread Natalie across the road and the central reservation, Natalie's lungs were as pink and pristine as they could be.

Natalie had not reached an age where she'd had cause to think about death very much. If the subject of an afterlife ever crossed her mind, it was only to wonder vaguely if heaven was where the hamster had gone. But she had no particular desire to be reunited with the hamster, and so was less put out than most would be when she didn't go to heaven after all, but was instead reincarnated as an ashtray.

There was a green marble ashtray in the living room. Once in a while favoured guests would be allowed to flick their ash into it, and at Natalie's birthday parties it was used to hold peanuts or sweets; most of the time it served as a pretty enough ornament. It was the only ashtray in the house anyway, so Natalie presumed this was the one her soul now inhabited — she had no way to detect her greenness or her marbleness, and only knew she was an ashtray in the first place because all the guests kept on grinding their cigarettes into her. Julie's mum was there, too, grinding away, all dressed in black and looking ever so mournful — Natalie could tell she wasn't *really* mourning, no-one but her parents were, but it was the right facial expression to wear at these sorts of do's. Natalie didn't much like it that all these strangers kept stubbing out burning sticks of tobacco into her — distant relations, Daddy's friends from work, people she'd never seen before and who really had no reason to care whether she were alive or dead. It wasn't that the stubbing hurt — she couldn't feel any physical sensation at all, no matter how hard she tried — but that the growing pile of butts blocked her already limited field of vision. She couldn't hear very much either – all the sound seemed to come from a long long way away, and nothing was distinct unless the speaker was standing directly over her – but it wasn't as if anything she heard was especially interesting, she heard the phrase 'sorry for your loss' so often it was nearly funny, but that was as good as it got. With nothing to see and nothing to listen to, Natalie drifted off to sleep; it had been a tiring day, after all.

The next thing Natalie knew was that she was being rinsed in the sink. There was a weird sense of vertigo as she came to, staring straight down a plughole, and then she was righted and could see it was her mother who was washing her. Natalie thought her mum might have been crying, but covered in water there was such a film over everything it looked as if the whole kitchen had been crying. Her mum set Natalie down upon a table, and then began tipping all the rubbish into the bin – the leftover food, corks and cocktail sticks, the now empty wrappers for pork pies, savoury eggs, and other sundry funeral food. Natalie saw her mum pick up a packet of cigarettes, and then freeze as she was about to throw it away; it clearly wasn't empty after all. And the mother just stood there for a while, looking down at the carton, all tense and rigid, and Natalie couldn't believe she could be spending so much time thinking about a *carton*, not really, and then the tears started, and Natalie saw at last that her mother *hadn't* been crying, not until now, she'd worked so hard all day at keeping it all in. Mummy took out a cigarette, and it was as if she didn't know how to hold it, she held it like she'd hold a pen or a spoon or a, or a *carrot* or something. And she put the cigarette between her lips, but just at the very tip, as if she didn't really want it there, and struck a match, held the flame to the end, and then fast pulled the cigarette away from her with a cough. She sat down at the table, not inhaling from the cigarette again, just tapping the ash on to Natalie every few seconds, tap-tap-tap even before any ash had formed. And the tears poured out in earnest, and her mum was close enough, or maybe just loud enough, that Natalie could hear them come out with a moan that didn't sound quite human. There she sat, crying, moaning, tap-tap-tapping, the burning ash sizzling against the damp. And with every tap Natalie could see that little bit less of her mum through the ash, but that was okay, she was beside her, they were together, and it was as if her mum was stroking her gently with the cigarette, and the smoke curled up into the air above them both. In came Daddy, and Mummy looked up – didn't say a word, not either of them – and when he approached her she suddenly threw her arms around his waist and held on to him tightly for a while. Then, although the cigarette wasn't yet finished, the mother ground it out. She took the father's hand and allowed him to lead her from the room. 'We'll finish clearing up in the morning,' Natalie thought she heard him say, and then he turned out the light, and for a while she saw and heard no more.

Natalie assumed that the next day her ashtray would be back doing its normal ornamental job in the sitting room. But instead she was left on the kitchen table. Her mother would sit with her, smoking and yet not smoking her way through the rest of the packet that had been left behind. And then, when that packet was finished, her mother would come back with a new one – first in a carton of ten, then in the regular size of twenty. For a while she'd tap at the ash as before, but Natalie could see her take puffs of the cigarette more often – awkward, rushed puffs, blowing the smoke out before it had gone in, the sort of puffs she'd seen Julie play at behind the bike sheds. But within only a few days Mummy had got better at that too; she'd hold in the smoke with more confidence, then let it out of her nostrils at her own leisure, thank you very much. Once in a while her father would appear in the kitchen, and sometimes when he approached Mummy she'd cling on to him as before, but it happened less and less often – it seemed to Natalie that the better she got at smoking, the worse she got at hugging. Natalie couldn't pretend she minded (although she did worry a little about how much her mummy's hair would smell, surely it must be rank by now), she was just so pleased that Mum wanted to spend so much time with her, that she *needed* her. 'Oh, God, Natalie,' her mother said once, very softly, but it was so close to her it was as if she were whispering in her daughter's ear, 'oh, God, why did you go?' And Natalie would have given anything to have told her mum she was well and happy and holding her cigarette for her, she tried so *hard* to move, to dance up and down the table just to show her. But she supposed it was a good thing she wasn't able to – a dancing ashtray might have frightened her mother, and wouldn't necessarily have been taken as evidence of her daughter's return from beyond the grave; it would, besides, have got ash and fag ends everywhere.

Eventually her Daddy stopped coming to see Natalie at all. She imagined at first he was simply somewhere else in the house, but, as the weeks went by, and as the mother began cooking straight-from-the-packet meals-for-one, Natalie realised he'd gone for good. She couldn't work out how; Julie had told her when *her* parents had split up there had been a lot of arguing and shouting and door slamming, but Natalie had seen none of that. It was true, she knew, that her view of the house was somewhat limited, but something as dramatic as a family breaking down surely would have been obvious even to an ashtray? If they *had* split up, she hoped it was nothing to do with her – but she couldn't see how it could have been, she'd been dead for *ages*. Maybe Daddy wasn't divorced, maybe he was dead too. Maybe he'd been hit by a bus, squashed flat, and turned into some bric-a-brac of his very own. With a start of fear Natalie would wonder whether in the sitting room Mummy would be now tapping ash into her father, whether she'd rather be stubbing out her cigarettes on him instead. But she didn't seem to be spending less time with Natalie. On the contrary. She settled for a brand she liked; she smoked as she cooked, as she washed up, as she made out the shopping list and put away the groceries. For a while she practised smoke rings, then just concentrated on sucking in and blowing out as much of the tobacco as she possibly could, right down to the very filter. Natalie began to realise that her mother wasn't mourning any more, she was enjoying her addiction. And she didn't need the special green marble ashtray, not really. Any ashtray would do.

One day Mummy brought another man into the kitchen. Natalie tried to work out if she recognised him – from her wake, maybe, one of those distant relatives, a friend of Daddy's from the office? Mummy gestured with the cigarette pack, and the man indicated he didn't mind her smoking, even lit the cigarette – 'You're a gentleman,' Mummy said. And they sat and talked about bland things for a while, and how much Mummy might be missing her dead daughter didn't get mentioned even once. The man suddenly got up and stood close by her, just as Daddy had used to do, and there was the same sort of charged silence; then he put his hands on Mummy's breasts, and they hugged and began kissing so hard, and he took her by the hand and pulled her from the kitchen – the cigarette once more only half-smoked, but this time nobody bothered to stub it out. And Natalie thought, that this is what *Daddy* should have done, if he'd gone for the breasts rather than standing there so morosely he might still have a marriage. And Natalie thought some more, and concluded that that man probably hadn't been a relative after all.

Mummy began cooking properly again. Not just meals-for-one, but things which had bits of actual food in them. She went jogging; Natalie saw her come into the kitchen wearing shorts, dripping with sweat, and *laughing*, something she'd not done in ages, not even when Natalie had been alive. And the strange man came back, she knew – he didn't go into the kitchen much, but those were the nights Mummy made dinners for two. And then, one day, Mummy took hold of Natalie, as she often did, and rinsed her under the tap. But this time she didn't put her back on the kitchen table and light herself an immediate cigarette – no, instead, she took her back upstairs to the living room. And Natalie thought as she was carried in her mummy's hands that Mummy *knew*, that Mummy at last realised that her dear dead daughter was in the ashtray, because she spoke to it, she actually *spoke* to it. She said, 'You've been a lot of fun, but you're not healthy, and I've got to pull myself together, I've got to move on.' And she smiled at Natalie, and Natalie would have smiled back if she could have. Mummy set her in pride of place in the sitting room, a lovely ornament. And when she married the stranger they allowed the guests to flick their ash into Natalie – but no-one ever filled her with nuts or sweets, because there were no children's parties to be had.

Extra Ordinary

I met a girl at college who said she didn't sweat. She'd tell people at parties, it was her way of breaking the ice. 'I think it's something to do with my pores,' she'd say. 'I think it's because they're too big, or too small, or something.'

Let me just stress that she wasn't trying to get sympathy, or get attention, or get anything as far as I could see. It was just a funny story. Becky Simmons probably *needed* a funny story at parties. She wasn't all that clever, and she wasn't all that pretty – nothing awful, but her teeth butted out a bit, and she was gangly, and she always seemed to be trying to mask one zit or another. The breasts were okay, but you know, there were better breasts out there.

'You don't sweat at all?' we'd ask. 'What, not ever?'

'No,' she'd say. 'The doctors say it's really odd.'

'That's impossible,' said Mary Haskell, who was one of the top biology students. 'Your body has to sweat, just to let some of the heat out. If you never sweated at all, you'd burn up inside. You'd *die*.' Mary Haskell may have been right, and she was a lot prettier and her breasts were bigger, but no-one cared because she was a bitch.

Even then Becky was too nice to lay into Mary. 'You're probably right,' she said to her, and gave her a smile as genuine as anything, 'you're the expert, not me. But the doctors do say I never sweat, and they do say it's really odd.'

At some parties we boys used to like to test Becky Simmons out. We'd do this if there wasn't enough alcohol to keep us busy – or, frankly, if there was too much. She didn't seem to mind. We'd try to make her as hot as possible, one of the lads got a hairdryer once and trained it close on her face for fifteen minutes. Or we'd all run around the house, up and down the stairs, up and down. We'd all get exhausted, dripping with perspiration and giggles, but Becky was as good as her word and would stay dry as a bone. 'I sometimes worry that all the heat is bubbling away inside somewhere,' she'd tell us. 'But then I think, what the heck.'

Behind her back the boys would say they'd be pretty sure they'd know how to get her sweaty, given half the chance. Matt Buckley said he had done her. He said he'd done a lot of the girls, and it was clear that even if he was making some of his conquests up, a few of the stories had to be true. 'I gave it my best shot,' he told us, as we all smoked and drank and talked about porn. 'I did a good job and everything. But, no, not a bit of sweat, and I was watching the whole time, I was really *staring* at her to see.'

I didn't think Matt Buckley had done Becky Simmons. She wasn't that sort of a girl. She never swore, never smoked, and only drank a little bit of alcohol if there was a lot of fruit juice on top. Besides, I was pretty sure Matt Buckley wasn't her type. I watched her a lot at those parties, and sure, she was *nice* to him – she was nice to everyone, was Becky – but she never gave him any special attention. No more than she did, say, me.

It's fair to say I had a bit of a crush on Becky. She just interested me somehow. I began going out with a girl called Janet, who just happened to be living in the same digs. Sometimes she'd invite me back to her place for sex, but I'd always tell her I'd rather we did it at mine; I didn't want Becky to see me with another girl. Janet broke up with me in the end, told me I was always asking questions about Becky, what she was up to, what music she liked, whether she ever talked about me. 'I'm special too,' said Janet, 'I'm really special.' Looking back, I suppose I didn't treat Janet very well. But then, I don't suppose she treated me that well either. No-one does at that age.

I promised myself at the end of the final semester that I should just *talk* to Becky, at least see if I had a chance with her. What was the worst that could happen? Besides her laughing at me and breaking my heart. I got a little drunk beforehand, I took her to one side, and I remember her smiling politely and trying not to recoil from my cider breath – and I thought, I should pull out now, do this later, and I thought, no, it's now or never. I asked her if she'd like a snog. I explained that I'd heard that snogging was really good at stimulating the sweat glands, maybe we should try it by way of an experiment. Or, you know, we could go and see a movie some time. Whatever was good for her.

And she told me I was very sweet. And she smiled at me and I could see that it wasn't that nice a smile, not with those bucked teeth, what did I see in her? I wanted to wrench open that smile, I wanted to press my lips against hers, I wanted to wrench that smile wide open and stick my tongue inside. She said again I was very sweet, she'd better not. The doctors said she had to start taking better care of herself. It might not look obvious from the outside, but really she was a bit disabled, something of a cripple. She was just a bit too *special* to take the risk of getting in any way intimate. She was just too special for me.

*

This Tuesday morning I saw her on the underground train. I recognised her at once. She looked very different, actually – older, obviously, but also more beautiful, the teeth looked tamed and flat beneath her mouth, the breasts had filled out. But I had spent so long thinking about Becky all those years ago I just *knew* it was her. She was sitting down at the end of the carriage, reading some sort of celebrity magazine. I was standing. At the next stop some of the commuters got off and made just that little bit more room allowing me to squeeze my way down the aisle towards her.

Even when I was standing right in front of her, really close, she didn't look up. She was too intent on seeing the photo exclusive of Mel Gibson's latest mansion. I felt my heart pound as I bent towards her. 'Becky?' I said softly. 'It is you, isn't it?'

She looked right up at me, guiltily, as if she'd been caught doing something bad. And her mouth opened, formed a perfect little 'o' of surprise.

'Becky Simmons?' I went on, because she wasn't going to say anything. 'You remember,' I floundered, 'I knew you...'

'From college!' she said, quite loud, delighted – and all the passengers around glared at her as if she'd said something rude. 'Of *course* I remember you! Well. How are you?'

She remembered the college bit, but I noticed she didn't say my name. I put her out of her misery, though, made sure I mentioned it casually in the very next sentence.

'Yes, yes, I remember,' she said, smiling. 'God. It's *good* to see you. God. *Weird*. So, how are you?'

'I'm fine,' I said. 'I'm married.' Like an idiot. But why not? It wasn't as if I was expecting anything to happen, was it? And a part of me was glad she knew, right then and there, knew that *some* girl had said yes when I'd asked her for a snog.

'God,' she said. 'Well done. I'm still waiting!' she laughed.

'I bet you don't have to wait long,' I said. 'If I can do it!'

'That's what I keep saying to myself!' she laughed again. 'I mean, not about *you* doing it. Why would I be saying that? But, you know. About finding someone.' Laughing.

'I bet you don't have to wait long,' I repeated. 'Well.'

'Well,' she said.

'I'm getting off soon,' I said. 'But this was great. Seeing

you again. We should do lunch some time, catch up.'

'Of course,' she said. And she named a restaurant off Covent Garden, said she could be there for one o'clock, was one o'clock all right for me? And I sort of stammered out a yes. 'You know where that is?' she asked, and I said, sure. But she gave me directions anyway.

'Great,' I said. 'That'll be lovely! What an unexpected... And you looking so well. Great!'

I'd misjudged how long it would be until we'd be pulling into the next station, and for a good forty seconds we just smiled at each other. 'So,' I said eventually, 'what do you... oh, here we are, I get off here.'

'See you later,' she said.

I stepped on to the platform, looked back, raised my hand for a wave. But she wasn't looking, she was back to Mel Gibson.

Once I was at work I kept having to leave my desk and check out my reflection in the toilet mirror. There was a yellow stain on my front tooth that I couldn't get rid of no matter how hard I rubbed at it with the hand towel. I sniffed my armpits and couldn't be sure whether I was smelling me or the basic toilet ambience. I asked my intern whether he had any fresh mints I could borrow, and he said no, and I said I knew it wasn't in his job description to run errands but would he mind popping out to the shops and getting me a tube of the extra strong, and I gave him a pound coin and told him to keep the change.

That said, I didn't really expect Becky to be there. But she was. Standing at the entrance. She wasn't gangly as I remembered, she was now definitely *tall*, statuesque even. 'Hello,' she said with a smile.

'Hello,' I said. All morning I'd wondered if I should kiss her on the cheek in greeting. I half made the motion towards one, but she anticipated me and kissed my cheek instead.

'I wasn't sure if you'd come,' she said.

We looked at the menu. I'd never been less hungry. 'It all looks good,' I said conversationally. 'I could eat it all. Choices, choices. Yum yum.' Shut up. 'Do you want a starter?'

'Better not,' she said. 'I'm trying to watch my weight.'

'I wouldn't have thought you needed to.'

'Oh, don't you believe it!' she laughed, and tapped at her midriff in mock irritation. We ordered and she went for something low fat and expensive. She took out a packet of cigarettes, offered me one.

'I don't do things like that any more,' I said.

'Really?' she said. 'Well.' She gestured with the cigarette. 'You don't mind if I...?'

'Go ahead.'

She looked nice there, smoking. It was still a little hard to imagine Becky Simmons holding a cigarette, but it suited her in an odd sort of way. She'd turn her head very politely away from me and blow out little puffs, as if to say she was only *playing* at the whole smoking thing, she was only a little girl, really. She smiled at me, and asked me what I did for a living. I told her, and she nodded intelligently, as if what I said meant anything. 'I work in sales,' she said.

'What sort of sales?' I asked.

'Oh, you know,' she said. 'Just sales. I do all right. Probably not what you'd have expected from a fine arts graduate, though!' She'd been a fine arts student, I had no idea. That hadn't been one of the things I had thought to ask Janet.

The food arrived, she stubbed out her cigarette, waved the remaining smoke away from me. 'Yum yum,' I said again, and once more wished I hadn't. 'How's yours?' I asked her before she'd even taken a mouthful. She was kind, though, didn't point that out, and told me it was very nice indeed.

'So, what's your wife called?' asked Becky.

'Yvonne.'

'Oh. From college?'

'No, Yvonne was much later.'

'Oh. Because I read somewhere, a lot of people meet their sweethearts at college.'

'Yes. Not me, though.' Sweethearts, I thought. What a lovely word, and how very Becky Simmons! I vowed to try and use 'sweetheart' in my future conversation as much as possible.

As she ate her couscous, sipped at her wine, thanked the waiter, and lit her second cigarette, I kept watching to see if she were perspiring. She wasn't. I was dying to know, I wanted to find out about it in as delicate a way as possible. 'How's the sweat thing?' I asked.

'You remember that.'

'Oh yes.' And I dropped my voice to emphasise care and concern. 'We were all very worried for you. It sounded so very serious.'

'I didn't know you were concerned!' she said. 'How sweet! Aww.' And she reached out to squeeze my hand, realised it was holding the cigarette, transferred the cigarette to the other, then squeezed mine with the original. 'How sweet of you,' she said again.

'But you look really well now,' I said, feeling a little boyish pang as she took the hand away again.

'Oh yes, I'm fine now. Well, I say fine. I'm not completely fine. I have to take care. They gave me an operation, you see.'

'Oh dear,' I said.

'No, it was good. It took a long time, though. They had to open me up. And they did something to my glands.'

'And that did the trick?'

'Oh yes,' she said, smiling that smile of hers. 'I'm back to normal now.'

'Good,' I said.

'I have to take showers a lot. After any physical activity.

Even just carrying the shopping home! That's my life, in and out of the shower.'

'That doesn't sound so bad.'

'But I did use to gush a bit. Oh, it was awful, actually. The doctors said it was only to be expected, really, but it felt dreadful at the time. You see, I had twenty-one years of sweating to catch up on. It had all been building up, you know, behind the pores. But it couldn't get out. And now, suddenly – whoosh! It was like a tap had been turned on. They put me in the bath, and as I lay there out it would pour, out of every inch of my skin. And I'd filled that bath in less than ten minutes.'

'Bloody hell,' I said.

'And as the bath filled up, they'd grab me, this would be the nurses, they'd grab hold and put me straight into another bath. Trying to catch all the excess water still gushing out of me with, you know, buckets. And then I'd fill that one, and then another, and then another. I was filling the baths too fast, they hadn't run out the first one before they had to put me back in it again.'

'Bloody hell,' I said, and 'Christ,' for good measure.

'And that wasn't the worst part. You see, all that sweat, all those gallons of sweaty water. They'd all got so *hot* in there. They were burning me up. So out would come the water, and I'd be screaming, because it was boiling, it *scalded* me, God, you wouldn't believe how much that hurt.'

I no longer trusted myself to say anything.

'But I'm okay now,' she said, 'really I am. I can sweat like anybody else. Hang on,' she said, and reached a finger to the top of her forehead, 'yes, here's some now.' She held it out to me, and I could see it glistening and, thank God, perfectly cool. I wasn't sure whether to prod it or sniff it or lick it off, and I did nothing, and Becky looked a little disappointed.

'Well,' I said.

'Well,' she agreed.

I felt I'd failed a test somehow. I asked for the bill. 'This has been lovely,' I said. 'We must keep in touch.' I knew she wouldn't see me again, but it was the thing to say.

'There's a hotel round the corner,' she said. 'Let's go there. That's the nice thing about jobs in sales, that you can take the afternoons off when you feel like it. Does your job let you have the afternoon off?'

I lied and said yes.

★

The receptionist asked us how long we were staying and what sort of room we would like.

'Just the one night,' Becky said. 'And a double bed.'

'I'll get this,' I said, taking out my Mastercard. 'My treat.'

'No,' she protested fondly. 'We went Dutch for the pasta, we'll go Dutch for this.' The receptionist didn't say anything.

We closed the bedroom door behind us, and there was the big bed, unarguably designed to be the centre of attention. She took off her coat, began to unbutton her blouse. I remembered I'd once been rather good at being the passionate lover, Yvonne had always got rather excited; I tried to recall how to start. I gave a low growl, and Becky looked at me in some surprise. 'I want to rip your clothes off,' I said. 'Come here, and kiss me. And I'll rip your clothes to shreds.'

'There's no need for that,' she said cheerfully. 'Look, the clothes are off.' And so they were. That was Becky Simmons naked, that was. 'But you can kiss me if you like.' Too late I remembered the unopened tube of mints in my pocket. She tasted of house red and penne arrabiata and stale cigarettes, but it was all right for that. Her tongue teased across my teeth, no doubt buffing up the yellow patch.

'I'll do whatever you want, Becky,' I said. 'I want this to be special.'

'There is one thing,' Becky said, and I braced myself. For all I'd just growled so sexily, I really really hoped that pain wasn't involved. 'If you could call me Rebecca. Sorry. But Becky is so...'

'No,' I said, 'I can do that, Rebecca.'

I took off my clothes. I considered kicking off the underpants, but then thought it would look silly. I nibbled at Becky's shoulder, and she gave a little grunt. I knew how much that turned women on.

'Actually,' she said, after a few minutes of this, 'we could dispense with the foreplay. If you like.'

'Whatever you say, Rebecca.'

So we had sex. And it was very nice.

Afterwards I rolled off, exhausted. She seemed very composed. 'Was that all right?' I asked.

'Oh yes, it was very nice.'

'Good.' And I looked her all over, but she hadn't even broken a sweat.

She lit a cigarette, and we lay there for a minute or two. 'See?' she said. 'You can see my scars. Where the surgeons went in to slice up my glands. See?'

I couldn't really. So she pointed with her finger, showing the first trace of irritation I'd ever seen in her, and yes, I could just about make out a few lines of fading pink.

'I expect they'll disappear in time,' I said.

'I hope not,' she said. 'They're part of me now. They're what I am.' She turned her head and did that cute blowing out smoke thing, but it no longer looked so girlish when I could see her breasts and her pubic hair.

'Shall we do it again?' I asked eventually.

'Better not,' she said, and smiled politely. 'Remember, my sweating problem. The doctors told me I had to take special care, I'm special.'

'You haven't sweated at all,' I said.

She didn't hear it as an accusation. 'No,' she said. 'How

funny. I sweat *buckets* with most men. But not you.' She swung herself off the bed, stretched, and I saw her perfectly dry body bathed in the afternoon light. 'I should have a shower,' she said.

I lay in bed all the time she washed in the bathroom. She left the door ajar, and I could see the clouds of steam come out. And I wondered whether the steam was escaping from her, from that volcano in her body, all that heat had bubbled out of her pores all blazing and boiling. The special heat that somehow I just hadn't tapped.

I thought of Yvonne. She wasn't special at all. She smelled of vacuum cleaners and liked to sing along to TV ad jingles. And my son Philip. Not top of the class in anything, not bottom either. Not special.

I decided to tell Becky I thought we shouldn't see each other again.

'I don't think we should do this again,' said Becky, as she stepped out to get dressed. She'd dried herself thoroughly, so even now I couldn't see her wet. 'But it was lovely. Do you want to use the shower before you go? I have to go now, but use the shower. You might as well. We're paying for it, after all.'

After she'd gone I wished I had told her. About the first night I had sex, with Janet on that horrible student bed. And that I'd thought of her the whole time, that I'd closed my eyes tight and pretended it wasn't Janet at all, hoping that Janet wouldn't say anything halfway through and knock me off my stride. Maybe if I had told Becky, it would have changed things that afternoon. Maybe she'd have felt more aroused by me inside her. Maybe she'd just have said I was sweet and said awww. Maybe she'd have sweated. But then I remembered that even in my fantasy, with Janet keeping her mouth shut through the whole thing, thank God, even then I hadn't managed to make Becky sweat. Of course not. That had been the point of her, hadn't it?

That evening Yvonne had cooked us all something with chips and baked beans. Philip wolfed it down and then went off to rush through his homework so he could play on his Xbox. 'Anything interesting happen at work today?' asked Yvonne.

'Nothing special.'

That night we both got into bed together, and I felt angry at her – she couldn't smell Becky on my body, couldn't see that I'd been within some strange sweatless beauty. 'Do you want to read for a bit?' she asked. 'Or shall I turn off the...?'

'Yeah, turn off the light.'

We lay in the darkness, and I thought Yvonne might already be asleep. I considered calling her sweetheart, just to see what it sounded like, but the idea was ridiculous. 'I love you,' I said.

'I love you too,' she said firmly.

And she turned to me and began stroking me. And I wanted to tell her I didn't have the energy, but she did that nibbling thing on my shoulder that I like, and miraculously the energy came back, and we made love long and hard and sweated like pigs.

Stuff We Leave Behind

And then, after all that. All that suffering on his part, and that boredom on hers, quite frankly – running out of things to say, looking around the ward for inspiration, at the nurses, the beds, the other patients, all of whom seemed so much more communicative than her own husband, propped up on the pillows with tubes running in and out in all directions. After all that, there was just one moment of tenderness.

He'd reached out for her hand, creeping like a spider across the sheets to find it. And he'd grasped on tight, tighter than she'd expected his strength would allow. 'This isn't the end,' he'd whispered. 'I'll wait for you. I'll be waiting for you.'

They hadn't been the last words he'd said, but they were the last words she remembered. They'd taken her quite by surprise. He had not been a romantic husband. It had simply not been that sort of relationship. A marriage built on regular meals, pyjamas in bed, and mutually accepted silences.

They told her that she'd soon be grieving, but what did they know, really? These were the same people who told her how proud she'd feel when she got married, how depressed she'd get turning forty, or how at the birth of her daughter she'd be overcome by an indescribable wave of love. None of those things had been true, so why should this? Indeed, if anything, she was only disappointed that his death hadn't affected her more deeply. But he'd been in hospital long enough that his continued absence was no disruption, and the funeral arrangements had been at worst an irritant not an upset.

About three weeks after she'd buried her husband she decided it was high time to throw out his old things. She had no desire to erase him from her life – it'd be impossible, even if she'd wanted to – after over forty years! – but she was never one to hoard old clutter. On the Saturday in question the sun was streaming in through the windows, and she knew to get the job done properly she'd need to clear out the attic; there was a single little skylight up there, and it was best she catch as much natural light as she could. 'Right,' she said, after she'd finished her breakfast, washed up her bowl and her spoon, dried them, then put them back in the cupboard, 'let's get to it.' She gathered a few black plastic sacks, and set to work.

At first she made good progress. The shelves were soon done – they'd kept their books separate, his were a few rows of sports almanacs and cheap spy thrillers. She dumped them into the bag for the charity shop. The wardrobe was emptied almost as quickly. For a minute she pondered whether his suits would be of any use to her son-in-law – but for the life of her she couldn't remember his size, and she certainly had never understood the man's taste, he'd married her daughter, after all. Into the charity bag with the clothes too.

Just the attic left. She allowed herself a cup of tea. Then she was up the stepladder and through the little trapdoor in the ceiling. Heaven only knew when she'd last been up here. Heaven knew too what had been squirreled away, but she could at least be fairly certain it was all to be disposed of; if she hadn't missed it in all this time, why should she need it now? The sunlight caught a cardboard box, on its side the name of a supermarket that didn't even exist any longer; it was full of her daughter's old toys and schoolbooks. They'd need to be thrown out too. But not today, she told herself. Get rid of the husband first. The daughter could be saved for later.

One thing she didn't recognise was the large tea chest. Even hidden by the shadows it dominated the room. She crawled towards it on her hands and knees, picking past the boxes that represented her daughter's childhood. She realised the chest was even bigger than she'd supposed – it stretched all the way into the darkest corners of the attic. She felt at the lid, doubting she'd be able to lift something that looked so heavy. But it opened with surprising ease. It was too dark to get even a clue what might be inside, and so, gingerly, she reached in her hand to find out. The hand didn't need to stretch far before it felt a bundle of paper. She pulled it out, turned it towards the light, squinted at it.

She was holding a package of envelopes, all tied together with a ribbon. All unstamped, all made out to her husband, and, she quickly realised, all in her own handwriting. She pulled at the ribbon and it was as if the envelopes, set free at last, burst into life – they spilled out over her lap and on to the floor. 'Damn,' she said, even though she knew it didn't matter, they'd be going into the sack soon anyway. She took the top envelope, opened it, and recognised the birthday card that she'd bought him earlier that year – a rather sober affair of a bunch of flowers that looked, she thought now, as if they'd seen better days. Inside was printed a perfunctory little verse, and underneath, in ballpoint pen, she'd written, 'from Dorothy.' The envelope underneath was also for a birthday card: some more solemn flowers, another 'from Dorothy'. She rifled through the others. How far back did they go? Valentine's cards too, from the days when they still gave each other such things – 'from Dorothy' said a few, and then, as she took some from the bottom of the pile, she saw 'love, Dot'. When did Dot become a Dorothy, when did all that love become a formal 'from'? She didn't want to count them, but it wouldn't have surprised her had every single card she'd ever given him been here, all tied up for posterity in a red bow. In one card she found she'd written 'I love you so much, thank you for being mine', something she couldn't even remember, something she couldn't even remember *conceiving*, and looking at the cover she couldn't tell whether it was for birthday or Valentine's, it was all the same thing.

When had he collected them like this? Every time she'd given him a card he'd taken it and – what? Scurried up with it to the attic when she wasn't looking? When she'd been out shopping perhaps, he'd be sitting in the armchair watching TV, as comatose as ever, and as soon as she'd closed the front door he'd spring into action and fetch the stepladder, dart up with his prize and store it away out of sight before she could get back. Why? She tried to remember how he'd react on his birthday when she gave him a new card to open at breakfast – but, no, he'd barely shown interest, he'd read it with a grunt, put it to one side, eat his toast without a thank you. Couldn't he have shown some excitement, if they'd meant that much to him, couldn't he have been a bit bloody *grateful*? She knew she'd hardly responded to her own cards, but at least she'd put them on the mantelpiece, at least she'd put on a show of caring, before putting them into the bin with the rest of the rubbish. But he really had cared, hadn't he? And she'd never known.

Almost without thinking she reached into the tea chest once more. And was surprised when her hand hit more paper. No more cards, she thought, surely not – and no, they weren't. She pored over her fresh discovery, nothing as ordered as before. Still in her own handwriting, but just scraps of paper this time. Shopping lists, little reminders she'd left herself to pay the gas bill. Half-finished crosswords from the local newspaper, little doodles she'd made when she couldn't solve a clue, all meticulously cut out and tied into this bundle of paper. Postcards she'd written on holiday to friends but never sent because she'd forgotten the address or run out of stamps – for God's sake, she found even *drafts* of postcards she'd never finished writing. She leafed through them all, all these words, and not one written *to* him, not one meant *for* him – but he'd collected them anyway, he'd kept them without telling her, he'd sentimentalised them. All the detritus of her life kept forever – and why? Why had he never told her? And with a dizzying sickness she wondered if it were her fault, that he'd loved her so much but been embarrassed to show her. He'd worshipped her, he'd *adored* her, and had had to spend all these years pretending he was so passionless, because he'd thought she'd have rejected him had she known. And he'd been right, she thought now, and God, she was crying, she hadn't cried for him since he'd died, she hadn't cried at *all* in *years*, he'd been right, she would have laughed at him had he said how much she meant to him, laughed or worse, much worse. And for the first time she was glad that he was dead, that he had died before her. So that he had never searched the house after she'd gone looking for signs his wife had secretly loved him, only to find nothing whatsoever.

With a start she realised she could hardly see the writing any more. It was getting dark and she must have wasted hours of daylight up here reading things she'd forgotten she'd even written. She dried her eyes as best she could, felt her way clumsily towards the small square of light that was the trapdoor. She knocked into a cardboard box; a doll fell out and croaked 'Mummy'.

She made herself a cup of tea with shaking hands, and in the sanity of the kitchen couldn't help but be angry again. Damn him, she thought, damn him – for making me cry, for making me care after all this time. None of this was her fault. He had been the one who'd stopped smiling, he was the one who had yawned when she told him about her day, until she'd just stopped telling him about her day, why should she? – he was the one who had turned her from a Dot into a Dorothy. It wasn't enough that he had spent these years chronicling their relationship, measuring the frost as it hardened over their marriage, over their love, over everything. He had done nothing to stop it, nothing. There was something which disturbed her about that tea chest upstairs, pouring out the details of their lives together, and *lying,* showing her a husband who was attentive and loving when she knew he had never been that. For two pins she'd not have gone back to it again. But the stepladder was still up, and she couldn't put the stepladder away because the trapdoor was still open, and she couldn't climb up the stepladder just to shut the trapdoor without admitting defeat. And she wasn't going to admit defeat. She already had a wardrobe empty, and three bookshelves cleared, and she wasn't going to be beaten by anything.

This time she took with her the flashlight she kept in the kitchen in case of power cuts. There hadn't actually *been* a power cut for several years, so she was pleased to see that the batteries were still working. The torch cut a narrow beam through the darkness, picking out the tea chest, lid still ajar, like an open mouth grinning at her. She made her way to it, her knees treading through the birthday cards and shopping lists still spilled around the floor. She felt momentarily guilty as she felt them scrunch and tear, but over her tea she'd decided she had to be hard about this. Her husband may have cared for all this stuff, but it was nothing to her, nothing.

And as she shone the torch into the chest, to see just what else might be inside… she suddenly realised what it was about it that had been bothering her. It was just too big. How on earth had it got up here? The trap door was far too narrow. Had there been a larger trapdoor once? – no, that didn't make sense, and besides, the chest was so large it was wedged in between the supports of the house, you'd have had to have removed the entire framework of the roof to have got it in here. Could her husband have built the chest himself, then? It was the only explanation – and yet, as she'd trained her torch on it, she could tell it was an antique, the wood was old and marbled and put together by a real craftsman. Her husband hadn't even been able to change a light bulb without assistance. And even if he'd kept his carpentry genius a secret from her – like so many other things, it seemed – how had he built it? When she went shopping, he'd spring into life, race up to the attic, and now not only ferret away every scrap of paper she'd ever written a word upon, but construct an enormous tea chest to house them all? It was ridiculous. But no more ridiculous than her uncanny feeling that the chest had been here *first*, and that the house had somehow been built around it. And no more ridiculous than her realisation, as she shone the torch inside, that it was still full to the brim. That she'd removed so much from it already, and yet it was still *full*; she couldn't have fitted those bundles of paper back inside, she couldn't have squeezed in a single card.

No more paper. The next items that she removed from the chest were old clothes. Blouses, skirts, dresses she didn't wear any more. Oh, they were hers, all right, she had no doubt about that. But she'd taken them to the charity shops, surely? That's what she'd always done when something no longer had any use, she'd put it into a black sack and pop them down to Oxfam, or to Scope, or that Trinity Hospice Centre on the corner. ...And *he* must have bought them. She'd left them there to be priced and put on display, and then he'd come along, he'd have sifted through all the second hand clothes, looking for the pieces that had once been his wife's. That she'd once worn against her body. And that she'd rejected, she no longer wanted – but that wasn't good enough for him, he *wouldn't* let them go, they were *his* now. Who was this man she'd married? What had he been after? And why – oh, God, why? – had she been unable to provide it? Why had he needed to turn his love from her altogether, and instead give it to all those things she'd possessed, all the irrelevancies of her life? She lifted an old skirt to her face and sniffed at it, wondering if that's what he'd done, sniffed at her old skirt in the dark, revolted and yet excited by the thought. She smelled only attic and mould.

And underneath the clothes – photographs. At first, just

simple photographs, the ones she could remember posing for. Christmas dinners, snapshots on holiday. She was always looking impatient. It didn't matter whether the background was the sitting room downstairs or Brighton beach, her mouth was still set in that unconvincing smile. But underneath these were *other* photographs. Pictures taken of her with her eyes closed – what, was she sleeping? Yes, she realised, that was it, and she suddenly felt cold – these ones had been taken of her as she slept in her bed. And still more, her face younger the deeper from the chest she pulled them – asleep in the same bed, but her cheeks less wrinkled. And then, not just asleep – look, here's a picture of her out shopping. Here's one of her at the supermarket, here's one walking down the street, here's another crossing the road. Different clothes, different ages, but all the same woman, all *her*, and all utterly oblivious that someone was following her. That someone was snapping away with his camera, someone stalking her even, yes, stalking her, it didn't matter that he was her husband, and then...

And then... And then she felt colder still, and her brain tried to make sense of it...

A picture of her at school. The playground. She recognised that girl she was talking to, she'd been her best friend, hadn't she, but now she couldn't even remember her name... Never mind the friend, what about *her*, look at *her*. How old would she have been? Thirteen, maybe fourteen. In uniform, with that pony tail her mother had thought was so smart, she'd cut her hair short as soon as she was able just to spite her. Then so pretty, but never knowing how pretty she had been, never knowing she would never look better. And never knowing that some man was secretly photographing her.

And her brain reminded her. She'd only met her husband when she'd been twenty. So where had he got these photos? How *long* had he loved her? How long had he been collecting her life?

STUFF WE LEAVE BEHIND

Still more photographs. Younger and younger, with her parents, with the Girl Guides, at her eighth birthday party, look, you can count the candles... Her husband had been only one year older than her. She *knew* that, it was a *fact*, she'd seen his passport, she'd seen his birth certificate, hadn't she?, yes, she was sure she had. So how was this possible? Had he been stalking her when he was aged *nine*? Had he latched on to her so young, and determined to make her his, had he wanted her from childhood and plotted to have her, had he loved her so much? And yet never let that love out, not really, never *shown* that love... And, no, wait, there were pictures going back still further. Such a little girl now, on her daddy's knee, in her cot, smiling in each one, look at her smiling. *That's* when she knew how to smile, smiling so naturally, that's how to do it. She knew she was only glancing at the photos now, digging even further into the tea chest, trying to find the bottom, trying to find if there even was a bottom, and, at last, touching hard wood...

And bringing out the last photograph. Beneath all the others. And looking at it with her torch.

And seeing that it's her. Of course, it's her, they've all been her. But it's *her* her. There she is. In an attic. By a tea chest. Lit only by torchlight. Her face is looking frightened, and so very old. The photograph has just been taken, it's still wet to her fingers, it's been taken *now*.

And she remembered the last words he'd said to her. And the way that he'd gripped her hand so tightly, so tight she had to prise his fingers off, thinking they might leave a bruise. And that toothy smile he gave, from a face that was so close to becoming a skull it was part there already, she'd fancied she couldn't make out where the tooth ended and the bone attached to it began. She remembered that grip and that smile and those words he'd said.

'This isn't the end. I'll be waiting for you.' And she gave a final shiver as the flashlight went out.

Damned If You Don't

'I want to make a complaint.'

And Martin felt a thrill of courage, and for just a moment the first sensation of actual happiness since he'd arrived in this God-forsaken place. Here he was, always rather a timid man – both in the bedroom and in the boardroom, which is why he'd never accomplished much in either, but Moira had never complained, bless her, and even if he'd never had the nouse to rise to managing director, like everyone else his age, at least he'd never been sacked or demoted or what was the word they used now, yes, *reassigned*, no, they'd always kept him on, he was just too solid to lose. Solid, that's what Martin was, steadfast, reliable. But timid. Never one to rock the boat. And yet, here he was, all five foot three of him, squaring up aggressively to someone who must have been at least eight foot tall. And that wasn't even counting the horns.

Of course, Martin realised, in that split second when he felt so brave, he wasn't being as brave as all that. He'd chosen this demon specifically. Yes, he was eight foot tall, but that was distinctly diminutive for a demon since the rest of them were much larger and more ferocious. And there was a blonde tuft around the demon's horns which made him look almost endearing.

The demon turned both of his red rheumy eyes on to Martin. He didn't encourage him to go on, but neither did he *discourage* him, which was all to the good. Martin floundered anyway. He'd been so intent on summoning up the nerve to start complaining he hadn't given much thought on how to continue.

'It's my roommate. I'm not happy with my roommate,' said Martin. 'I didn't even know we'd be *getting* roommates. I haven't shared a room with anyone in forty years, not counting Moira. And Moira was bad enough with her snoring, I used to have to wear ear plugs. I don't suppose I could have a room to myself? No, okay, too much to hope for. But if I'm going to be here for a long time, and I think that's the idea, I should at least get a better roommate. Not that one. It's just...' and here he ran out of words for a moment, and then found a feeble conclusion, '...not on.'

The demon looked as if he were going to say something very cutting, then changed his mind, deciding that eternity was long enough as it was. 'Martin Travers,' he boomed.

'You know my name?'

'I know everyone's name. Your roommate has been especially selected for you.'

'Right,' said Martin. 'I see. Right. And how...' and he felt a bit of the old fire coming back; he'd come this far, he might not get the courage again, 'how exactly was he chosen? A lucky dip or, or, or what? I mean, I'm just saying. I don't think there was much thought to it. That's all.'

'Your roommate is very clean,' said the demon.

'Yes.'

'Doesn't smell. A friendly personality. Snores much less than this Moira of whom you speak.'

'Right. Good, I'm sure...'

'Frankly,' said the demon, dropping some of the booming cadence from his voice, 'you're in Hell, and you could have done a lot worse, mate.'

'But he's a dog.'

'He is indeed.'

'I'm not trying to make a fuss,' said Martin. 'But I deserve a human at least. Surely. I mean, I could do better than a dog. I'm not a, for God's sake... I'm not a murderer or anything...'

The demon shrugged. 'Everyone's equal here. No segregation based on gender, race, age, sex... or species.' He grunted and leaned forward confidentially – Martin felt a little nauseous as he was caught in an exhalation of fetid breath. 'Personally, I preferred it in the old days. Lutherans on one side, Calvinists on the other, and never the twain shall meet. What we've got now...' He waved a claw disparagingly at nothing in particular but the whole denizens of Hell, 'It's just political correctness gone mad.'

'The thing about dogs is they make me itch.'

The demon sucked air through his teeth in what was actually intended to be a gesture of sympathy, but sounded instead like a terrifying death rattle. Martin recoiled as if he'd been struck.

'I'll see what I can do,' he rumbled. 'Okay? But I'm not promising anything.'

'Thanks,' said Martin. And unsure what else to do now, nodded, made an attempt at a friendly smile, and went back to his room.

The demon watched him go. He wished all the damned would leave him alone. All the bigger demons laughed at him about it. It was that tuft of hair over the horns that did it. Every night he'd shave it off, but by morning the bloody thing would always have grown back.

★

The dog was waiting for him.

'Are you all right?' he said. 'You just took off without a word. I was worried.'

The funny thing was, it was only if you looked at him full on you could tell he even was a dog. Try out of the corner of your eye, or stand to him sideways, he seemed to be just another faded soul bouncing around in eternal damnation.

'I'm sorry,' said Martin. 'I was just a bit... you know.'

'I do know,' said the dog. 'It takes a while to get used to! Don't worry about it.' And he gave a friendly little smile, then panted cheerfully with his tongue hanging out. 'What's your name?'

'Martin,' said Martin.

'Nice to meet you, Martin,' said the dog politely, and offered his paw to shake. 'My name's Woofie.'

'Vuffi?'

'No, Woofie. I'm German.'

'Ah.'

'Yeah.'

They smiled politely at each other.

'I've never been to Germany,' said Martin.

'Oh, it's nice,' said Woofie. 'Well, bits of it.'

'Yes.'

'Rains sometimes, mind you. And gets a bit nippy in the winter.'

'Same as anywhere, I suppose.'

'Yeah, I suppose,' said Woofie, and smiled. 'Still, I liked it.'

They smiled politely at each other again, and Woofie even affected a friendly tail wag. Martin would have done the same, had he had a tail.

'Anyway,' said Woofie. 'I don't want to get in your way. You know, but if there's anything you need...'

'Thanks.'

'Make yourself at home. Well, it *is* now. Do you have a preference...?' he added, nodding at the bunk beds.

'Oh, I don't want to impose,' said Martin.

'It's no problem. Whichever one you want. All these years here, I've been in both. I'm happy either way. Don't worry,' Woofie said, perhaps seeing the involuntary look of disgust on Martin's face, 'I don't moult. And they're clean sheets.'

'Well, I suppose the top one might be more fun,' said Martin. 'If you're sure you don't mind.'

'Hey,' said Woofie generously, 'I know what it's like to be the new guy. We've all been there. Anything I can do to make it easier. There's a spare wardrobe over there, it's all yours. Washbasin in the corner.'

'What about the toilet...?'

'We never need to go,' said Woofie. 'Funny that. First couple of days I was here I was frantic looking for the litter tray, til I realised I didn't need one. And yet they give us a washbasin. I've never quite worked that one out.'

Woofie politely offered Martin use of the sink before they went to bed, but Martin let him go first. He watched his new roommate wash his fur, and brush his fangs, and a part of him thought he was about to scream and the scream would never stop, *I can't be in Hell with a dachshund.* Woofie wiped the sink clear of his gobbets of toothpaste, looked up at Martin. 'It's free when you want it.'

As Martin washed, he looked into the mirror. He stared at this timid little dead man, standing at five foot three. And if he tilted his head all the features he recognised vanished, and he saw a soul like any other. Every day, he realised, he'd look in this mirror when he washed, and he'd never be able to forget that he was dead, that he'd only ever been meat hanging on a frame, and that the meat was now rotting and the frame could be seen underneath. That's why Hell came equipped with washbasins. Not because of the sink, but the mirror. Martin sighed heavily, and all the stale meat of his face wobbled, and the soul framework dimmed a little. He heard Woofie let out a little snore, already asleep and dead to the world. And he didn't know why, but it reassured him, just a bit.

*

For the next few days, Martin waited for the tortures to start.

'It doesn't quite work like that, though,' said Woofie. 'I'm not saying there *aren't* tortures, but I've been here for ages and no-one's started on me yet. I don't like to say anything in case it reminds them.'

In the mean time there were the shopping malls to wander around. None of the shops were ever actually open, but Martin didn't have money to buy anything anyway, and it was reasonably good fun to look through the windows. There was a nice local cinema which screened films every evening, some of them even only a few months after general release. And Woofie kindly invited Martin to join his bowling team. They'd all go bowling three or four nights a week, and some of the players were really rather good. They were all dogs, and seemed a little reserved around Martin because he was a human. Martin felt a bit offended by that – if there were any qualms to be had, he should be the one having them. But none of the dogs said anything for Woofie's sake, and after Martin bowled his first strike, after a week of practice, all their congratulations seemed genuine enough.

'It's like the holiday village I once stayed at in Lanzarote,' said Martin. 'Hell isn't so bad.'

But of course it was.

'What are you in here for?' Martin asked his roommate once, as they were getting ready for bed. He wasn't especially curious. Just making conversation.

It was the first time he'd ever seen Woofie irritated. 'That's not a very polite thing to ask, Martin.'

'Oh. I'm sorry.'

'It's okay.'

But a few days later, as they were riding the mall escalator up and down for kicks, he asked him again.

Woofie sighed. 'Tell me what *you're* in for first.'

Martin was more than happy to do so – in fact, he'd just

been waiting for the excuse to let it all out. 'It's because I don't believe in God, apparently. They told me that when I arrived.'

'Uh–hum.'

'The thing is, I thought I *did*. I went to church most weeks, you know. Always thought there was some sort of higher presence or something.'

'Uh–hum.'

'Turns out I only believed I believed. But actually I didn't.'

'They hate it when you're wishy-washy,' said the dog. 'You'd have been better off not believing in God at all. They'd have respected that.'

'I wouldn't have gone to Hell?'

'Oh yes. But you'd have been able to sleep in on Sundays.' And then Woofie told Martin the reason why *he* was in Hell.

Martin was surprised and impressed.

'Don't be impressed,' said Woofie. 'It's nothing to be impressed about.'

'It seems a bit unfair,' suggested Martin gently.

'It *is* unfair. Most dogs go to Hell because they weren't kind to their masters. They bit them. Or wouldn't come when they called. Or wouldn't chase the sticks they'd throw. Dogs not doing what dogs are meant to do.'

'Yes, I can see that.'

'And I'm here because I *didn't* bite him. Frankly, I was damned right from the start. If I'd been lacking in my dogly duties, straight to Hell, no questions asked. But as a good dog, loving and patient to my master, I was serving Adolf Hitler.'

'So, really,' said Martin, 'it's just guilt by association.'

'Yeah,' said Woofie. 'When he told me to fetch a stick, I was just following orders.'

'Did you tell them that?'

'Of course I did. They said that's what *everybody* said. Throughout history, the same feeble excuse. So,' and he gestured with his paws at Hell, 'this is where I finish up.' As it turned out, he was gesturing at the time towards a Virgin Megastore, but the point was still made.

'I can see why you'd be bitter about that,' said Martin.

'Oh, I don't know,' said the dog, and he shrugged. 'If I'm going to be damned anyway, it might as well be for something impressive. ...It *is* impressive, isn't it, really?' he asked shyly.

'It is impressive.'

'I said you looked impressed.'

'You did and I was.'

'You know Strudel the poodle, who won the bowling last night? He'd belonged to Goering. I mean, just think. Bloody *Goering*. How embarrassing.' Woofie allowed himself a proud smile. 'If you're going to be in Hell because you were once the prized pet of a Nazi, better to be Hitler's than some jumped up SS Kommandant with ideas above his station.'

'I take your point,' said Martin, and for a moment felt embarrassed that the evil which had sentenced him had been so banal in comparison.

'I can't stop looking back,' said Woofie. 'I feel guilty. Of course I do. I think, if only I had been a better dog, maybe I'd have been a more calming influence.'

'No,' said Martin.

'If I'd distracted him for just one more hour with my squeaky toys, that would have been another hour he wasn't dreaming up death camps...'

'You can't think like that,' said Martin. 'What could you have done? Nothing, you could have done nothing.'

'I hope this won't make a difference between the two of us,' said Woofie. And he reached out for Martin's hand with his paw.

Without thinking twice, Martin squeezed it. 'Of course not,' he said. 'It doesn't. Really, really.'

Martin didn't bring the matter up again. They bowled

together as usual, watched the same movies, took turns to use the washbasin. And, if anything, Woofie seemed more relaxed around his roommate. The polite friendship was replaced by something warmer and more honest; Woofie let down his guard and beneath the affable doggy exterior there was a really sharp sense of humour. His mocking impersonations of the rest of the bowling team, all done behind their backs, used to have Martin in stitches – they were cruel, but so accurate, especially the way he imitated Rudolf's stutter or Ludwig's limp. And it all helped single Martin out as his *special* friend, the one he would never laugh at privately, the one that he truly took seriously. Martin felt quite proud of that.

'You may as well get it over with,' said Woofie one night. The lights were out, but Martin couldn't sleep, and he was pleased to hear the voice of his friend rise from the bunk beneath him. 'Ask me what he was like.'

'Who?'

'Who do you think? Come on. Everyone always wants to ask. It's all right.'

'All right. What was Hitler like?'

'He was okay,' said Woofie. 'Quite generous with treats. Didn't like me lying on the bed, but was usually good for the odd lap. Even as I got older and fatter, he never minded me climbing on to the lap for a cuddle. He wasn't a bad master at all. Of course,' he added reflectively, 'he had his bad days. When he got things on his mind, and he did a lot, actually, as time went on. Then sometimes he wouldn't find the time for walkies. But, you know. He did his best.'

There was silence.

'And at this point everyone asks whether I knew I was being fed and petted by an evil man. Go on, ask it.'

'I don't want...'

'It's all right, really.'

So Martin asked the obvious.

'I was his first dog, his childhood pet. So you've got to

bear in mind that when I came on the scene he hadn't done anything yet. Well, anything that was particularly *evil*. He'd done a few things that were *naughty*, but really, refusing to eat your greens, or reading under the bed covers after lights out, or graffitiing over pictures of Otto von Bismarck... I mean, you wouldn't say that was especially untoward. I know what you're going to say. That surely I could have seen *something* there. The seeds of the man to come. Say it, you might as well.'

'Did you see the seeds of the man to come?'

Woofie paused. 'Do you know, Martin, no-one's ever asked me that before?'

'Really?'

'I'll have to think about that.' And so he did. And then, at last, the voice gentle in the darkness:

'It's not as if he ever had the chance to discuss matters of state with me. But I don't think he'd have been ashamed. I dare say he'd have explained the need to burn the Reichstag, or invade Czechoslovakia, he'd have explained the concentration camps. I'd have only had to ask. I honestly think he was just doing his best. Muddling through, like the rest of us. Trying to be a good person. I'm not saying all his decisions were *good* ones. And that he didn't get carried away. Who wouldn't, you or I in the same position, who wouldn't? But people think of him as a demon. And he wasn't. Well, we know what demons look like. And he was just a man, you know. Just a man with his dog. Like you and me. Well, like you, anyway. Yes,' Woofie said softly, as he thought about it, 'Adolf Hitler was a lot like you.'

'Thanks,' said Martin, and meant it.

'Why didn't you want to ask? No-one else has left it for so long.'

'I just supposed,' said Martin, 'that it must get a bit irritating. Always being in his shadow. People never asking you about *you*, only the famous person you hung out with.'

There was silence for a while.

'But I was in his shadow,' said Woofie. 'I was his dog.'

More silence. For a while Martin thought Woofie had fallen asleep. And then:

'Thanks, though. That's really thoughtful of you. Thanks.'

'That's okay.'

'You're my best friend.'

'You're my best friend too, actually.'

'We can cuddle if you like,' said Woofie. 'I don't mean anything funny,' he added hastily, 'just cuddling. If you like. I mean, there's nothing funny about a man and his dog sleeping together, is there? If you like.'

'I'm not sure there's room,' said Martin slowly.

But there was room, if Martin leant into the wall a bit. And Woofie wasn't very big, he curled into the spaces left by Martin's body as if they'd always been designed to fit together like this. If Martin laid against Woofie sideways he was rubbing against his soul, but face on he could feel his fur, and the warmth of it was more comforting than he could have believed.

'Good night, Martin,' said Woofie softly.

'Night.' And within minutes Martin heard the snoring that told him his new best friend was asleep. And he had only a few moments to realise how reassuring that snoring was, how much gentler than Moira's, how much more *right*, before he was fast asleep too.

★

'Good news,' boomed the demon. 'You're being transferred tomorrow morning.'

Martin tried to work out how he should respond. 'Oh,' he said eventually.

'Well, don't look too bloody grateful,' muttered the

demon as he stomped off. He was having a rotten day already. Since he couldn't shave the tufts of fur round his horns, he'd set about plucking them out with a pair of tweezers. This only succeeded in drawing attention to them still further, and the overall effect made him look a bit camp. He rather suspected – accurately, in fact – that behind his back in the staff room the piss was being ripped out of him quite mercilessly.

Martin wondered how he should break the news to Woofie. But that was the one thing he needn't have worried about. He was waiting for him when he got back, the body unnaturally tense. Martin thought he might have been crying.

'Hello,' said Martin, for want of anything better to say. Then, 'I'm sorry.'

'Was it something I've done?'

'No. No, that's not it.'

'What is it? Just tell me what I ever did that was wrong.'

'It's not you, Woofie. I'm sorry. It's *me*. It's my fault, it's me, I'm sorry.'

Woofie looked so sad, with his big dog watery eyes boring into him. Martin wished he'd be angry – bark at him, nip at his ankles, *anything*. Anything other than this quiet and this hurt.

At last Woofie said, 'Is it because of the whole Hitler thing?'

'No,' Martin hastened to reassure him. 'It's because you're a dog.'

Silence.

'It's nothing personal.'

Silence. For the first time since he'd met him, the dog made Martin itch.

'So it's not because of what I've done. It's because of who I am.'

'Well. Yes. Sort of.'

Woofie stared at him. 'That's sick.'

'Yes,' said Martin. 'It is. I'm sorry. Is there... is there anything you'd like? Anything I can do, or...'

'No,' said Woofie. And then he changed his mind. 'Yes,' he said gently. 'I'd like my bunk back. The top bunk. My favourite bunk. And all to myself. Please.'

So that night Martin slept on the bottom bunk. Woofie hadn't spoken again all evening, and he stared up at the little sagging mound from the bed above him, and he wanted to touch it, *prod* it, just to get some sort of reaction, even to have an argument, just so there could be an ending to this. But he didn't dare. In the morning, Woofie seemed kinder, even to have forgiven him.

'Best of luck, Martin,' he said, and offered him his paw.

'And best of luck to you too,' said Martin warmly. 'And thank you for everything.' He made to give him a little pat on the head, but Woofie stepped backwards instinctively. He'd gone too far.

Martin's new roommate was a human called Steve. Steve was very polite and almost friendly. He didn't give Martin the top bunk, but really, why should he have? It turned out that Steve was a rapist. But, as he told Martin, it had only been the once, and it was a long time ago, and he felt very sorry about it. And besides, Martin didn't know the child in question, so he decided not to be bothered about it.

And Steve let Martin hang out with his friends. At the shopping malls, at the cinema, at the bowling alley. It had been a long time since Martin had spent time in the company of humans, but he soon adjusted. Inevitably there were occasions when he'd almost run into Woofie: the first time was a bit awkward, and he could see that Strudel would happily have jumped at his throat. But Woofie barked something in his ear, and with bad grace Strudel turned his back on the fair weather human and got back to his ten pin bowling. And that was the worst of it. After that, whenever Woofie or Martin realised the other was near, they'd simply not make eye contact as discreetly as possible. It was never not embarrassing – but it was an embarrassment that Martin could cope with with increasing ease as the years went by.

It may have been on his third or fourth Christmas in Hell that Martin received a card. 'Something addressed just to you,' said Steve with a sniff, as he handed it to him. Most of the cards would say 'Steve and Martin', and one or two might be for 'Martin and Steve'. Never Martin on his own.

'Dear Martin,' it said. 'Long time no speak!' And the exclamation mark dot was a happy face, just trying a bit too hard.

Martin took a breather from hanging the tinsel – Christmas decorations are always very popular in Hell – sat on the bunk, and read the card properly.

Dear Martin,

Long time no speak! How are you? It's been ages.

This is just to wish you a merry Christmas, and let you know an old friend is thinking of you. Because we are old friends, aren't we? I know we've lost touch, but I didn't want you to think there were any hard feelings. There really aren't. I only want the best for you. I only ever did.

I catch sight of you every once in a while, and I keep meaning to say hi. But either you look very busy, or I'm very busy, so it never happens. Which is so silly! We must catch up one day. That'd be lovely.

All the old gang are well, and send you their best.

Lots of love, Woofie.

And the 'love' had been written with a hesitancy that made it all the more emphatic. And then, in a different pen, there was a P.S.

P.S. Look, if you're up for it, and I'm sure you have other plans anyway – but still, no harm in asking. We're thinking of having a party at New Year's. Nothing very fancy. If you've nothing better to do, and I dare say you have, do come along!

And then, same pen, but written later:

I miss you.

Martin reread it. He wondered if he should send a card back, but really, Steve took care of all that.

'Shall I hang it with the others?' said Steve, reaching out for it.

'Sure,' said Martin. 'Why not?'

And then, some time in January, the announcement came.

Hell was getting too full. There simply wasn't the space for many more damned souls. So someone had decided they had better send an emissary to God, and find out what should be done about it. And when he came back, the emissary said that he'd looked long and hard, and it turned out there *wasn't* a God after all. He wasn't sure there had never been one, but if there had, he certainly wasn't around any longer. And this had caused a bit of consternation – who was going to solve the overcrowding problem now? – until it was realised that his non-existence solved the problem in itself. After all, it seemed hardly fair to be damned for not believing in God if it turned out you were, embarrassingly enough, absolutely right.

Martin was told he could leave immediately.

'Where am I going now?' he asked. 'Heaven?'

It turned out he was going to Surrey.

★

The day the dead came back to Earth was one of mixed emotion. Everyone seemed overjoyed to see their loved ones return; there were a lot of tearful reunions and a lot of street parties. The government weren't really sure how to react until they realised that on the whole everyone was very happy about it, so decided in the end they were happy about it too, and acted as if it had been their idea somehow.

But no-one had quite anticipated that the dead weren't going to go back again. Had it just been a flying visit, then fair enough. But by the end of the week most people really felt that they'd outstayed their welcome. The government picked up on the prevailing mood and quickly asserted that they'd *never* been happy about this, that they'd had nothing to do with it whatsoever. And even that new measures would soon be taken against this unwanted invasion of the immigrant dead.

When Moira first saw Martin again, she hugged on to him so hard that he thought she'd never let go. She'd still kept all his clothes and belongings, suitcases full of old nick-knacks that she couldn't bear to part with. She said everyone had told her to give them all to Oxfam, and when she'd refused, well-meaning friends had got rather angry with her and worried about her mental health. 'So I got rid of them. I've been very lonely. But I knew you'd come back for me.' Martin was touched. He didn't want to point out he wasn't back because of her at all but a bureaucratic quirk. 'Thank God you came back.' And that there was no God to thank, and if there had been there wouldn't have been the bureaucratic quirk in the first place. They made love that first night, and for several nights afterwards, something they hadn't done much even when he'd been alive. And it was surprisingly nice, but not so nice that he minded when they sank back into their usual platonic domesticity. Within a week he was lying in bed next to her, blocking out the snoring with ear plugs. And in the dead of night, when all was still, he could almost believe that he'd never died and been to Hell at all.

At work, however, they weren't so accommodating. For old time's sake, the boss generously gave Martin ten minutes out of his hectic schedule. 'And it is hectic at the moment!' he told Martin. 'Busy, busy, busy! Well, I needn't tell you. You know what this job's like, you've lived it!' Martin was told that they would *love* to take him back, they *really* would, but they just *couldn't*, not in the present climate. 'You can hardly expect to take a leave of absence that long, without any warning, and expect your job waiting when you get back.' And besides, the boss admitted when pressed, not everyone felt very comfortable working alongside corpses. Not the boss himself, of course. But even Martin must admit, being one himself, there was something funny about the way they looked. Whereas once he'd been respected for being so reliable, so solid – now, in a very real sense, he wasn't solid any more.

See the dead face on, and you could just about pretend they were normal – that they were living and breathing like all right-minded people. But turn your head to the side and you could see the soul, that all of this skin and bone and individuality was just a façade. It wasn't a thing anyone liked to be reminded of. And it meant that the dead were instantly recognisable. By and large the living would ignore them, some would glare at them with obvious hostility; there were even incidents of target beatings by gangs, but outbreaks of violence became rarer when it was realised you couldn't do anything to kill them. Within weeks the worst that a dead man walking the streets might expect was to be spat at.

Once upon a time, if you'd wanted to separate a race from the rest of society, to make a people stand out and be judged, you'd bring out the yellow badges, you'd start shaving heads. Woofie's masters had done it. But no-one had to isolate the dead; with their souls flapping about for all to see, they'd done it to themselves. And the worst part of it was that they felt ashamed of each other too. A dead man seeing another dead man would turn his eyes in the same way as a living man would; once in a while there might pass a look of sympathy, of understanding, but they'd hurry on, not daring to talk to each other, not daring to reach out and say 'I am one of you'. As if for fear that the vacancy in their eyes, the deadness that had so much more to do with the heart no longer beating and the lungs no longer filling, might be what you looked like too.

Moira didn't like to mention to Martin the fact that he was very nearly two-dimensional. But even her discretion started to irritate him. She'd try to ignore it at first, then to make it go away. She'd make him his favourite meals, fried and fatty, and she'd say it was because she loved him, that she'd missed cooking for him, that she just wanted him to be happy. But he saw the truth.

'You're trying to fatten me up!' he said.

Moira blushed, and admitted that she thought he could do with a little padding out, his body might lose some of its *flatness*, if only just...

'But the food doesn't go anywhere. I eat it, then it vanishes. It doesn't stay in the stomach, I don't have a stomach. For God's sake, I can't even shit.'

Moira cried, and said he'd changed, he'd never used to be like this, he didn't love her any more since he'd changed.

And he wanted to say of course he'd bloody *changed*, he'd died, hadn't he? He'd died and gone to Hell, and she *hadn't* died, she'd just stayed cosily alive, what had they got in common any more? He'd gone to Hell and fallen in love with someone else, he'd fallen in love with Hitler's dog. But he couldn't say this, even Martin couldn't be so cruel. It gave him no pleasure to see his widow crying all the time, it just revolted him. 'I can't even shit,' he repeated numbly. And then, as an afterthought, 'I want a dog.'

Moira pointed out he didn't like dogs. He was allergic. They made him itch.

'I want a bloody dog,' he said, 'that's all I bloody want. Get me a bloody dog.'

They called the new dog Wuffles. Martin had wanted to call it Woofie, but couldn't quite do it, it was all a bit too raw. Maybe in time he'd rename it, he didn't suppose the dog would mind. Moira had wanted to name him Snoopy, but Martin calmly pointed out that was a bloody stupid name, Snoopy was bloody stupid. Besides, Snoopy was a bloody beagle, wasn't he, and this wasn't a bloody beagle, it was a bloody dachshund, you stupid bitch, it was a bloody sodding buggering dachshund. And then he kissed her gently on the forehead and told her she'd done well, it was a lovely dog. And if she could now bloody well leave him alone to play with it.

The thing was, Wuffles didn't like Martin. He *loved* Moira — he'd wag even at the sound of her voice, wait outside the bedroom door for her, was never happier than when she was petting him or stroking him or touching him. From Martin he'd just recoil. Martin supposed he could see his soul, the same as everyone else. And he quite respected the dog for it — at least it wasn't a hypocrite.

Still, he'd try. He'd take Wuffles out for walks — *drag* Wuffles out for walks, pulling the resistant pet by the leash until it had no choice but to follow. They'd go to the woods. Martin would find a nice fat stick, and throw it.

'Fetch,' he'd say.

Wuffles would just stare at him blankly.

'Fetch,' Martin would repeat. 'Fetch the stick.'

Wuffles would look to where he'd thrown it, look back at him, then lie down. He wasn't going to chase after a stick. Not for *him*. For his mistress, anything. But for this flattened dead man, the dog refused to follow orders.

One day Martin dragged the dog to the car instead. They drove far far away. He opened the passenger door. Threw the stick he'd brought with him.

'Fetch,' he said.

But Wuffles made it clear that if he wasn't prepared to chase a stick in the woods, he certainly wasn't inclined to do so on the hard shoulder of a motorway. So Martin pushed the dog out of the car anyway, and drove home without him.

Moira was distraught. 'It's all right,' he reassured her.

'He'll be fine. There are lots of rabbits for him to chase out there, probably. And if he *isn't* fine... He was a good dog, he never bit or scratched. He loved his mistress. So at least he can be sure he's going to a happy place.'

Martin never saw Wuffles again. But when a few weeks later he opened the door to a dachshund who had rung his doorbell, he thought that his unwanted pet had tracked him down. That he'd have to take him on an even longer journey up the M1.

'No, no,' said the dog. 'It's Woofie. How are you, Martin?'

'Woofie,' repeated Martin. 'I didn't recognise you.'

'Well, it has been a long time. Can I come in?'

Once inside, Martin asked his old friend whether he wanted anything to eat or drink, wanted to sit down, wanted anything, really. 'No, I'm fine,' said Woofie. 'Nice place you've got here. Very cosy.'

'It's not mine, it's hers,' said Martin. 'It's nothing to do with me. How did you get out of Hell?'

'Oh, they're letting all sorts out now. I wouldn't be surprised if the whole thing hasn't shut down before too long.'

'And how did you find me?'

Woofie smiled. 'A dog can always find his master. If he wants to hard enough.' He let his words sink in. 'You do know you're my master, don't you?'

'Yes,' said Martin.

'I only think sometimes. That if I'd met you. Right from the start. If I could have given my love to *you*, and not to Hitler... I'd never have gone to Hell in the first place. I could have been great. And I think, too, that with me there beside you, you wouldn't have gone to Hell either.'

'No,' said Martin.

'We could have been great, you and I. We could have been great.'

And Martin kissed him. And he knew that what he was

kissing was a dog, and that it was a *dead* dog, but it was all right, it didn't matter, it was all all right.

'Let's get out of here,' said Martin. And he got his coat, locked the front door, and put the keys through the letterbox. He considered leaving a note for Moira – but really, what would he have said?

And man and dog went out together. They had no money for food, but that was okay, they had each other. They'd sleep when they got tired, on park benches, in shop doorways, wherever they could cuddle up. And people would avoid their gaze on the street as always, and some would still spit at them. But together man and dog had a strength. They would stare down their persecutors. They showed they weren't ashamed.

Early one morning they were shaken awake by an angry farmer. They'd decided to spend the night in an empty barn – the straw was scratchy but warm.

'Get out!' screamed the farmer, with a fury that was mostly fear. 'Get off my property!' And he jabbed at them with the handle of his pitchfork.

'There's no need for that,' said Martin. 'We're going.'

'You're filth!' the farmer shouted after them, as Martin and Woofie walked to the door with as much dignity as they could. 'You dead bastards. You dead perverted... and on my property! You're filth!'

And, quick as a flash, Woofie turned round, leaped up, and tore out his throat.

Martin looked as surprised as the farmer, who, eyes bulged in shock, reached out for a neck that largely wasn't there, before pitching forward on to his face. The blood sprayed across the straw.

'Oh my God,' said Martin, bending down. 'He's dead.'

'Good,' said Woofie. 'Now he knows what it feels like.'

'Oh God, oh shit,' said Martin.

'Come on, let's go,' said Woofie.

★

They walked in silence for a while. Martin kept looking at his hands, and every time he did – yes – they were still smeared with blood.

'Oh God,' he said at last. 'It was an accident. It was an accident.'

'It wasn't an accident,' said Woofie. 'I all but bit his head off.'

'Oh God.'

Nothing more was said for a few minutes. A man walked towards the pair down the footpath. He gave them the customary glare of hatred and contempt. And then he saw Martin's bloody hands, and the way Woofie openly snarled at him, and there was blood there too, right on the jaws – and he hurried on.

'What's going to happen to us?' Martin moaned.

'What are they going to do? Send us to Hell? Been there, done that.'

'Oh God.'

'Hitler was like this, you know,' said Woofie. 'The first time he had a Jew killed. Well, that's it, Woofie, he said. If I'm right, then I have made a blow for justice and the common man. But if I'm wrong... If I'm wrong, I'm damned forever.

'And do you know what I said? What I whispered into his ear. Oh, he couldn't hear me, of course. Dogs can't talk. But I whispered it anyway.

'"If you're going to Hell for one Jew, then why not for a hundred? For a hundred thousand. For six million. If you're going to be damned anyway, at least be damned for something impressive." I'd rather be damned for being Hitler's dog than Goering's. Do you understand?'

'Yes,' said Martin. 'Oh God. I understand. Oh God.'

'There isn't a God,' said Woofie. 'Stop saying that.'
'Sorry.'

'Do you realise by how much the dead outnumber the living? Do you? Thirty to one. And yet *we're* the outcasts. We're the ones who are spat at. How long do you think that can go on for? How long *should* it go on? Martin?'

'What?' said Martin weakly.

'How long?' demanded Woofie.

'I don't know.'

'Then think about it,' said Woofie sternly. 'For once in your life, just think.'

And Martin thought.

'But we mustn't hurt them, Woofie,' he said eventually. 'We can't do that. We should just put them... I don't know. Out of harm's way.'

'For their own good.'

'For their own good, exactly. Somewhere safe. Promise me, Woofie. Promise me, whatever happens. That what we'll be doing is good.'

Woofie promised, Martin smiled, and on they walked. A man and his dog, making plans.

Favourite

The first surprise was that my younger brother phoned me at all. The second was what he had to say.

'Mum's dead,' he told me, and burst into tears.

'Now calm down,' I said. 'Are you all right?'

'Of course I'm not all right! Mum's dead, and I'm never going to see her again. I had all these chances to see her, so many chances, and they're all wasted now, I used them up.'

'Okay,' I said. I took the phone to the armchair, settled down. I could see this conversation lasting quite a while. 'Okay,' I said again, once I'd got myself comfortable, 'how did all this happen? Tell me about it.'

'The leukaemia,' he said. 'The leukaemia's finally got her.'

'I didn't know she had leukaemia,' I said.

'Yeah, well, there's lots that you didn't know. I suppose I just didn't want to tell you. I suppose you've had it easier.' From anyone else that might have sounded like a rebuke, but not my baby brother. He was just telling the truth.

'It all sounds pretty horrible,' I said sympathetically. 'Leukaemia's a rotten way to go, I expect. So it wasn't a shock, or anything, was it? I expect, at the end, you must have felt a bit of relief.'

'Well, yeah,' he admitted, 'but that's not the point, is it?'

I supposed not, and he began crying again.

'When did all this happen?' I asked.

'Last Thursday.'

'Thursday? Mum's been dead the best part of a week, and you wait until now to tell me...'

'I've been feeling very down,' he said. And although I couldn't see him, I knew he'd be sticking out his bottom lip, just like he always did as a kid. You'd tell him off, he'd know he was in the wrong, and out would pop that lip, right on cue.

'It doesn't matter,' I said, although it did, and I couldn't help but feel a little hurt. 'I just would like to think you could turn to me if you needed me. I'm here for you, sweetie. I love you.'

'I know,' he said. 'I know you are.' The bottom lip was still out, I could all but hear it on the end of the phone, quivering. 'Oh, Connie,' he said. 'I'm never going to see Mum again. I'm *never* going to see my own *mother*... *again*.'

There was a lot more talk like this, but eventually he hung up – he was calling long distance, he said, and it was peak rate, and he'd forgotten he'd been the one who'd phoned. He thanked me again for listening, it had helped him a lot. I didn't think I had helped him, actually, he sounded just as upset as before, but I didn't like to argue. Before he went he threw me one last titbit. 'It's not fair,' he said. 'That's what gets me. I'm the youngest. You and Anthony, you had bags more time to spend with her than I did. It's just not *fair*.' And there was no answer to that.

After he'd gone I paced around the house for a bit, and then decided I really ought to call Anthony. I couldn't remember the phone number, and had forgotten where I'd written it down, so it was nearly an hour before I dialled the number and heard his voice.

'Hello?' Anthony said.

'Hello, Anthony,' I said, feeling strangely formal. 'It's Connie.' And added, unnecessarily, I hope, 'Your sister.'

'Oh, hello, Connie,' said Anthony.

Anthony was my elder brother. I spoke to him even less frequently than I did my younger. The last time would have been the previous Christmas. First we'd stopped doing presents, then we'd stopped the visits and the cards. The phone calls were the only thing we had left, a few awkward minutes grabbed some time between the Queen's Speech and the turkey.

'I just heard from Kevin,' I said, quickly, as if eager to explain why I was breaking protocol and phoning him when there were no decorations up. 'He said Mum's dead.'

'Yes, I know,' said Anthony. 'He called.'

'Oh,' I said. 'When was that?'

'Let me think,' he said, and did. 'Thursday.'

I felt put out by that, and couldn't help but give a disappointed 'oh.' And then a 'he's only just phoned me,' which sounded a bit pathetic and needy.

'We're brothers,' he said. 'Brothers are closer, aren't they?' And I thought, no, not really. You've never much liked Kevin, he was eight years younger than you and when we were kids that was too much of a gap, at best he'd been an irrelevance, at worst something you could be cruel to. I was quite certain Anthony didn't like Kevin. And I'd been pretty sure Kevin didn't like Anthony either.

'How did he sound to you?' I asked.

'How did he sound to *you*?'

'Well,' I said, 'he was pretty upset.'

'Oh, for God's sake,' said Anthony, 'he was unbearable with me. Crying down the phone. He just has to get a grip. Did he cry for you?'

I slipped right back into the role I'd played when we were children, lying for Kevin, trying to protect him. 'Not very much.'

'I bet he did,' said Anthony. 'I bet he cried during the whole call. He has to get a grip. I mean, what is he now, twenty-eight? He has to get himself some sort of job, some sort of life, he can't be the baby forever. I said to him he should pull himself together, find a job, stop being so irresponsible.'

'You didn't say all that to him on Thursday, did you?' I asked. 'I mean, Mum had just died and everything...'

'Yeah, maybe I went a bit too far. But I'm right, Connie, you know I am. He was always Mum's favourite, right from the start she spoiled him. I think he'll be better off without her, stand on his own two feet. And no, I didn't say *that* to him on Thursday,' as I began to interrupt, 'I'm not totally insensitive.' He thought for a bit. 'All this grief,' he said, 'it's so ridiculous. All this wailing and gnashing of teeth. I shan't be that way when Mum goes, I tell you. I'll show a little more dignity.'

I asked him what he meant.

'I've been through so much worse already,' he reminded me. 'It's nothing to lose a parent, you *expect* that. But my wife died, and she was so young, and *that's* difficult.'

I'd bumped into Anthony's wife by accident out shopping only a few months ago. We'd had a coffee and a chat. She'd told me that getting away from Anthony was the best thing she'd ever done. 'He means well,' she'd said, 'but, God, he's bitter.' Of course, I hadn't told Anthony I'd seen her. It wouldn't be right.

'How's work?' I asked, changing the subject.

'It's all right,' he said shortly, meaning it probably wasn't. Anthony worked as a beautician and hair stylist – and, in fact, wasn't gay, and resented the idea people thought he must be. He carried that resentment into work every day, his wife had told me, which is why all the women's faces he worked on always came out the other end looking so grumpy. As she said, bitter.

The change of conversation, the attempt at ordinary pleasantries, was a signal to both of us that this phone call had outlived its usefulness. Before I hung up, I told him what Kevin had said about it not being fair. 'Well,' said Anthony. 'It isn't, is it?'

FAVOURITE

★

The next day after work I drove over to my parents' house. I'd been the only one of their children not to have moved far away, but I still didn't visit as often as I should have. I rang the bell, and Dad answered the door.

'Hi, Dad,' I said. 'How are you?'

'Oh, I'm fine,' he said, and gave me a kiss. He let me in, took my coat, asked me how work was going.

'I heard about Mum,' I said. 'Kevin phoned me.'

'Oh dear. Was he very upset?'

'He was a bit.'

'Did he cry a lot?'

'Yes.'

'Oh dear.' Dad bit his lip. He'd never really known what to do about Kevin – he'd been Mum's favourite, not his. 'Well, I suppose that's to be expected.'

'Is Mum around?'

'Yes, of course,' said Dad. 'She's in the kitchen. I think she's making gingerbread men.'

When I went into the kitchen, Mum looked happy enough. She was covered in flour, and wearing her favourite apron, one that Kevin had given her for Christmas a few years back. 'Hello, sweetie,' she said. 'I'm making gingerbread men!'

'Yes, Dad told me.'

'I think this lot are going to come out rather well.' Mum only made gingerbread men when she was trying to avoid thinking about other things. The times we were going through our school exams, the time when Anthony was in hospital to have his tonsils out, that horrible month when she found out Dad was having an affair and for a while we all thought the marriage might be over... we'd all been drowning in gingerbread men back then.

'I heard about you and Kevin,' I said.

She stopped dead in mid-bustle. Smoothed down her

apron. 'Yes,' she said quietly, 'I thought you must have.'

'Leukaemia.'

She nodded. 'Very unpleasant. Is he all right? No, don't tell me. I'm better off not knowing.'

There was quiet for a while. She managed a smile, but it was a little guilty, I think. Then clucked her tongue, said to herself, 'Well, that's that over,' and got back to her baking. I watched her for a bit.

'It must be hard for you,' I said eventually. 'Kevin was always your favourite, wasn't he?' It was meant to be sympathetic, not be an accusation of anything, but it all came out wrong.

'Your father and I didn't have favourites.'

'Not Dad, maybe. But you did.' I remembered the little story she'd once told us. How she'd always wanted a boy, more than anything in the world. But she'd got it a bit wrong with Anthony, he was her first child, she was awkward, maybe tried too hard. She knew she'd do better with her next one, but that had been a girl, me. So she'd given it another go, and out had popped another boy, her perfect boy, this time he was just right. And as we watched she'd lifted him in the air, because Kevin was still very young, and given him a kiss.

'God, did I tell you that? God, that's awful. I was joking, Connie. Sweetie, it was a joke.' But it wasn't. And Anthony had known it, and I had known it, and by God, Kevin had certainly known it. 'Poor Kevin,' she said.

'He'll be all right.'

She nodded briefly, went back to the oven.

'It just seems so cruel,' I said suddenly, and my voice may have been a bit too loud. 'The whole lot of it.'

'Is there anyone special in your life yet?' she asked me. 'Some man? You'd be so pretty if you tidied yourself up more. Put on a face, did something with your hair.' But I didn't want to talk about that.

FAVOURITE

She gave me a gingerbread man, still warm from the oven. I bit off its head. It was too sweet, she'd put too much sugar in, she always put in too much sugar. 'Nice?' she asked, and I nodded. 'I wish you could take some of these to Kevin,' she said with a sigh. 'I know how much he loves them. They're his favourites.'

I said nothing. Ate the rest of its body, torso and feet, just to be polite.

'Will you be going to my funeral?' she asked me. 'Will you see Kevin there?'

'I doubt it,' I said. 'I doubt he'll even invite me. Why should he?'

★

But, in fact, Kevin did invite me. I was quite taken aback. But I checked at work, found out if I did some early shifts I could take the day off without eating up my holiday time, I was happy with that. When I got to the church I looked around for Anthony, but couldn't see him anywhere. With a little buzz of pride I realised that Kevin had invited me and not his elder brother, that I was favoured after all. It put me in a good mood for the whole service.

Mum had never been a religious person, and nor, I thought, had Kevin. But he stood up at the lectern and read some very nice verses surprisingly well. They were all about death and life and eternal love. I doubt he got the proper meaning across, but they certainly sounded very sad and moving. I told him so afterwards, and he thanked me for coming.

'It's a pretty good turn-out,' he said. I looked around, but didn't recognise anybody. Friends of his, I supposed, or a part of my mother's life she'd shared with him not me.

'How are you holding up?' I asked. He nodded solemnly, as if this were an answer. He looked weak and vulnerable, but then he always looked weak and vulnerable. Right from the start he was the sort of person who invited you to protect him or to persecute him. Mum and I had protected — just about everybody else had gone the other way.

I remembered the way he was bullied at school; he'd always be coming home with a grazed knee, or his lunch money stolen, always crying. I'd decided to do something about it. One day I'd waited for the most regular of the bullies, laid into him with my fists, secured from him not only the money returned with interest but the promise he'd never bother my brother again. Kevin had been furious. From now on, he'd told me, crying, always crying, his life would be a living hell, the kid who needed his *sister* to protect him. 'It'll be humiliating,' he'd said. 'I hate you.'

Now we stood together, and I didn't know what to say to him, and he didn't know what to say to me. And I smiled kindly and took his hand and squeezed it, and he nodded solemnly once more, doing the whole orphan thing. Being so brave. And I felt a flash of Anthony's impatience, for God's sake, you're twenty-eight years old, and watched with disgust as he began to cry. 'It'll be okay, sweetie,' I said.

Mum's body was in an open coffin. She'd been made up and looked pretty, if a little exhausted. I suppose that's what the leukaemia does to you, it must really wear you out. She certainly looked older and feebler than the Mum I knew. I said you could see it had been a struggle for her, she was at peace now. And Kevin said he knew it was best for her, it was selfish to wish she was still alive, but he couldn't help it, he *was* selfish.

The body was cremated, and Kevin was told he'd be given an urn of her ashes. 'Would you like some of them?' he asked me kindly. I thanked him, of course, but told him the ashes should be his.

'Have you seen her recently?' Kevin asked me in a hush. 'I mean, is she all right?'

FAVOURITE

He shouldn't have asked, and he knew it. What could I say? 'Mum's dead, Kevin,' I told him. 'They're putting her in an urn.'

★

It was maybe a year and a half after that that Mum died for Anthony. There'd been a cyst, apparently, and everyone had assumed it had just been a trivial thing. But the cyst had grown and ripened and spread and felled Mum dead in her tracks. Thank God it had all been a lot quicker than the leukaemia. I sent Anthony a letter of condolence, and his thank you reply was very stiff and cool – but since everything Anthony ever wrote to me was stiff and cool, I read nothing untoward in that. And then, a few months later, he phoned me up and said he was unexpectedly in the area – could he buy me lunch?

There was a little Spanish place he said was his favourite, we could have tapas. And it struck me that only Anthony could have favourite restaurants for a part of the country he never visited. I made an effort before going to see him, washed my hair, put on make-up. I knew he wouldn't mean to, but he'd sit there critically and judge me, it was his job. I arrived and he was already there, drinking a glass of wine. He was immaculate, of course; he looked sleek and groomed and shiny, and I thought he'd probably plucked his eyebrows.

We automatically shook hands, then realised we were related to each other, and kissed cheeks.

'You look well,' I said.

'So do you,' he replied smoothly. And frowned. 'But if I could give just a little advice...?'

'If you want.'

'Clear and simple is a good choice, keep it natural. But you can overdo simplicity, you know. You could stand to wear a little more make-up.'

'I am wearing a little make-up. Look.'

'I'm just saying. There's a pretty face under there, it just needs bringing out.'

'Look. I've got lipstick on, and some mascara too. Look.'

'All right. I'm just saying. It's just that the boyish look suits some, and not others. And you could stand to look a little more feminine.'

We ordered some tapas. He spoke to the waiter as if he knew him.

'I'm sorry about Mum,' I said. 'How are you holding up?'

He thought about this, finished chewing, then plucked an olive stone from his mouth. 'It's been very odd,' he said. 'I actually cried. Do you know, I actually cried.' He shook his head, in some amusement. 'It's true. I'd wake up, tears would be coming out of my eyes. Streaming. Most peculiar.' He popped another olive into his mouth.

'Only to be expected,' I said. 'Mum being dead and everything.'

'Why is it expected, do you think?' And he bored those eyes in to me. Yes, the eyebrows were plucked, I'm sure of it.

'I don't know,' I floundered. 'You'll never see her again.'

'Oh, no, that's not it,' he replied, and I felt put in my place. 'I'm always prepared for that. Every time I'd see Mum or Dad, I'd always say goodbye to them as if for the last time.'

'Right,' I said.

'Because you just don't know, do you? What's around the corner. That comes of having a wife who's died so tragically. Even the two of us, when we say goodbye after lunch, I'll say it as if it's for the last time. Just to be sure.'

'Right,' I said.

'No, all the crying was something more *psychological* than that. More profound, from within me. You know, when I reached my eighteenth birthday, I thought, that's it, I'm an adult now. Things will change, I'll feel different. I'll *be* different. But I wasn't different at all. And then, when I got married. Now it'll happen, I said to myself, walking up the aisle. I took Nicola to the Algarve, and for the whole honeymoon I waited in vain for adulthood to kick in. With Mum's death, I think maybe I'm finally there. I feel, at last, that I'm a man.'

I was going to say 'Right' again, but stopped myself. I watched as he deliberately skewered another olive on to a stick, aiming exactly for the very centre.

'And my work's improved,' he said. 'I think there's a new maturity to it. Everybody says so. Well, most people anyway. The ones who count. They say that within my celebration of life there is now a recognition of death. It's very fulfilling. I mean,' he went on, twisting that stick into the olive, twisting it on ever further, 'there's still room for development. I'm interested to see what will happen to me when Dad dies. But, you know, I'm happy now,' and he *did* look happy, actually, and that was a good thing, I supposed, 'there's no rush, I can wait.'

'You should call Kevin,' I said. 'Have you called Kevin? Now you've both lost Mum. It's something you should talk about.'

'I must do that,' he agreed.

'And we should keep in touch. You know. More than we do.'

'We must.'

He smiled at me indulgently then. 'That's the thing about you,' he said. 'You always want to put people *right*. Make sure we're just a happy family.'

'Oh,' I said. 'Do you think so?'

'You're just like Mum. You look a lot like her, you know. Or you could do. If you just took a bit of care, wore a bit of make-up, did a bit of work to your hair.'

'Yes, you said.'

'I could help you make more of yourself. I'd be glad to.

Free of charge, of course. Well, save materials. Free labour.'

And all I could think of was Mum lying there in that coffin, all made up to look pretty before they'd burned her, her hair neater than it had ever been in life, her cheeks pink and lips red to hide the pallor – because she must have been pale, mustn't she, underneath? And it was silly to care because it wasn't as if she were *my* Mum, not exactly. And I couldn't tell Anthony, because it wasn't exactly his Mum either.

'Thanks,' I said. 'I'm fine.'

'I know you are, sweetie,' he said. 'I was just saying.'

I offered to pay for the meal; it seemed only fair, since he was the one who was mourning. And he insisted we go Dutch. We kissed on the cheeks as brother and sister would do, and then somehow ended up shaking hands anyway, that all went wrong somehow. And he said goodbye to me as if it were the last time he'd ever see me, and I wondered if it might be.

*

Mum and Dad died for each other at exactly the same time. There was a car crash. The policeman told me they wouldn't have felt anything.

I tried phoning Mum, because I knew she'd be upset. And when there was no answer I began to get worried. A few hours later she called me from a phone box. 'It's a bit embarrassing,' she said. 'But obviously your father and I can't live together any more. Can I stay with you for a bit?' I picked her up in the car, and she flung her arms around me. 'Oh God,' she said. 'It was horrible. Our heads passing through the windscreen like that. I don't care what that policeman said, it really hurt.' She reached out and took my hand tightly; I couldn't steer the car properly when she did that, so I pulled over to the kerb – I didn't want her dying in a car crash twice the same night. 'You're the only one left, Connie,' she said. 'You're the only one left.'

FAVOURITE

I don't have a big house, but it has a spare bedroom, and I'd naturally assumed it could easily accommodate any visitors should the need arise. But in all the years I'd lived there the need never had arisen, not even once. It was full of boxes: old school books, clothes I hadn't worn since I was a girl, dolls. I did my best to stick everything into the back of the wardrobes. 'Thank you, sweetie,' said Mum. 'Oh, thank God for you, thank God for you.' She took my face in her hands gently, stroked my cheeks. 'I'm going to need more wardrobe space,' she said.

For the next few days she didn't do very much. I'd go off to work in the morning, and by then she'd already be up, watching television, spread out on the sofa in her nightie. When I'd come home she'd still be there, watching repeats of soaps she'd already seen earlier that day. Sometimes she'd perk up and ask if she could help with anything – tidying up, making dinner. Then she'd cry with frustration when the vacuum cleaner wasn't the same model she was used to, or when the cutlery wasn't in the drawer she'd expected.

'Your father was a wonderful man,' she'd tell me from time to time. 'There never was a man more kind, more gentle, more tender.'

Of course, I went to see Dad. It was no surprise he didn't want to know how Mum was getting on, I knew how awkward that would be. 'I've found someone else,' he said. 'I'm happy.' I didn't tell Mum, but she found out anyway. 'That shit,' she said, and began to sob. 'He was just waiting for me to die. He couldn't keep his hands to himself even when I was alive.'

It seemed churlish to mind Mum staying with me. She did her best. She tried to keep out of my way, not make any mess. And the insomnia wasn't her fault, and certainly she could hardly have crept around the sitting room any more quietly. But it was knowing she was there at all. I'd lie in bed at three in the morning, seething as I heard her tiptoe down the stairs, open cupboard doors in the kitchen so gently. Cry to herself in such a quiet selfless little sob.

One night I got up to confront her. She was in the kitchen making gingerbread men. There was flour everywhere, flour that I knew she'd have cleared up before morning. She started at me guiltily.

'I didn't disturb you, sweetie,' she said. 'I didn't, did I?'

'No,' I answered truthfully. 'What are you doing?'

I helped her to cut the little gingerbread figures, I put a smile on every one. 'What do you think happens when we die?' she asked me suddenly.

'I don't know, Mum,' I sighed.

'I mean, when you die to *everyone*. When there's no-one around any more who knows who you are. No-one who remembers you. Do you think we just vanish forever? I think we do. I think we must do. If there's not even a *memory* of who you were, what choice do you have?'

'I don't know.'

'Oh, Connie,' she said, and stroked my face with floury fingers. 'Oh, sweetie. Who's going to remember you? How many people can you die for, when no-one knows who you are? Oh, sweetie, what ever will become of you?'

One day I came home from work to find a man sitting with Mum on the sofa. He was in his early thirties, wore glasses. She told me she thought he was reasonably good looking, and I could do much worse than let him take me on a date. I didn't know what to do. I apologised to the man, and he said it was all right — in fact, he *was* rather lonely, and he wasn't doing anything that night; my mother had showed him a photograph of me when I was a little girl, and he appreciated I had aged in the mean time, but I was certainly his type. So he was up for the date if I was. He told me his name was Mike, and he shook my hand — then, as an afterthought, he kissed me on the cheek as well. I took Mum to one side and asked her where she'd found him, and she said it was the supermarket. For a moment I thought she meant she'd *bought* him there and I was confused, but Mum laughed and said, 'No, sweetie, he's a greengrocer there. He was serving behind the counter. Seriously, sweetie,' she whispered, confidentially, 'he's a catch. You can never have too much fruit.'

Mike waited as Mum took me to the bathroom, did my make-up, fluffed my hair. 'You look so pretty,' she cooed.

We went to a local restaurant. Mike didn't buy one of the expensive wines, but the one up from the one up from the house red. It was quite nice. I realised that life selling fruit in a supermarket was more interesting than I'd have imagined, and he had many funny anecdotes to tell me. I tried gamely with anecdotes of my own, and he was a gentleman and laughed at the end of each one. Then he took me home and shyly said he hoped we could do it all again some time soon. And I said okay, and gave him my phone number. Then Mum said, no, no, what's the point in that? 'Don't spare my blushes!' she laughed. 'I think you should go to bed together right now! Life is fleeting, and you never know when it'll be over. Just grab every chance you've got.'

We made love, and it hurt a bit, but not as much as I was expecting. Mike said sorry, and I could see he really meant it, so I told him it didn't matter. I thought he might then have gone home, but he didn't. We lay there together for a while, not really knowing what to say. 'Your Mum's nice,' Mike ventured at last. I told him I was going to the toilet, and he said okay. And I asked if he wanted anything, a drink or anything, anything to eat, but he said he was okay.

Downstairs my Mum was making gingerbread men. She was very excited.

'I think he's lovely,' she said. 'He reminds me of your father. So kind, so gentle, so tender. But it's up to you, sweetie. What do you think?'

She went to the cupboard I used to keep my baked beans in, and took from it a plate. She plonked a gingerbread man on to it. 'Here,' she said. 'Fresh from the oven.'

I bit its head off. 'You've been using salt again, Mum,' I said.

'Have I?'

'Yes. It looks the same as sugar, but really, it's not.'

But I ate the rest of the body, just to be polite. And I cried.

'Ssh,' said Mum, and took me in her arms. 'It's okay, Mummy's here. Mummy's here.' And at that I couldn't help it, I cried all the louder. 'You were always my favourite,' she told me. 'You were, baby. Sweet sweet baby. All the others have gone, but you stuck by me. I love you. And I'm never going to leave you, not ever.'

I thanked her, said good night.

Mike was upstairs, no doubt waiting for me to come back to him. And Mum was downstairs, committing unspeakable acts in the kitchen. So there was nowhere for me but the garden. It was cold and I couldn't stop shivering. And I delivered up a prayer, of sorts, my first since I was a child. For anyone who might care to listen.

Oh God, I don't know how I'll react. How I'll mourn, whether I'll cry, whether I'll go numb. Whether it will be a passing fleeting moment, and then all will seem as it was. You can't know until it happens to you. But please, God, please. Let me know what it feels like. To find out how I'll be when my mother dies.

Static

When Ernest went into his sitting room that morning, he found that his television set had been bleeding.

Of course, it could all have been much worse. What if he hadn't gone into the room until the afternoon? What if he hadn't gone into it at *all*? He didn't always feel like the sitting room. It had too many memories, none of them unhappy, but you don't always want memories crowding in on you, even the happy ones. Besides, it seemed silly to have a room just for *sitting*, if he wanted to sit there was always the kitchen, there was a perfectly good chair in there, and the stove made the place warm.

But he *did* go into the sitting room, and he was alarmed. 'Oh dear,' he said. He might easily have come out with a swear word, so great was this alarm, but he always rationed his swearing for really special occasions. 'Oh dear,' he said again.

Not to overstate the problem: it wasn't a *puddle* of blood. It didn't look as if anyone had been butchered on the carpet. But you'd have been hard pushed to have written it off as anything as trivial as a speck either. It sat there, bright but undramatic, probably no more than three centimetres in diameter, already drying into the faded taupe with which Lizzie had chosen to furnish the room so many years ago. With a heave that hurt his joints, Ernest bent down and looked at the underside of the television. He couldn't see where the blood had spilled from, and it might only have been a little cut – certainly it didn't seem to be bleeding any more. Better to be safe than sorry, though. He fetched a Tupperware bowl from the kitchen, and stood it on the red patch so it could collect any more drops. And then he thought for a bit, removed the bowl, and scrubbed at the red patch hard with a wet flannel and soap. All he succeeded in doing was in making the patch a little pinker and a lot bigger. He sat the Tupperware back down in the middle of it, and had another think. And he went for the telephone.

The repair shop said they didn't like to make home visits – couldn't he bring the television in? And Ernest explained that he was elderly and had a bad hip. Then the repair shop said that they'd send someone out, would Thursday afternoon be any good for him? And Ernest said that it was really terribly urgent, his television set was *bleeding*; admittedly, the blood had stopped now, but there *had* been blood, and that couldn't be good, could it? And the repair shop went silent. Then said they'd send someone round right away.

That said, the repair man was a disappointment. 'I can't repair it.'

'Oh dear,' said Ernest. And 'Why not?'

'Well, look at it,' said the repair man. And gestured, as if it were obvious. 'Look how *old* it is. That must be twenty years old, that must.'

'It's forty-eight years old,' said Ernest. He knew exactly when he bought it. It was in that month just after he'd married Lizzie.

'Forty-eight?' The repair man was incredulous. 'My parents aren't that old! You've got a TV older than my parents!' And he laughed with the gusto of the very young who cannot conceive the world in any way predates them. Ernest smiled politely. He wondered if the repair man, with his young parents and his stud earring and his blonde apology for a beard, thought he was an adult. He probably did.

'Is it blood?' asked Ernest. 'I thought it might be oil.'

'TVs don't run on oil,' explained the repair man. 'That

doesn't make any sense.' Ernest wondered whether the blood made any *more* sense, but didn't say anything. 'They're not cars,' the man went on, almost sneering. 'You don't put *petrol* in them. That's not the way they work, is it?'

Ernest said he supposed not. 'What should I do with it now?'

'We can sell you a new TV.'

'I don't want a new TV.'

'I don't mean *new*. I mean, second hand. But very good, you know. Cheap.'

'I'd rather you fixed this one.'

The repair man sighed. 'Look, even if I could... and I can't, you know, it's the parts, they won't make the parts any more. It'd be very expensive, you'd be better off starting from scratch... I mean, I'm amazed it still works at all. It does work, does it?'

Ernest didn't watch television very often. It hadn't picked up ITV in years, but that didn't matter, neither he nor Lizzie had ever watched anything on the commercial channel. BBC1 had recently become something of a snowstorm – you could see that *something* was there, but it was hard to hear what over the gale of fuzzy spots. BBC2 still worked, though. Most of the time.

The repair man made another offer – he could give Ernest a bit of a discount. They had lots of TVs in stock, he explained, they were a TV shop. Had a whole raft of new features, too, like plug-in aerials and remote controls and this new thing called colour, Ernest wouldn't believe he'd lived without them. And Ernest was very polite, said no thank you, and steered the man to the front door. He paid the call-out charge, said goodbye, then went back to the sitting room.

'Well, that didn't do much good, did it?' Ernest had never spoken to his television before, and even as he did so he told himself he shouldn't make a habit of it. But it seemed somehow appropriate. And 'Oh dear!' he said, still not swearing. 'You're bleeding again!' And so the TV was. Three spots of blood now lay in the bowl, small but very red and unarguably *there*.

Ernest wondered whether it'd been his fault. Maybe he'd used the television too much, he'd exhausted it. And then he reasoned that he hadn't watched it in days, that couldn't be it. Then he worried himself all over again – maybe he'd not used it enough? Maybe it was because he'd neglected it. He stood in front of it, aching with indecision. 'Sorry about this, old boy,' he said. 'Hope this doesn't hurt.' And he turned it on with a click.

It took a few seconds for the screen to warm up. He turned the knob, and found himself BBC2. It wasn't crystal clear, but then, it was never crystal clear. The snooker was playing, and Ernest always enjoyed the snooker. He thought he should keep watching for a bit, try to ascertain whether or not the picture had got worse since he'd last watched it. And to see whether that snooker chap could pot the pink. As he sat down in the armchair he idly wondered whether it was Ray Reardon – but then, he supposed Ray Reardon had probably retired, which was a shame as he'd always liked Ray Reardon. The man who may or may not have been, but on balance probably wasn't, Ray Reardon did indeed sink the pink, but came unstuck on the black – and Ernest never did find out what his name was, or whether he won the game at all, because he soon dozed off.

He woke to the telephone ringing. And felt immediately guilty. Dozing off in front of the television! That's what Lizzie used to do – he used to laugh at her a lot for that. Always affectionately, she knew that, she'd always laugh back. Her mouth would be open, and she'd be snoring, drowning out whatever was being broadcast. And Blackie, she'd be cuddled up to her mummy, seeing Lizzie on her favourite armchair was a red rag to a bull, Blackie could never resist, she'd have to cuddle up, and she'd put her paws over her face as if she felt ashamed to be caught dozing like that, and she'd be snoring too, it was like a little whinny. With Lizzie snoring and Blackie snoring you really couldn't hear a thing, and Ernest would laugh at them, and they'd laugh at him too – well, Lizzie would, anyway. And here he was, doing the same thing! The shock of the phone, and the rush of the memories, made his head spin for a moment.

'Dad? Are you all right?'

'Yes. Yes, I'm fine.'

'Are you sure?'

'Why wouldn't I be?'

'You took a long time answering the phone. I had to ring off, try again.'

'I was asleep,' said Ernest, and immediately regretted it. Now Billy would think something *was* wrong.

'But it's two o'clock, Dad.'

'I know,' said Ernest, who didn't, in fact.

'In the afternoon. You shouldn't sleep in the afternoon. You know what the doctor said.'

'No,' said Ernest. 'What did the doctor say?'

'He said you shouldn't sleep in the afternoon.'

'What is it you want, Billy?' asked Ernest, hoping it came out kindly.

'We haven't seen you in a while. The family. We thought we might pop over.' And see if I'm all right, Ernest supposed. 'And see if you're all right,' added Billy.

'I'm all right, I'm always all right,' said Ernest. 'Have you been speaking to anyone? Has anyone said I'm not?' Ernest thought hurriedly. 'That repair man. You've been speaking to him, haven't you? Did you phone him? Or did he phone you?' Ernest couldn't work out what was worse – that his son would be employing a repair man to spy on him, or that a repair man would be spying on him and telling his son by his own volition.

'I don't know what you're talking about, Dad. What repair man?' So Ernest told his son the whole story. It just spilled out, and even as he told him he knew he should shut up, keep it all to himself, it'd only be more reason for Billy to come over.

'Bleeding?'

'That's right,' said Ernest. 'It's not bleeding much,' he added hastily, but the damage was done, he knew that.

'That doesn't sound right, Dad. Televisions shouldn't be doing that sort of thing. How's the video? Is that still playing all right?'

Billy had given his parents a video recorder for Christmas a couple of years back. Well, as Billy had said at the time, it wasn't *really* a present – it was just an old cast-off, the family were upgrading their own, and rather than just sling it out he thought that Mum and Dad should have it. They'd never used the video recorder. It was in a box in a cupboard somewhere, Lizzie had packed it away, she took care of things like that. She had taken a look, and said that the television was too old – it wouldn't have the right lead sockets or what-have-yous, but that they mustn't tell Billy, it had been such a kind gesture. Ernest agreed, but he hadn't thought it was a *particularly* kind gesture: it wasn't as if they had any videotapes to play on it anyway.

Ernest thought for a moment about all the things Lizzie had put in cupboards – he wouldn't have said they had that many cupboards, but Lizzie had certainly put away a lot of things over the years, so they must be bigger than they looked. He'd have to go through them one of these days, see what was there. The thought gave him a sick feeling in his stomach, and he was almost pleased to realise his son was still talking nonsense down the phone at him. If he listened to Billy for a bit, it might distract him. 'What?' he said.

'I said it sounds like it's broken. You should sling it out, Dad. Just sling it out.'

Ernest said he didn't want to sling it out; there was far too much slinging out going on these days. What with Blackie and with Lizzie and with, what was her name, Jane, yes, Billy's own wife, Jane, you can't keep slinging out everything when it gets broken, what about trying to mend things for a change? And Billy started to argue, and Ernest said he was sorry, and he *was* sorry, it was none of his business, of course. And he looked around desperately, trying to find something urgent that could end this phone call, get him free – and that's when he saw the television actually *leak* blood, no longer dripping in red but spattering out thick and black, and Ernest hung up on his still protesting son.

The blood lay in the bowl, warm, sticky like tar. Again, Ernest wondered whether it really *was* blood, but when he put his fingers to it they came away with the same tell-tale coppery smell. BBC2 was still playing snooker, but there was interference now; the picture kept strobing, as if it were in distress. Ernest quickly turned the knob to off, and then looked at the ailing set uncertainly.

He wished Lizzie were here. He often wished Lizzie were here, of course – but never quite as fiercely as he did now. She would know what to do.

On the shelves in the bathroom were a whole array of medical bits and pieces, most of them bought by Lizzie so probably now out of date. Ointments, tablets in all different colours, painkillers which should be taken with food, some to be taken after food, and some others to be taken as far away from food as possible. These were all useless, of course; if his television didn't have the right socket for a video recorder it clearly wouldn't have one for paracetamol either... And for just a second Ernest wondered whether his thoughts were altogether rational, but then he found a whole box full of plasters and put the worry out of his head.

Lying beneath the television set, Ernest struggled with the sticky covering of the bandages, trying to pull them from first one finger then another. He still couldn't see where the TV's wound was, but the greater quantity of blood at least gave him a better clue, and he liberally pasted all possible areas with

Elastoplast Extra. He felt a growl in his hip, and he crawled out on to the carpet, caught his breath.

Lizzie would have been so *good* at this. She was never fazed by the sight of blood, not hers nor anybody else's. He remembered that evening when Blackie had started coughing. She'd been dozing on the armchair as usual, making her little whinny snore – she'd been dozing and whinnying rather a lot recently. At first they had both laughed, because the coughing had woken her up, and the expression on Blackie's face had been so scandalised – she'd always been a haughty dog, and that such an ugly sound could have disturbed her, and, even worse, that the ugliness had come from *her*, clearly appalled her. When they'd seen, though, that she'd been bringing up gobbets of black, and Ernest had begun to panic – what was going on, what should they do? – it had been Lizzie who had taken charge.

'Go and get a towel,' she'd said. 'Go on.' And she'd cradled Blackie's head, wiped the glop from the mouth without a qualm, comforted her.

'Is it blood?'

'It's bile. And bring me the phone. I'll need to call the vet.'

They'd stroked Blackie to calm her down, but she'd clearly been in some distress. And whenever they thought the coughing had stopped, that their dog had miraculously been restored to full health, off she'd start again. 'I've made an appointment, first thing tomorrow morning,' said Lizzie. 'We'll have to keep Blackie in the kitchen tonight, close the door so she can't get out.'

'Why?' asked Ernest.

'It'll be easier to clean up the bile if we keep her off the carpets.' He'd carried Blackie down the stairs in his arms; such a big dog, such a dead weight. Normally Blackie would have cried and scratched to have been shut in the kitchen: she'd both cry and scratch merely to be shut away from her rightful place, at the foot of her mistress' bed. But she didn't make a sound of complaint as he'd closed the door on her, leaving her her favourite rug and her favourite cushion and her favourite squeaky toy. In the morning Ernest had opened the door, and Blackie didn't appear to have moved from where he'd put her. Just for a moment he had a horrid thrill that she might have died in the night, just unexpectedly, she might have saved them the bother of having to... – but no, when he'd called her name she'd raised her head slowly and incuriously. By the side he'd seen further traces of brown black gunk.

'It's the kidneys,' the vet had said. 'There's really not a lot you can do.'

'Oh dear,' Ernest had replied. His wife hadn't said anything, her mouth set in hard decision.

'Can't you fix her?' Ernest had gone on. 'I mean, I know there are kidney transplants and things...'

'Not for dogs,' the vet had said. 'Blackie could struggle on for a while longer, I can give some medicine. But the quality of her life would be drastically reduced, and she'd never be comfortable. I think you should strongly consider putting her to sleep.'

Ernest had made to protest, but 'Do it,' Lizzie had said suddenly, and he'd shut up.

The vet shaved Blackie's foreleg, and all the time Lizzie and Ernest had stroked Blackie's head, reassuring her. 'It'll all be all right soon,' Lizzie had promised her, 'no more pain soon.' There was a syringe, it was in and out, and before Ernest could change his mind, before he could say, no, wait, this is wrong, we're not trying *hard* enough, Blackie seemed to stiffen then slouch, and her eyes grew harder. And greyer. And wetter, or maybe that was just Ernest's.

'They didn't have the parts,' he said to himself now, as he put a fresh Tupperware bowl underneath his poor sick television. 'They didn't have the parts, you see.'

The next morning the plasters had come off. The blood had seeped through, made them sodden, and they'd fallen into the Tupperware with the rest of the matter. At first Ernest was heartened to see that the blood was red rather than the thick black he had been dreading – red seemed so much healthier somehow – but to counter that, there was rather a lot of it. When he'd gone to bed, the bowl had had no more than a few specks in it. Now it was lapping at the rim.

Ernest found a bigger bowl – one from Lizzie's brief but fondly remembered cake-baking exploits. And he was washing out the older one when the doorbell rang. He was still in his pyjamas, and wasn't expecting anyone.

'What do you want?' he asked Billy. And it wasn't just Billy either – there was his wife, and those two children.

'I told you I was coming today, Dad,' said Billy. 'Don't you remember?' He stepped past him into the hallway. Billy looked frail and a little feminine, and not unlike his mother. It hurt Ernest to be reminded of how she'd once looked; and it hurt him even more to see her features cut off, rearranged, and pasted so inaccurately upon this ineffectual man standing there. Standing so awkwardly, as if he were a stranger, as if he wasn't even his son. 'You're in your pyjamas,' Billy pointed out.

'I know.'

'Yes. Right.'

And after him trailed the two kids, barely concealing their disinterest, and then the wife. Oh, no, she wasn't the wife, was she? That was the other one, before he'd got the divorce.

'Hello,' he said to the children, wishing he could remember their names. 'Hello,' he said to the woman who wasn't the wife, and therefore wasn't called Jane, he mustn't do that again.

'We've brought you presents, Dad,' said Billy. And, indeed, the two children were each laden down with a cardboard box. 'Put them down here, kids. That's it.'

'Would you like a cup of tea?' asked Ernest.

'I'll make some tea,' said the woman, and disappeared into the kitchen. This left Ernest with nothing to do but be drawn back to the cardboard box, which, he supposed, was the idea. 'What is it?' he asked, when Billy opened the first one and took out some gadget or another.

'It's an answering machine,' said Billy. 'You know, for the phone.'

'Why would I want one of those? Nobody phones me anyway.'

'That's not true, Dad,' Billy said patiently. '*I* phone. I phoned yesterday, and you didn't answer, I had to phone again. And it would make me feel much happier, if that happens again, that I could leave you some sort of message. No, don't do that,' he said to the children. Ernest didn't want to see what they'd been doing.

'If it makes you happier,' said Ernest, not, he felt, unreasonably, 'then it's more a present for you than it is for me.'

'If you say so, Dad,' said Billy with a sigh. The woman emerged from the kitchen with tea. 'Shall we go to the sitting room?' he suggested.

'When can we go home?' one of the children asked its mother, as it flopped into Lizzie's favourite armchair.

'Ssh,' she said, 'not yet.'

'But I'm bored,' said the child.

Ernest stole a look of worry at the television set in the corner. He supposed it was resting, and if it were sick, it needed all the rest it could get. He didn't want its peace disturbed.

'And here's your other present,' said Billy, with just a hint of playfulness. 'Ta-dah!... There you are, you see.'

It was another television. Newer, shinier, smaller, and a damn sight more plasticky than Ernest's own.

'I don't want it,' he said.

'Come on, Dad,' said Billy.

'I already have a television set,' said Ernest.

Billy laughed. 'This old thing?' he said. 'You had that when I was a kid!'

'Forty-eight years,' said Ernest. 'I bought it the month after

I married your mother.' It had been one of those little peculiarities in her that he had never got used to. Most of the time she'd been so practical, so careful with money. But once in a while, right up to the end, she could surprise him, could indulge in a bit of a 'splurge', as she'd called it. The honeymoon had worked out cheaper than either of them had expected. Both of them supposed that the sensible thing would be to put the leftover in the bank, but Lizzie had grinned at him a little wickedly and said, 'Well, we *could* be sensible. Or we could just splurge out and buy ourselves a television set.' He'd laughed, but she'd been serious, and so that's what they'd done.

He supposed it was the thing that had kept their marriage fresh. All those little surprises. 'I've got cancer,' she told him one day.

'Oh,' Ernest had said. 'Oh dear.'

'I don't know what can be done, my darling. I don't know, I'm sorry.' And she'd kissed him with so much tenderness, and he'd hugged on to her. He hadn't wanted to cry, he had to be the strong one – and, looking back, he supposed she'd felt exactly the same thing.

A few nights later he had been lying next to her in bed. After that hug they hadn't mentioned the cancer again. As if ignoring it would make it go away. 'You know I'm dying,' she'd said to him in the dark.

'I don't want to think about it.'

'I know, darling. I know you don't. But it's there.' And she had held him close. 'I'm not going to get better, you know. I'm only going to get worse. I've been reading up on it in the library.'

'You think you know everything,' Ernest had said to her, not without spite. 'But you don't.'

'It would be easier, it seems to me,' she'd said there, in that thick darkness, and it had seemed to Ernest to get thicker, to make his head swim, 'if we just stopped it now. You could, you know. You could give me a kiss. Say goodbye. And put a pillow over my face. And that'd be an end to it.'

Ernest couldn't, and wouldn't, he said he couldn't and wouldn't...

'I know, darling,' Lizzie had said, perfectly placidly. 'I know.' His poor Lizzie, who'd never even smoked, dying of lung cancer.

'I'm popping into the garden for a cigarette,' said the woman who wasn't married to his son.

Billy waved her on with a smile. One of the kids ran out after her. The other was too busy wrecking the armchair. Billy moved towards the old television, sick and neglected in the corner, and no doubt trying to sleep through all the noise. 'What are you doing?' asked Ernest. 'No.'

'I'll unplug this one, put the new one in. My God, it's ancient. You said yourself, it was broken.'

'I said it was bleeding,' said Ernest. 'Not broken. Look at the bowl underneath.' But, of course, he'd just changed bowls, this one was fresh and clean. 'I said, don't!' he said, more sharply, and pushed his son back. Billy looked at him in surprise. 'I bought that with your mother,' he said. 'I bought it with her.'

Billy stared at his father for a few seconds. 'I miss her too,' he said at last.

'You have no idea,' Ernest almost spat. 'You have no idea. You had your wife, what was her name...?'

'Jane.'

'Jane. That's it. And then you threw her away. Her and the grandchildren, you threw her away. And now you're here with another woman, and children who aren't even your own. It's all fucked-up.'

'Dad, Graham's still here, he can hear you...'

'It broke your mother's heart. It did. She said to me, why'd he sling her out, Ernie, why'd people just sling things out? She never forgave you, you know. Not ever. Not even when she died. The last thing she said to me, and I was there when she died, I stood over her, she said, I'll never forgive Billy, never.'

Billy breathed long and hard through his nose. Ernest wasn't sure that the boy was going to cry, or punch him. One or the other, he thought, do get on with it. This kid of his, this kid who had kids of his own, and kids that weren't *even* his own, what sense did that make? This kid of his, who looked like Lizzie reassembled by an idiot.

But the Lizzie look-alike didn't cry or punch; he finished that funny breathing thing, then bent down, back towards the television. 'We'll just swap these over,' he muttered. 'Then we'll get out of your way.'

'Don't touch it,' said Ernest. 'You'll hurt it. It's sick. If you must give me a television, for God's sake, put it in the kitchen.'

Billy straightened up. 'You don't want a TV in the kitchen, Dad. This would be much more comfortable. With your nice chair, look...'

'There's a perfectly nice chair in the kitchen. I want it in the kitchen. Leave my old set alone. Put the new one in the kitchen.'

'William, just put it in the kitchen, if that's what your father wants.' So said the non-wife, stepping back through the door.

'Right,' said Billy. 'Of course. Fine.' And he picked the new TV up, carried it downstairs without another word.

There was silence in the sitting room as Billy worked away. 'Thank you, Jane,' said Ernest at last. The woman ignored him.

'Mummy, I'm bored,' said a child, who may or may not have been the one called Graham.

'I know. We'll be going soon.'

And indeed they were. 'That's the answering machine plugged in,' said Billy. 'And the TV. Shall I show you how to...'

'No,' said Ernest. And he closed the door behind them.

Ernest all but ran upstairs to the sitting room, as fast as his hip would allow. 'I'm sorry,' he said to the television. 'We're alone now, I'm sorry.' There was still no blood in the Tupperware bowl, and for a moment Ernest thought his poor patient had come to no further harm.

But when he turned it on, he saw that the snowy fuzz that was BBC1 was no longer just grey. It was red too. And getting redder. All the dots of static fizzing in a frenzy, punching themselves against the screen, punch punch. And Ernest watched with horror as the screen began to bulge out under the pressure of them all, and a hairline fracture traced its way from one diagonal to the other, and then...

...out gushed the blood. Red and black, thick and coppery. It exploded out, over the room, over Ernest. 'Oh dear!' he cried, and then, because he'd let it out anyway, so why not? 'this is fucked-up, this is so fucked-up.' It felt good to say that, to admit that truth at last after so many months of pretending everything *wasn't* fucked-up, he felt so much better as he stood in the centre of his sitting room, his pyjamas dripping with the blood of an elderly television set. He even allowed himself a smile.

Ernest waded over to the TV. 'Do you feel better now too?' he asked, putting his arms around it soothingly. 'There, there,' he assured it, 'better out than in. It'll be all right now.'

He felt he should dry himself off, but knew too that it would be heartless to abandon his poor television when it was suffering so badly. How would it look, him being so perfectly well and happy, to be worried about his personal *cleanliness* of all things? And it wasn't unpleasant, this sensation of blood, on his hands, in his hair, even in his mouth: it warmed him, calmed him. So he stayed in the room. The blood could wait, all this mess, the gunk over him, over the new answering machine (was it?), over Lizzie's favourite armchair... He wouldn't abandon the invalid now.

He remembered how, near the end, Lizzie had begun to cough blood. 'Never mind,' she would say, as she would dab at her mouth as pertly as if she'd been eating chicken, 'never mind.' But, of course, he *did* mind, how could he not mind? Sometimes in the night he'd wake next to her, find her pillow drenched in the stuff. She'd asked him to move to the spare room so she wouldn't disturb him, but he'd refused – he'd wanted to take care of her. And he'd only relented when she'd said it was for her sake, God, please, Ernie, it was for her, it was for *her*.

She'd come to his room one night. Stood at the doorway, silhouetted against the landing light. 'What is it?' he'd said. 'Are you ill?' Which was, even looking back, a pretty stupid thing to say.

'I don't want to go back to the hospital tomorrow,' she'd told him. 'I'm sick of it. If I go in,' she'd said, 'I'll never come out again. This isn't how I want to go.'

'No, Lizzie,' Ernest had said, and then cried. 'I can't do it. I can't do to you... what we did to Blackie. I can't.'

She'd climbed into bed next to him. 'No,' she'd said. 'We could just go, though, couldn't we? Just get in the car, and go.'

'Go where?' he'd asked.

'Somewhere else. Anywhere else. And never come back. No more hospitals. We've got lots of money saved, we could have a splurge, couldn't we? We could splurge it all out.'

'It'd kill you,' he'd said.

'Yes,' she'd said. And she'd said no more, but spent that night with him after all. And the next morning he'd taken her to the hospital, just as they'd always planned. And Lizzie had been right – she had never come out again. He wasn't there when she'd died a few days later. He'd wanted to say goodbye, be beside her bed when it happened. But you can't be there all the time, can you?

Ernest woke up, found he'd been dozing again. His television was on, but the static behind the split glass looked reassuringly grey and normal. His stomach growled. 'I'm going to get some lunch,' he told the television. 'But I shan't be long. I promise.'

STATIC

In the kitchen he found some bread, and some butter. Ideal for a sandwich. He also found the new television set. He'd forgotten it was there. 'Ugly little thing,' he told it.

He picked up the remote control, turned it over in his hand. And then – and he didn't think he'd pressed any of the buttons, but he supposed he must have – the television sprang into life. It was clear and it was sharp and it was *colourful*, my God, there was more colour on that screen than you got in real life, but principally it was *loud*. 'Shut up,' he told it in alarm. He stabbed at all the buttons he could find. He didn't hit the one to turn it off, but he did succeed in turning down the volume. 'Keep quiet,' he hissed at it angrily. 'There's a sick television up there, and it's better than you. And I don't want it getting any funny ideas that you're its replacement. That wouldn't be nice, would it?'

And then he fell silent. Stared at the screen, his sandwich forgotten.

It was BBC2, and it was the snooker. The table was green – oh, it was such a green, you could imagine this was a snooker table only played upon by angels! Someone was lining up a shot, and with the perfect clarity of the image Ernest could see it wasn't Ray Reardon, this man was young and short and scruffy even in his dinner jacket.

But it was the *balls*. The white and the black and the pink and the... so many reds, so many, all like the apple the Wicked Queen gave Snow White in that film, but nine of them, so plump and shiny and red you could *bite* them. He looked at the red on his arms and clothes, the blood from upstairs, and it wasn't nearly so impressive.

The snooker player sank a red. And then a brown. Everyone applauded. Ernest had to sit down.

All these years, with his black and white television, he'd never been able to tell the red and the brown apart. It had caused some confusion. But Ernest knew that you could work out which was which, so long as you were patient, so long as you used your brain. The brown was put back up on the table, but the red, once potted, stayed down. Not knowing whether the player had miscued as he cannoned into the ball in question lent an extra soupçon of suspense to the game that Ernest knew he wouldn't have experienced seeing the game live – his snooker, in all its monochrome ambiguity, was *better*. And here was this new television. This colour television. Making it all so *easy*. Explaining everything. As if its viewers were children. Idiots. To be patronised. Ernest looked around the kitchen, considered the rows of Tupperware bowls he'd been using. No, he'd need something heavier. The saucepan, that would do. He drove it hard into the television screen. Into all its colour and clarity and condescension. It fizzed and popped and banged.

When he went back upstairs, he saw that the snooker was playing on his black and white set as well. Though he hadn't changed channels, as far as he could remember. But it was a different game – look, this time it was Ray Reardon. That was good. Ernest preferred Ray Reardon.

'Hello, Ernie,' said Ray Reardon.

'Hello, Ray,' Ernest replied.

'I'm in such pain, Ernie,' said Ray. 'So why don't you take that saucepan of yours, and smash my snooker-playing face in? Put me out of my misery.'

'All right,' said Ernest. And he lined up the saucepan, as if swinging a golf club. Come on, Ray gestured, come on, it'll be all right. And then frowned as Ernest lowered his arms.

'I can't,' said Ernest.

'Why not? You murdered that TV downstairs.'

'I know,' said Ernest. 'But I can't. I can't let you down the way I did Blackie. Or the way I did Lizzie, either. I suppose,' he added, a little embarrassed, 'I love you, Ray. I suppose that's what it is.'

Ray stuck out his bottom lip, then rubbed his eyes, making boo-hoo gestures. Then he winked to show he was only kidding. And his face faded back into the snowstorm.

'Bye, Ray,' said Ernest.

He dropped the saucepan. He knew he wouldn't be needing it. And he went close to the television, knelt before it. He put his arms around it the best he could, gave a squeeze to its unyielding bulk. 'I love you,' he said once more. And he slept happily, a man who feared he'd never love again.

He was woken once more by the sound of the telephone. He stretched his arms painfully, surprised he'd slept in so uncomfortable a position that soundly. He decided to ignore the ringing, cuddle back next to the television, and snuggle. But the answer phone kicked in.

'Hello, Dad? It's me. Look, I... I'm sorry about yesterday. I wasn't in the best of moods, I think, the kids were driving me mad, and I... I'm sorry I snapped at you. It was silly. Look, I don't know but... I thought I'd come over again. Just me this time. Would that be okay? Just the two of us. We haven't talked, not really, I thought we could talk. About Mum, I miss her, you know, I know you do too... well, obviously. And I can show you how your new TV works. Hope it's okay, it's not new or anything, just an old cast-off, didn't want to sling it out. And I'll take away that old one for you. ...I love you, Dad. Don't say that enough. Must say it more, I think. Love you.'

And the voice clicked off.

'Shit,' said Ernest. He looked at the room, all the blood, all the mess. 'Shit,' he said again. And then, 'Come on, we haven't much time.'

The television set wasn't as heavy as he'd expected. But as for all the leads and plugs – it was like spaghetti back there! Ernest didn't have time to work out which wire connected to what, just pulled out as many as would set the television free, and hoped for the best. With a grunt, both arms stretched as far around the box as they could go, he took it from the table on which it had sat so many years. And puffing, ignoring the pain in his hands, in his back, the *screaming* pain in his hip, he edged towards the stairs. One foot shuffled forward, then the other. It looked as if he were dancing.

When he reached the top of the steps he was able to balance the television on the banister rail, catch his breath. It reminded him of having to carry Blackie to the kitchen, all those years ago. 'But I'm not taking you to the vet's,' he promised the set. 'You'll see.'

Halfway down, the doorbell rang. Ernest froze. Peering through the banisters, he saw the face of his son fractured and misshaped through the frosted glass.

'I'm not letting them take you now,' whispered Ernest.

Billy had parked out front. But it was all right. It was fine. Because Ernest's car was in the garage. And he could get into the garage by the side door, and if he were quick, Billy would never notice. His muscles protested – they couldn't *go* any quicker. But Ernest insisted. No-one else was going to be slung out. There was going to be an end to all slinging.

'Dad?' he heard, as Billy knocked against the door. 'Dad, are you in there?'

But Ernest had reached the car. He had to set the television down for a moment as he fumbled for his keys – he marvelled at his thin fingers, how bruised and squashed they now looked. But he didn't feel anything, not a thing. With a final heave, he lifted the television into the passenger seat. Smiled at it. And then, with a sudden wave of concern, he pulled the seatbelt across it. 'Got to keep you safe,' he said, as he climbed in next to it.

'Where are we going?' the television didn't ask.

'Somewhere else,' said Ernest. 'Anywhere else.' He turned the ignition, the car pulled out of the garage. He thought he caught sight of Billy's surprised face at the front door, but he couldn't be sure – he was travelling *so* fast, after all, so very fast, never faster. 'And we'll never come back,' he said, as he put his foot flat on the accelerator, and sped away onward to freedom.

No Looking Back

They brought in his wife's body, already stiff as a board, and the music was turned off and the dancing stopped and some of the guests gasped and one of them even screamed. And the first thing he thought was, oh God, that's *ruined* the wedding party, and we haven't even cut the cake yet. And the second thing was, what about the honeymoon, those tickets were non-refundable, could he go with someone else, no, no, that would look terrible. It wasn't until the third thing that it hit him – he should be much much more distressed, surely, this was his wife who'd just died, his *wife*, they'd only been married a few hours, he should feel *something* – and then he realised he was shivering, and he must be in shock, that would explain why these thoughts were so callous, and he was so grateful he began to cry. He cried so much they had to give him a sedative to shut him up.

'There's nothing we could do,' a bridesmaid told him later. 'She was dancing barefoot, got bitten by a snake.' He hadn't known she was the type to go barefoot dancing – he supposed that was one of the things he would have learned about her in the years of wedlock, years now denied him.

Everyone was very sympathetic for a while. At work his boss would smile at him fondly, and his boss wasn't the sort to do *anything* fondly, let alone smile. And the honeymoon *was* refunded after all; it wasn't company policy, but the woman on the end of the phone had felt so sorry for him that she'd pulled a few strings. And, so very easily, life went on. He felt bad, of course – but mainly he felt bad because he didn't feel much worse. He'd expected that the grief would have left him reeling, but on the contrary he was quite composed, even (but only behind closed doors) flippant. At the funeral he said his piece very well, and everyone in the church looked at him kindly – even more so, he thought, than they had when he'd got married in the same spot just ten days previously.

'It needn't be the end,' said his mother-in-law confidentially. He'd been doing that wake thing of making sure he took condolences from everyone, and he'd thought he should give his in-laws-that-weren't a bit of extra attention.

'What do you mean?' he asked.

'You can get her back from the Underworld. It's true,' she said, perhaps because he looked so unconvinced, or just plain reluctant, 'I got Arthur back. Didn't I, Arthur?'

'She did,' said Arthur, his mouth full of sausage roll.

'You go down to Hades, get ferried across the River Styx, pass Cerberus, the two-headed dog who guards the gates of Hell. And make your case to Pluto, ruler of the dead. You can't *keep* doing it,' she added. 'You can't just bring back *anyone*, willy-nilly. You have to give a good enough reason. But, you know, he's fair.'

'And what was your reason?' he asked.

She looked surprised. 'Well, I *loved* Arthur, of course. So much. I mean, I couldn't live without him. Could I, Arthur?'

'She couldn't,' agreed Arthur, and smiled, his lips flecked with crumbs of pastry and sausage meat.

'You could get our daughter back,' she said, and prodded him affectionately. 'It has to be you.'

So he went to the entrance to the Underworld. It wasn't hard to find. It wasn't the sort of thing that would be marked on a map, but everyone seemed to know where it was. And everyone seemed to expect, too, that he'd be going down there, that as grieving husband this was his mission. 'Good for you,' they'd say, 'bring her back safe!' His boss smiled and patted him kindly on the back and told him that once he'd returned they should talk about a nice promotion; a healthy raise and more responsibility was just what a family man deserved.

He followed the tunnel into the bowels of the earth, round and round and deep and down. He was ferried across the River Styx. He passed Cerberus, the two-headed dog who guards the gates of Hell. He saw a lot of the damned, some in chains, some in lakes of fire, their faces indistinct. I wonder if I'll have to make a speech, he thought, or whether it'll be like a quiz, with multiple choice answers. And before he knew it he was in front of the king, the ancient god, so huge he blocked out the sky.

'Speak,' boomed Pluto. 'What does one who is living seek from those who are dead?'

'I was hoping to get my wife back.'

'Can you see this wife of yours amongst the sea of souls around us?' And as he looked, he realised that no, he couldn't, that all the dead looked the same, grey and drab and featureless, it would be impossible to... oh, no, there she was waving, 'Here I am!' she cried, 'over here!'

'That'd be the one,' he said, and pointed.

'Very well,' said Pluto. 'Make your case. But know this. You have one chance to convince me of the power of your love. If you fail, she will forever stay within my realm and you shall never see her again.'

So this is it, he thought, and stood forward, cleared his throat. 'Well, you see, we were at the wedding...'

'Your wedding?'

'What? Yes.'

'Sorry, your *own* wedding?'

'Yes.'

'That's awful,' said Pluto. 'God. Of all the things to happen.'

'Yes. Well, she was dancing near this snake or something...'

'No, you've said enough. Losing her on your own wedding day, that's really out of order. Of course you can take her back.'

'Oh,' he said. 'Don't you want any more? To check how much I loved her?'

'Well, you *do*, don't you?' said Pluto. 'I mean, you must do. Otherwise, why would you have gone through with the wedding in the first place? No, no, you take her home, and best of luck to you both. But just remember,' he added, as a warning, 'you must walk on alone, and she will follow. Whilst you are underground you are still in my domain, and if you so much as look back at her she will fade away and be lost to you forever.'

He walked the long climb up the tunnel. At first all he heard behind him was distant footsteps, and he could imagine that perhaps Pluto had tricked him, that it wasn't his wife following him at all but some other. But soon she could rein in her excitement no longer, and he recognised her familiar chatter.

'Oh, I *knew* you'd come for me! Just as Mummy did Daddy. And it's so romantic! All the girls are going to be *so* jealous, I mean, they were jealous enough that I was getting *married*, but once they know I've been rescued from Hell, they'll all go green with envy!'

And he thought, this was meant to be the test. The point at which he put his feelings on the line, found out whether or not his love was wanting. Because he still didn't know, couldn't know, at first he'd just been so grateful a girl was happy to date him in the first place, that she didn't run away when he wanted to kiss her, that she not only wanted to see him again but would actually be looking forward to it! So there was all that relief, everyone else in the world seemed to have someone to go out with on a Friday night, someone they could call their own — but was that relief actually *love*, really *love*, was it really? He'd proposed, or rather she'd let it be known that he *could* propose, so he had — and even as he'd done so, he'd thought, this is a big step — maybe it's big enough that it'll jolt my feelings a bit, I can find out whether I *need* this girl or whether she's somebody I just put up with because it's the right thing to do. But nothing changed, nothing became clearer, the whole engagement passed by in the same bland blur. The church ceremony had been no good either, he'd really wanted the vicar to give him a good grilling at the altar, demand to know what he really felt, but all he got was the standard do-you-take, to-have-and-to-hold, in-sickness-or-in-health, on and on, it was pretty clear what he was *supposed* to say, but did he feel it? And, he'd thought, here in Hell at last he'd find out. He'd have declared what he thought of his wife, and the King of the Dead would have listened impartially, he'd have judged and he'd have *known*. And either way it would have been fine, if it *was* love then that would have been great, he'd have taken his wife back to the land of the living with so much pride, he actually *loved* and here was the proof! And if it wasn't love, if it had never been love... well, that would have explained a lot.

God, she was still talking. 'And we'll have children, one of each, oh, not right away, but *soon*, within the year, I think. And we'll send them to the best schools and they'll wear the best clothes and it's just going to be lovely!' And he looked around.

She stopped talking. Froze with sudden fear.

'What are you *doing*?' she hissed at last.

'I'm just tying my shoelace,' he said. And then decided in that case he really ought to stoop.

'Turn the other way! Not this way, the other!' And he did.

They both stood there in silence for a while. 'Have you faded away?' he asked eventually.

'No,' she said.

'I thought you were supposed to fade away.'

'Maybe they didn't notice. Maybe they felt sorry for us, let us off.'

'Perhaps we should get someone, it's only fair...' he said, and began to turn his body around again, and she shrieked at him to stop. And again, silence.

'Shouldn't we keep moving?' eventually she asked, a little coldly.

'All right.' And so they did. This time his wife kept quiet, so that was a relief of sorts – but it meant he had to keep checking she was still there. 'Have you faded yet?' he'd ask, and each time she replied she sounded ever more irritable. And at last they broke into the daylight, they were safe, they were free, and death couldn't take her back. And even if she were still a *little* cross with him she was so relieved to be alive again that she hugged on to him and kissed him.

They didn't go on the honeymoon; now he had that promotion he couldn't afford all that time off work. But they managed a very pleasant four nights in the Cotswolds. They'd go for walks, eat pub food, and make love in a double bed that creaked at the slightest movement and couldn't help but make them laugh. And she was all right, he supposed he *did* love her, really, even though she never excited him, even though she never did anything as outrageous as dance barefoot again. It wasn't until Christmas that the looking back incident was brought up. The wife had her parents to stay, and they were all relaxing in front of the television after a particularly festive dinner.

'Did I ever tell you,' giggled the wife through her sherry, 'that time he rescued me from the Underworld, he looked back?'

'He looked back? At *my* daughter?' The mother-in-law was scandalised, and Arthur harrumphed disapprovingly.

'I didn't look back,' he said. 'I dropped something.'

'You wanted to tie your shoelace.'

'I tied my shoelace, that's it. I didn't look back. She's

here, isn't she?' But although no more was said, there was a noticeable frost in the air as they all settled down to play Trivial Pursuit.

Within the year they had a son, and within the year after that a daughter. They moved to a bigger house. 'Take care crossing the roads,' she'd say to the kids, or, 'Don't play too rough, now. If anything happens to you, Daddy won't be able to save you – he'll probably only look back.' And the children would laugh at a joke they didn't understand, but which had been repeated so often they *thought* they did.

One day, when the children were just too old to play with any more, he decided to buy himself a pet.

'What on earth do you want a *snake* for?' his wife all but shrieked. 'They're dangerous!'

'Oh, don't be ridiculous,' he said. 'There's no poison in it, it's had its sacs removed.'

'Yeww,' said the girl. 'Daddy, it's gross!' said the boy.

'I'm not having it in the house,' said his wife. 'Over my dead body.'

'Fine,' he said. And he put its tank in the garage. He got a little freezer for the garage too, that he could keep the snake's food in. He'd spend more and more time in the garage now, after a hard day running things at the office he'd sometimes not bother to go inside the house at all. He'd take out the little frozen mice he'd bought from the pet shop, 'yum yum,' he'd say to Snakey, he'd hold them by their tails, and they'd be stiff as a board. And he'd feed Snakey by hand, and how he'd watch as the mouse was swallowed whole, how it'd be sucked round and round and deep and down until it disappeared completely.

So Proud

It had taken her long enough to get used to the idea he was her boyfriend. She kept on expecting him to open his eyes, realise there were other girls out there, prettier, smarter, go with them instead. And then that day he'd proposed, right out of the blue, and amid the excitement and the pride she'd also realised she'd have to start thinking of him as a fiancé now, it'd be another adjustment to make. But now here they were, they'd done the registry office, both families had got together without incident, there'd been none of the clashes they'd been expecting – hey, even the weather had stayed bright for the photographs. And as the cameras were trained on them, she looked at him, and thought, *husband* now, got to think of him as *husband*. That sounded good to her, the most right so far. He smiled at her, and she could see in that smile that he loved her; she'd got him now, *husband*, he wasn't going to get away. And in the relief of that moment, in that triumph, she realised at last that she loved him too.

There wasn't to be a honeymoon, they couldn't afford it. Maybe one day, he said, when they were rich. And she'd agreed, and pictured that in a few years' time, in a hotel in Marbella, somewhere with a beach, they'd look back and say, *this* is our honeymoon, and laugh, because by then they'd be rolling in money, *every* holiday could be a honeymoon. But there was still a treat in store, far better than a honeymoon could offer. His parents had spoken to her parents, and together they'd bought them a flat. It was a small flat, there was no point in pretending otherwise, but it was theirs, and they wouldn't be in anyone's spare rooms any more. They climbed the stairs, unlocked the door, and they stood on the threshold of their new home. He asked, jokingly, if she wanted to be carried over the threshold, and she, jokingly, said yes. And because neither of them could quite be sure how much the other was joking, they did it anyway; she lay back in his arms, and he heaved her bulk into the tiny kitchen. They both felt a bit self-conscious afterwards.

He said it really was *very* small, this place. Not enough room to swing a cat! And she laughed, and said they'd just have to make sure they didn't *get* a cat then, and he laughed, and said he didn't like cats anyway, he was allergic, and she laughed again, but realised with some little shock she'd never even known that, were there other things about him she didn't know? He looked at the hand-me-down furniture and the hand-me-down wallpaper and said it would have to do for the moment, they'd do better later. And he took her to the hand-me-down bed, and there they made love. And it *felt* like making love, too, she'd always thought of it as just sex before, something you did guiltily in the spare room hoping the parents wouldn't hear, but now he was her *husband*, wasn't he, and this was their home, wasn't it, this was Making Love. As he bounced around on her she imagined this was what Mummy and Daddy got up to, how they'd done it all these years, mature, legal, sanctified by wedding contract and local registrar. She squealed with pleasure throughout the whole thing, even when she really wasn't feeling very much any more, even when frankly it was all over and the two of them were spent.

Maybe it was the squealing, or maybe the added frisson of being newly wed. But within a few days she realised she was pregnant. She called her mother to ask her advice, but her mother wasn't much help – she said the whole wretched business had been rather a long time ago, and she was really doing her best to forget all about it, thank you. The wife

SO PROUD

didn't mind; she liked the idea of another life inside her, and she wondered whom it would most look like, herself or her husband. The husband didn't look too happy when she told him though. He pointed out there wasn't even the room to swing a cat, hadn't he said they couldn't swing a cat? And a baby was even bigger than a cat, most likely. And the wife laughed and said they'd just have to take care not to swing the baby, and he sulked a bit and said it wasn't funny. And he asked her whether she really intended to go through with this, to alter their marriage so drastically even before it had started. Wasn't she thinking of aborting it? And she hadn't been, actually, but now she *did* think of it. She made herself a cup of tea in their hand-me-down kitchen with the hand-me-down kettle, and applied her mind to the notion. And she concluded it'd be rather a shame, wouldn't it? – and they'd never find out which of them the baby most looked like, she was looking forward to that, that would be the best bit. It'll be all right, she assured him, trying to coax him out of his sulk, they had each other, and they loved each other, and this baby was a *result* of that love, they'd love it too and care for it and not swing it around the cramped flat. They made love again that night, and the wife had to give him credit, the husband certainly put in as much effort as he normally would, you would hardly guess he was so angry.

The leaflet she got from the library was packed full of information and lots of colourful pictures. The wife thought the cartoon drawings made it all look very exciting, and could hardly wait to see what she was going to enjoy the most – the morning sickness, the strange hunger cravings, or watching her own belly button pop out. But she didn't have to wait the nine months she'd been promised. That Friday evening, as the married couple sat in front of the portable television, her waters broke. She told her husband she felt the most extraordinary urge to *push*, but he told her she was being ridiculous and went into the kitchen for a Diet Coke. But she pushed anyway, she lay on the floor and pushed and pushed, and she did it all very quickly; he hadn't made it back from the fridge before she gave birth. She felt it suck out from between her legs, and then the sort of physical relief she associated with having a really good belch. And she got to her feet to see what her new baby looked like. Her husband, on his return, almost dropped his Coke can.

It wasn't what either of them had expected. It wasn't a baby, or not a human baby, at any rate – instead, they were looking at a Chesterfield sofa. The wife couldn't help but wonder how something so big had been hiding in such a small place – because this wasn't one of your *small* Chesterfield sofas, no, this one was at least six foot long and three foot tall. It was covered with some strange thin gloop, and the wife worried that it might stain the leather upholstery – but it was all right, it was like cellophane wrapping, it came off in one easy tug. Now both husband and wife could see that it was a very good sofa indeed, high quality stuff, that – and the leather was coloured a fashionable dark green. Neither of them quite knew what to say for a while, until the wife remembered the leaflet she'd been reading, and suggested they cut the umbilical cord. So the husband dutifully went back into the kitchen for the scissors. And as he cut away, the wife looked her new baby over, from every angle the cutting would allow, and couldn't help but feel a little disappointed. The Chesterfield sofa didn't much look like *either* of its parents.

At first it was pleasing to have such a fine quality piece of furniture. The hand-me-down pieces they'd been left by the flat's previous owners were serviceable, but not at their best – the single armchair was fraying at the sides, and if you sat too close to the left armrest you risked being jabbed by a loose spring. The Chesterfield sofa, on the other hand, was luxury indeed. It was far more comfortable even than their bed, and one evening the husband began to make love to the wife on it, and only stopped when she pointed out it made her feel slightly weird having sex lying on her own offspring. But the richness of the green leather only showed up how drab everything else in the flat was by contrast – it looked strange and alien against the peeling pink wallpaper and the threadbare stained carpets. And it was clearly too big for the sitting room; the only way they could position it was diagonally from one corner to the other, and even then it was hard for the wife to see the television screen; it blocked so much light from the window it made the whole flat seem dark, small, and dingy, even more so than it really was. So the husband told her that they'd have to get rid of it, such class simply wasn't for them, and the wife reluctantly agreed. Late one night he brought some of the lads home from work, and they heaved it out of the flat, down the stairs, and into a skip they'd found further up the road. The sofa all but filled the skip, but the lads had done it under cover of darkness, no-one had seen them do it, so it was all right. And the wife noticed immediately that her husband's mood lifted, he seemed more relaxed than before. They made love that night and it was passionate and it was good, she squealed for all the right reasons this time, and she thought as she lay in his arms afterwards that she could get used to this. She could get used to not having a baby after all if this is what marriage could be like. And she told him that, and he looked so pleased, and even though he was very drowsy he put his tongue in her mouth and they made love all over again.

So when she found out she was pregnant once more he nearly hit the roof. He asked her what on earth she thought she was playing at. And she told him she hardly thought she was the *only* one responsible here, and burst into tears. And he said sorry, sorry, and put his arms around her, and said it was okay, it was *nobody's* fault, they'd just have to take even more precautions in the future, that was all. And maybe it would be all right anyway, maybe it was just another bit of furniture they could chuck in the skip, they must keep their fingers crossed. And it *was* another bit of furniture. Some time on Wednesday, whilst her husband was at work, she became the proud mother of an escritoire. She didn't know it was called an escritoire, mind you, so she had to be a bit vague when she called him on his mobile, and when he came home early he didn't know it was called an escritoire either. The husband sighed, and asked what they could want with a writing desk, he never wrote anything anyway. And she showed him all the drawers, and the place you could put your pens, and the lovely design on the mahogany, but he wasn't impressed. He said that if she was going to propagate furniture, couldn't she at least come up with something that was actually *useful*? They needed so much stuff, why not just pop out a couple of chairs or a table? He said he thought it was embarrassing anyway, he'd better call the lads from work, see if they wouldn't mind carrying the desk to the skip, but if they began to suspect all this unwanted furniture was coming from his wife's belly he'd be a laughingstock. He went as far as to say that had he known he'd been marrying someone who was a bit abnormal in the baby department, he might have had second thoughts. She cried and said that maybe *he* was the abnormal one, not her, it might be his sperm not her eggs, and he said no, he knew *perfectly* well that he could produce babies, did she really think she'd been his first? There was tons she didn't know about him, *tons*. And they both fell silent because they'd said too much, and then she asked him if he had a child she didn't know about, and he reassured her that it hadn't got as far as that, they'd dealt with it, it was okay — but he went on to mutter under his breath, just loud enough for her to hear, that he was pretty bloody sure all that palaver he'd been through hadn't been for a king-size sofa or some fancy writing desk. And then the lads came.

As the lads were about to lug the offending escritoire down the stairs, one of them asked the husband whether he'd be prepared to take twenty quid for it instead. The husband narrowed his eyes suspiciously. Why would a spot welder

SO PROUD

want a writing desk? What was in it for him? And the lad buckled and admitted he knew someone – not that well, mind, so this was a bit of a gamble – who liked to buy up posh furniture once in a while. The husband went very quiet. The lad asked if he wanted the twenty quid, and the husband said no, he didn't want his twenty quid. And the lad said, all right, should they put the desk in the skip then, and the husband said no, he thought he'd hang on to it after all. And the lad said, sod you then, and that the husband mustn't think he'd come out late at night again and have his time wasted like that, and the husband rudely assured him he wouldn't want him to. There was a banging of doors as the lad left, taking all the other lads with him, and had the escritoire been a human baby it would undoubtedly have started crying – but, because it was an escritoire, it didn't. The husband looked at the desk thoughtfully, as if for the first time. He pulled out the drawers one by one, turned them over, gave them a proper inspection. It almost made the wife tear up with joy to see him being so paternal at last. And then he said he was going to phone in sick for work the next day – he had things to do.

When the wife woke the next morning the husband had already left – and the escritoire had gone too. But he didn't bring it back with him. Instead he brought back a Chinese takeaway for them both. A bit of a treat, he called it, he thought they deserved to splash out. He announced that he'd sold the writing desk for three hundred pounds – three hundred! – and he beamed at her as if expecting a round of applause. The wife didn't want to let him down, so gave as congratulatory a look as she could muster. Her husband explained that their son turned out to be a genuine antique from the reign of George III – that was the 1700s, you know – and the dealer had been very keen to get his hands on it. The wife asked how it was possible their son was from the 1700s when he'd only been born yesterday, but the husband huffily asked her what she thought he looked like, a furniture expert?

After she'd polished off her sweet and sour prawn balls, the husband led her to the bedroom. She started to get out their precautions – one for him, one for her – and he shrugged, and said he didn't think they needed to worry about precautions *too* much.

The next time she fell pregnant he didn't get angry at all. On the contrary. He brought her cups of tea, kept asking how she was, wanted to make sure she didn't overexert herself. And he'd nuzzle her swelling belly, kiss it, and whisper to it – what are you going to be when you grow up? What are you going to be? Over the next few weeks she produced a grandfather clock, two sixteenth century tea chests, and an ornate dining table designed to seat a party of twelve. Every time they'd appear, pushed and pushed, after so much *pushing* the wife thought she'd burst, he'd unwrap the covering gloop and snip the cord like a kid opening a Christmas present. There were many more Chinese takeaways, and the wife began to associate the taste of sweet and sour with the nausea she always felt after giving birth. And it wasn't just Chinese takeaways the husband would buy; bit by bit, the hand-me-down furniture was replaced with fresh items he'd get from Argos. But every new item she'd produce from her stomach still somehow made them look as drab as the hand-me-downs, and a bit more plasticky to boot. In the bedroom the husband would become more experimental – wonder if they'd produce different types of furniture if they had sex in different positions. They did it standing up and were soon blessed with a Victorian standing lamp. They did it on all fours, and out came a whimsical framed portrait of four dogs playing poker. He invested in a lavish edition of the Karma Sutra, and was delighted with the gold statuette of Vishnu she delivered, so very exotic.

One evening, in a daze of sweet and sour, she told him that she missed the set of brass toasting forks he'd sold that day to buy their dinner. He looked perplexed. Told her patiently that they had no *need* for toasting forks, brass or otherwise. She agreed; but added softly that they were their children, weren't they? Right down to their little brass handles they were their children, and she missed them. He told her that she couldn't possibly *miss* something she hadn't even had until one o'clock that afternoon; she was being illogical, it was just her post-natal depression playing up again. And she supposed that was true. In the same way that she couldn't help but feel there was something different to their love making now. She'd lie beneath him, watching as he bounced around on top – well, whenever the Karma Sutra allowed bouncing – and she'd zone out a little watching his face, the gritted teeth, the rolling eyes, the spit, all that effort, all that work. It didn't seem like it had anything much to do with her any more. She no longer felt the urge to squeal; if there was any squealing to be done, he'd be doing it, and it'd be a squeal of avarice. But when she tried to bring this up, as delicately as possible, she'd be told the same thing. Illogical. Post-natal Depression.

And then, one day, something truly miraculous happened. She'd just given birth to a four-poster bed, and thought little of the fact – she coolly admired all the frills and drapes, but she'd long ago taught herself not to get too attached to things like that. It was a big bit of furniture, it all but filled the room, and the wife wasn't sure how her husband could get it to the dealer. But, she considered wearily, that was *his* problem, *his* part of the job, let *him* deal with it. She tried to swallow down the inevitable taste of sweet and sour sickness that took her after a delivery, no matter what she ate before it. And was about to go into the kitchen, make herself a cup of tea, when she felt something fall out of her body and hit the floor with a dull clang.

It was a kettle, she saw. Not an especially nice example of kettledom, the stainless steel a little rusted. Not antique either – her Mum's one was just the same, and she doubted that predated the seventies. Under normal circumstances, the kettle would be a disappointment, you'd be lucky to get a fiver for it. But sitting on the floor next to the opulent bulk of the four-poster bed, it looked laughably banal. Probably no better than the hand-me-down kettle they had in their hand-me-down kitchen.

But it looked like her.

She'd all but given up looking at her children for any signs of resemblance, to see whether they took most after Mummy or Daddy. However impressive it might have been on its own terms, the four-poster bed was really just another four-poster bed; she knew intellectually it was of her flesh, but she felt no bond to it. But the kettle was something else. She couldn't work out why they looked so similar; the spout didn't look like her nose, the handles were nothing like her ears. Maybe it was just because it a bit tarnished, a bit dirty, and it wouldn't go for much in Oxfam.

'Peek-a-boo,' she said to the kettle, and smiled. 'Peek-a-boo!'

And she knew then that she was going to be all right. She could cope with all of this. Produce children who weren't going to be her children. Live with a husband that she knew less and less day by day. Make love that wasn't love at all. If she could just have her little daughter by her side, see her face whenever she needed to, remind herself what this whole family thing was supposed to be about. Was she a daughter, maybe he was a son...? She picked up the kettle gently, ever so gently. Daughter. Definitely daughter. How lovely! Up to now all the furniture had been boys.

She'd got her now, *daughter*, she told herself, *daughter*, and she wasn't going to get away. She cradled her in her arms, and the baby kettle gave a sigh of calm that quite broke her heart. She wouldn't tell the husband, this was all hers, she was all hers. And she took her into the kitchen, kissed her softly, and shut her in the cupboard.

The Storyteller

Tell me a story, she'd say, and although I didn't know any stories, not really, I'd always try my best. Up on my knee she'd clamber, and at eight she was just a bit too big to sit there comfortably, she'd have to hold on to me tight. And she didn't need to worry, I wouldn't have let her fall, not for all the world, not for all the tea in China (and I don't even like tea!), but it made me feel proud to feel her arms around my waist, so I didn't discourage her, no. What sort of a story would you like, I'd ask, and it was a sort of a joke, because I didn't know any stories, not really, and she'd laugh. Sometimes she'd ask for a scary story, and I'd put on my scary voice, my extra deep voice which wasn't remotely scary and only made her laugh – no, Daddy, *properly*, she'd say, but I knew she didn't mean it because she was laughing so hard. Sometimes she'd ask for an adventure story, something with a lot of action, or a mystery story. The only thing she didn't *ever* want was a romance story, but I'd ask her anyway, because I liked the way she'd roll her eyes in disgust and stick out her tongue and go bleurgh, it made me laugh and that made her laugh; it was another joke, really, she liked my jokes. But most often she'd just cut to the chase and ask for a *funny* story, tell me a funny story, Daddy. And I could put on my silly voices and make little jokes, she was the only one ever to get my jokes, so that was fun for both of us.

And, of course, she hadn't stayed eight forever. And nor would I have wanted that, I'm not an idiot, that would have been absurd. But, I don't know. It could have lasted a little longer, surely?

She hadn't phoned for a while, so I was pleased to hear her voice, of course. But a little nervous too, she always did that to me. 'Hello, Claire,' I said.

'I need to speak to Mummy,' she said.

'All right,' I said. 'How are you? How's the world of, ah, academia?'

'Just get Mummy right *now*.' And she sounded so angry I was more than happy to oblige. She couldn't be angry with me, though, could she; the last time I'd seen her, that last Christmas, she'd been angry with me about something or other, I could no longer remember what – but that would have blown over by now, surely?

Anna came to the phone but I didn't hover, she hated it if I hovered. I went into the sitting room and pretended I was doing something. I heard a few noises of sympathy, a few 'how terrible's and 'of course's.

'Claire's on her way home to see us,' she told me.

'Oh,' I said. 'That'll be nice.'

'She's in a right state. She said her boyfriend's dead.'

'God,' I said. And then, 'How?'

'She didn't tell me,' Anna said, a little impatiently. 'She was calling from a mobile, she didn't want to spend too much money.' Which was fair enough. 'Can you pick her up from the train station in about an hour?'

At the end of each term I'd meet her from her train, and always be struck by how different she'd look. It's hard to put my finger on why; it wasn't as if she'd ever *do* anything dramatic to herself, I mean, Claire was a good girl, she'd never been through that teenage thing of putting metal studs through her nose or dyeing her hair pink. No, Claire had always rebelled in stronger, subtler ways. Each time I'd see her, every six months or so, she'd just stand there outside the station with her bags and just look so *adult*, distressingly adult, really. More composed and harder faced and further and further away from the Claire who'd been mine.

This time she didn't look composed at all. 'Oh, Daddy,' she said, and gave me a big hug. She'd been crying a lot on the journey, quite obviously, and her cheek was wet against my shirt. But she wasn't crying *now*, and I couldn't help but feel no matter how upset she was she probably could have found time to have dried her face at some point. It felt good to have her there, though. I patted her back a little.

'It's okay,' I said. 'You're home now.'

Which wasn't quite true yet, of course; and that was a shame, because it meant we had to disentangle and get into the car. 'Put your seatbelt on,' I said automatically.

'Yes,' she snapped. 'I do know.'

We drove in silence for a bit. I didn't quite know how to bring up matters which were clearly rather delicate. And I didn't want her to start crying again. 'Mum said that your boyfriend isn't very well,' was the best I could come out with.

'He's dead,' she said dully. 'And he wasn't my boyfriend.'

At least she wasn't crying. 'Okay,' I said.

Once home she flew into Anna's arms, and she stayed there for ages. And I thought, well, no more hugs for me, not now she's got her Mummy. But then she burst into tears, so I felt a bit relieved. I don't like tears, they make me nervous. Even way back, when Claire was a kid, the tears had been Anna's territory, not mine. I was there for the funny stories and the laughter.

'Sit down,' said Anna, leading her sobbing daughter into the kitchen. 'I'll make you a nice cup of tea. And you let it all out.'

'Yes,' I said. 'What happened? How did he die?'

'It was a car accident,' she said.

'Oh *no*,' said Anna. 'How terrible.'

'Oh dear,' I said.

'And it wasn't a quick death or anything, Mum,' Claire continued. 'He went to hospital, and it took *hours* for him to die. It's even worse than you imagine.'

'How terrible,' said Anna. 'Which boyfriend was this? This wasn't the one we met? You know, at that thing?'

'Mark,' said Claire.

'It wasn't Mark?' asked Anna.

'No, and Mark wasn't really my boyfriend anyway, not really.'

'Oh well, I'm glad it's not Mark, I liked him,' said Anna. 'Sorry,' she added immediately afterwards. 'So, which boyfriend was this?'

'Claire says he *wasn't* her boyfriend,' I said. And I wanted to go on to say that, seeing he wasn't, I couldn't really see what all the fuss was about, but wisely decided to keep that to myself.

'He was my fiancé,' said Claire.

We took this in.

'When you say "fiancé",' said Anna carefully.

'God, we were engaged and everything! Don't you believe me? God. Look. Look, he bought me a ring. Look.' So we did. I don't know why, I was expecting something plastic from a Christmas cracker, maybe. But, no, it was a *real* ring, real metal and stones, the whole bit. It looked too big for her little girl finger.

'Well,' said Anna.

'Good, isn't it?' said Claire, holding it up so we could appreciate it properly.

'You didn't tell us you got engaged,' I said, and it wasn't meant to be even the slightest dig, but she took it as one anyway, and said, 'God, I'm telling you now, aren't I? I wanted it to be a surprise. I wanted you to be proud. But now he's gone. My *husband*!' And she screwed up her face to squeeze the tears out, and waited a few seconds for them very patiently, and then out they came.

'What was his name?' asked Anna tenderly.

'Jake,' blubbed Claire.

I didn't know any Jakes. 'That's nice,' said Anna.

'What about his surname?' I asked.

'What? Why?'

'I don't know,' I said. 'I was just curious to know, if you had got married, what your new name would have been.'

And she cried all the more loudly, Anna gave me a look, and I thought to myself, it was sort of a *joke*. No-one got my jokes any more.

Anna and I left her watching television, and went to make dinner. 'We'll have risotto,' she said, 'it's her favourite, that'll cheer her up.' We wouldn't ever have made a risotto, not just for ourselves – Anna went to the supermarket once a week and loaded up the car with frozen meals. I asked if I could help, and Anna looked a bit surprised, then said that if I really wanted to I could chop up some vegetables. So I did.

I chopped up onions and peppers and leeks and a stumpy looking courgette. 'Any more?' I asked, because I remembered how much I liked chopping, I could have chopped all night, but Anna told me that was the lot. 'That's a shame, I was rather enjoying that!' And Anna told me, in that serious quiet voice she sometimes uses, that she didn't think we were supposed to be *enjoying* anything.

I went back to see Claire. 'All right?' I asked.

She nodded, eyes still on the TV. 'Your screen is much bigger than the one in my digs. I'd forgotten. It's weird.'

'Dinner's ready!' said Anna cheerfully, and brought in a bowl of it, big and steaming.

'No, Mum, I couldn't,' said Claire. 'I'm mourning.'

'It's your favourite.'

So Claire tucked in anyway. 'This is much better than student food,' she said at one point, and reached out to touch Anna's arm. 'Thanks, Mum, you're a really good cook.'

'If there's anything you want to talk about...' said Anna.

'I don't.'

'The accident or anything...'

'No, I don't.'

'Okay. But you know we're here if you ever do.'

'Or,' I added helpfully a few seconds later, 'if you don't.'

So we ate in silence. Until at last Claire put down her fork with an angry clatter. 'God,' she said, 'just because I don't want to talk, doesn't mean you shouldn't! It's *weird*. Just carry on as normal, please!'

But this *was* normal. Still, to make Claire feel better, Anna and I had a little go at conversation. I talked about work, and she talked about weather, and we were relieved when Claire's plate was empty and she went back to the TV.

We both took her up to her old bedroom. I don't suppose it needed both of us – or either, come to that, she wouldn't have forgotten where it was. But we stood in the doorway together as Claire looked around. The room seemed barren and unloved; the walls still had blu-tac marks that I hadn't been able to scrape off when I'd taken down her pop posters.

'I hope it's all right,' said Anna. 'The sheets are clean, but they haven't been washed in a little while.'

'It's fine, Mum,' said Claire, and gave her a hug.

'I'll put everything in the wash tomorrow.'

'Yes. But it's fine for now.'

'Sweet dreams,' I said.

'Wait a minute,' said Claire. 'Where's Freddie?'

And I wondered whether he was some other dead

THE STORYTELLER

boyfriend she'd not told us about. 'Who's Freddie?' I asked.

'Freddie's gone, darling,' said Anna patiently. 'Don't you remember?'

'No. Remember what? No. I didn't say you could take Freddie.'

'I asked you if we could take your old stuff to Oxfam, you said yes...'

'Yes, I remember that, but not Freddie. I wouldn't have let you take him.'

'Who's Freddie?' I asked.

'I'd have specifically told you not to get rid of Freddie,' said Claire, and she began to cry.

'I'm sorry, darling,' said Anna at last. 'It was a mistake.'

'Yes.'

'It won't happen again.'

'Well, it can't, can it?' She dried her eyes.

'Sorry.'

'Who's Freddie?' I asked.

'The teddy bear,' said Anna. And, oh yes, I remembered. Claire hadn't liked it being a teddy bear, she said she didn't know anybody called *Teddy*. So I said that it should be a Freddie bear, there was that boy in her playgroup called Freddie, wasn't there? Maybe she'd like to cuddle up to a Freddie every night. And she'd rolled her eyes and stuck out her tongue and gone bleurgh, but said she'd call him Freddie then, because that's what *I* wanted.

'We can get you another bear,' I said. 'I'll go to the shops and buy you another one.'

And Claire just stared at me, and so did Anna, but it wasn't as if I'd been the one who'd taken the wretched toy to Oxfam in the first place.

Next morning I went to the sitting room to read the newspaper. Claire was already there, sprawled across the sofa.

On Saturday mornings the sitting room was *my* territory, just as it became Anna's in the late afternoon through evening. I honestly didn't know what to do.

Claire didn't look at me.

'You watching this?' I said. It seemed to be some sort of kids' programme; lots of twentysomethings were bouncing across the screen pretending they were even younger.

'Yeah,' she said.

I stood there for a while. Eventually she looked up at me in irritation, then studiously turned her attention back to the television. One of the hyperactive twentysomethings had calmed down enough to introduce a pop video.

'You all right?' I said.

'Yeah.'

I didn't know where to go. There was the kitchen, but Anna was there with *her* newspaper, she wouldn't want me. There was the bedroom, but that was absurd. So I put on a jacket and went for a walk. It was surprisingly mild for the time of year.

On Tuesday night, before Anna put out the bedside lamp, I asked her how long Claire would be staying.

'Ssh! She'll hear you!' Which I thought was rather unlikely, as I'd been whispering. Mind you, if Anna and I ever talked in bed we *always* whispered, it was just something we'd do, so I suppose it must have felt like normal volume. 'If it's bothering you that much, why don't you ask her?' she whispered even more quietly than usual, and rolled over.

So the next day I did.

'Why?' she asked, looking up from some game show. 'Is it a problem?'

'No,' I said. 'I just suppose you've got essays to write and things, haven't you?' She looked at me blankly. 'And there'll be some sort of funeral, won't there?'

'I'm not going to the funeral,' she said flatly. 'Jake's parents don't want me there.'

'Oh,' I said. 'That's a shame.' I thought about this for a little bit. 'Why not?'

'You tell me,' she said. 'I haven't even met them! They can't accept that their son loved somebody else. I think they're sad.'

'Yes,' I said, 'I expect they are.' But I realised that she'd meant 'sad' in some sort of pejorative sense, so shut up.

'They want family only. That's a joke. Jake couldn't *stand* his family. And anyway, I was far more his family, wasn't I? I mean, we were engaged.'

'Mmm,' I said.

'I was going to be his wife. The mother of his children.'

'Ah,' I said. 'You aren't really, are you...? I mean, that's not why...?'

'No, Dad,' she groaned, and rolled her eyes in that way she used to. 'God. We took precautions. Honestly. Jake wore a condom, and I'm on the pill.'

'That's nice to know,' I said, rather gently, I thought. 'All the same,' I stumbled on, 'you know, all this sitting around the house, and crying, and things. There are other ways to grieve, you know. And I'm sure Jake would want you to get on with your life.'

She glared at me. 'Don't even pretend you know what Jake wanted.'

'I'm sure he'd have wanted the best for you, that's all.'

'Don't think you can speak for Jake. Not ever.'

'Right,' I agreed, 'I promise never even to consider putting myself into Jake's shoes again.'

'It may not have been a long relationship,' said Claire, and the word 'relationship' sounded comically adult coming out of that little kid's mouth, 'but that time we were together is the most precious time of my life. We packed more into those three weeks than you and Mum have in your whole lifetime.'

'Hang on,' I said. 'Three weeks?'

'Yeah,' she said. 'Our first anniversary will be on Friday. Then it'll be a full month.'

'Three *weeks*?'

'It wasn't as if I'd just met him, Dad. We'd been friends for *ages* before that. But you can just fall in love with someone, and know it's *right*, can't you? I mean, not love at first sight, but say third or fourth. Oh, what's the point in asking you?' as she went back to the television, 'If you can't understand what I'm saying, you're just *sad*.'

'Well,' I said. 'This is fun.'

'Yeah,' said Claire. 'Just great, Dad.'

Anna had suggested we spend some time together. 'You don't seem to be talking at all,' she'd said, 'and I think that's worrying, I really do. Aren't you worried?' I'd dutifully said I was a little worried, yes. 'Go to the supermarket together, here's the shopping list for the week. Have a bit of quality time.' I could see Anna *must* have been worried; the supermarket run was her province altogether, jealously guarded from husband's help – she must have been close to panic to relinquish that so willingly.

Without discussion Claire and I found a way to make the partnership work. She'd be in charge of the list, and pick the necessary groceries off the shelf. And I'd be in charge of the trolley, wheeling it down the aisles she told me to wheel it down, and waiting whilst she criticised all that we ate, drank, and cleaned ourselves with.

'I mean, this for example,' she said, looking at the nutritional information on the side of the cereal box. 'It's pretending that it's good for you, low calories and everything. But it's synthetic rubbish.'

'Your mother likes it,' I said.

'She wouldn't if she tasted *real* food. Once you get

what's real, you never want anything else. Jake used to say that anybody who bought stuff like this were morons.'

'That's nice,' I said placidly.

'Oh, don't give me that,' said Claire, with a weary sigh. 'I wasn't calling you and Mum morons. I was just saying. God, don't take it all so personally.' She had me wheel the trolley down to the frozen food. 'I wish you could be more environmentally friendly. I don't know, everyone can do their bit. Jake was just trying to save the planet, that's all.'

'He sounds great, really he does,' I said. And she looked at me, searching for even a trace of sarcasm, but I really believe there wasn't one, I believe I actually meant it. 'I'd have loved to have met him. I'm sure we'd have got on.'

She thought about this for a moment, and then laughed, not unkindly. 'No, you wouldn't have, Dad,' she said. 'No, you really really wouldn't.'

It was shortly after that that her mobile phone rang. 'Hello?' she asked cautiously. Without a word to me, just a hand raised vaguely in my direction, she took the phone down to the end of the aisle so that I couldn't hear her but dozens of strangers buying pork loin could hear her instead. I watched her for a bit; then somehow I felt guilty, and I looked at the nutritional information of the breakfast cereal she had such contempt for.

'All right?' I asked, as she stomped back.

'I don't want to talk about it,' she said. 'It was Mr and Mrs Dunderdale.'

'Who's that?'

'Come *on*. Jake's parents.'

'Oh, right.' Claire Dunderdale, I thought. No, she'd had a lucky escape. 'Are they inviting you to the funeral?'

'No,' she said, glowering. 'They want the ring back.'

But by the time we got home again the glowering had stopped and the crying had started once more, there was a whole river of tears and snot, and I wondered why I'd ever been so nervous of her crying, I'd seen so much of it, I suppose you get used to anything eventually. I was doing my best to be sympathetic, really I was.

'I thought you said he *bought* you a ring,' I said. And Anna glared at me as she hugged her daughter in her arms, shielded her from me and the Dunderdales and anything resembling common sense.

'It was his Mum's,' she said, between sobs. 'He said she'd wanted him to give it to his fiancée one day. Well, I am his fiancée, aren't I, aren't I? So what's the problem?'

'Maybe I can sort it all out,' said Anna, with a smile. 'It all seems a lot of fuss over nothing.'

'It's not nothing...!'

'No, I know it isn't. What's their phone number? I'll see if I can't sort it all out. I bet I can.'

She came back a few minutes later. 'Did you sort it all out?' I asked her.

'Claire, darling,' she said. 'I really think you should give the ring back.'

'No,' said Claire.

'Now, come on, darling.'

'No,' said Claire. 'It's *my* ring. Jake gave it to me. Jake loved me, he's the only man who's *ever* loved me, and he gave me a ring, and I'm not going to give it back. Because I'm the only one he *ever* loved, he said that, and so if I give it back, it'd be a betrayal, wouldn't it? Wouldn't it?'

'Not really,' I said.

'He *loved* me,' she all but spat. 'I mean, yes, he loved them too, I suppose, but not really, not in the same way. I mean, you don't *choose* to love family, do you? You just get stuck with them. You say you love them, but it's just because you've got used to them, you get used to anything eventually.'

'She said Jake took a lot of her jewellery. Did he give

THE STORYTELLER

you anything else, darling?'

But Claire ignored Anna as she warmed to her theme. 'I can't believe that bitch. I mean, her son is *dead*. He's *dead*. And that should be enough, but oh no, she's worrying about a bloody ring. God. I mean, how petty is that?'

'I think she must be hurting a lot,' I said gently.

'Well, what about me? *I'm* hurting, aren't I? I'm hurting.' She paused for a few seconds, and then she went on, with all the anger and the hate drained from her voice, and that made it all the worse somehow, 'I can't really do with being worried about other people's feelings any more. I've got problems of my own. Does that sound selfish?'

Neither Anna nor I answered.

'I've made some risotto,' Anna said.

One night I got up and went to Claire's bedroom. I watched her sleep from the doorway, it didn't seem right to venture any further in. But she looked so small and young, and her eyes were closed and all that coldness was closed behind them. And I knew that if I gathered her in my arms she'd be eight years old again, she'd clamber on to my knee maybe, make me tell her a story maybe, maybe a funny story.

Anna came to find me. 'What are you doing? You'll disturb her.' And I didn't reply, because it was fairly obvious what I was doing, and that I couldn't disturb her, wouldn't, not for the whole world, not for all the tea in China. (And I don't even like tea.)

'Come back to bed,' she said gently, and touched my arm briefly, and then, 'You've got work tomorrow.' But I stayed there a while longer, I don't know how long. After all, it was all nothing to Anna, this sleeping Claire, because the waking one loved her and wanted her. The sleeping Claire was mine, the one I knew still loved me, deep down; let Anna have the daytime Claire, the night Claire was my territory.

'Today's the funeral,' Claire announced one morning. 'So I want you both to be a little understanding, please.' We did our best. Even Anna gave her a wide berth.

But every so often Claire would come and find us anyway. Always crying, or, if not, on the brink of tears at least. 'They might be cremating him right now,' she'd say. And then, an hour or so later, 'He might be being burned to bits as we speak.'

'What time's the service?' I asked.

'I have no idea,' she replied.

'Ah.'

One time she came to us and said, 'He might be ashes by now. I bet he is. I bet Jake is ashes. And I bet she doesn't give me any of them. And I deserve them, I have *rights*. If she sets the police on me because of the stupid ring, I'll just set them on her because of the ashes. The bitch.'

'I can't bear it,' said Anna to me eventually. 'To see her suffering so much. All that suffering. She must have really loved him, don't you think?'

'Oh yes,' I said.

I went to find Claire in the sitting room. 'I don't want to talk, Dad,' she said. 'I'm busy mourning.'

'Yes, Claire, I can see that you are.' But I carried on anyway. 'You know,' I said, 'jealousy is a really ugly thing. Sometimes you think you've got a good excuse for it, it can really make you hurt. But that doesn't change anything.'

'I'm not jealous,' she sneered. 'Jealous of *her*? She can keep her bloody ashes.'

'Not you,' I said. 'Me.' And she looked at me at last.

And I told her about Anna. How the doctor had said last year that she had a tumour. Just over a year ago, how time flies. He thought we'd caught it in time, maybe, but he didn't want to raise our hopes, because that'd be a cruel thing to do, wouldn't it, he'd put her in for surgery as soon as he could, immediate surgery. Immediate meaning three weeks. It was ovarian cancer, Anna would have to have her ovaries cut off or whatever it is they do, and I told Anna it was okay, it wasn't as if we'd wanted any more kids anyway, and she'd squeezed my hand tight and actually laughed, she'd got the joke and laughed. And for those three weeks things were different, she let me help her, she'd let me bring her cups of tea, I'd cook dinner with her, I'd do the supermarket run. I began to feel useful again. And we talked, we found we had things in common after all, who would have thought. We even discussed going on holiday together, once the operation was all over and the ovaries were all over, we hadn't been on holiday in years, I brought some brochures back from the travel agent, Venice looked nice. And Anna had the operation, and we knew the odds were about even, really, not terrible but you wouldn't *bet* on them, and Anna said she thought she should be cremated, she'd heard it was more environmentally friendly, we try to do our bit. And, of course, she *didn't* die, she recovered, and that was great, but we didn't go to Venice either, and that wasn't so great, and I'd thought that all that *use* I'd felt might actually mean something. But it didn't, we went right back to the way we were before, worse maybe. All that silence we'd had, all that distance, it was all just waiting to move back in, it turned out we didn't have anything in common after all, and if she'd died on that operating table maybe that would have been the best time, I'd been so in love with her that day. I'd spent the day just walking around the hospital, they told me to go home but I couldn't, what if I were to lose her just now we'd fallen back in love again, but I should have, I should have. I could have been the one mourning, I could have been free. And instead here was Claire, my own daughter gets to mourn and not me, my own *little girl*, so of *course* I was jealous, it shouldn't have been Jake that died, it should have been Anna. It should have been Anna,

I could have had people tiptoeing around *me,* and being understanding to *me*. And Claire had had such a short relationship, but maybe that was for the best, if Anna had been taken from me after only three weeks, Christ, how I would have *loved* her, before we'd stopped talking or touching. Three weeks, or any time within the first two years, to be fair, I'd loved her so *much*. Where had all that love dribbled away to? And we'd only stayed together for Claire, for our daughter, but she'd grown up and gone away and come back as hard as nails, and she wasn't worth it, frankly, she hadn't been worth it.

I don't think I told her all of that, actually. But I told her enough.

Claire was angrily flinging all she had into her rucksack. 'No,' said Anna. 'Calm down. Don't leave, not like this. Oh, darling, darling. Calm down, *please.*'

'You had *cancer*,' said Claire, jabbing a finger at her. 'You had cancer, and you didn't even *think* to tell me!'

'I didn't want to worry you,' said Anna feebly.

'You might have *died*, and I'd never even had the chance to say *goodbye*. I have *rights*, you know. I have bloody *rights*.' She marched towards the front door. 'Well, if the cancer comes back, and it does sometimes. I don't want to know. All right? You've had your chance. Goodbye.' And then she doubled back, gave me a brief hug. 'I still love *you*, Dad.'

'Wait,' I said, 'I'll run you to the station.' But she turned and went, slamming the door behind her.

I looked at Anna. Her face was wobbling, it couldn't get any words out. I watched it try. 'But...' she managed at last.

'Shut up!' I said. And I slapped her. It wasn't a hard slap, and I know that the cry she let out was one of surprise, not pain. Immediately I wanted to apologise, but I knew if I did that I'd lose all the advantage I'd gained. I mustn't back down now. '*Never* talk to me like that again. Never. Do you understand?'

She said she did. So I went upstairs.

I sat in Claire's bedroom for ages. I don't know how long. Hours, probably. The day wore on, it got dark. I heard Anna outside at one point, hesitating, probably deciding whether to knock or not. She didn't.

I closed my eyes very very tight, so tight my head swam.

'Tell me a story, Daddy.'

I looked at Claire, and my heart leaped to see she was eight years old again.

'Daddy's not in the mood for stories, darling. Sorry, darling.'

'Oh, please, Daddy,' she said. 'I love your stories. I shan't sleep without a story. *Please.*' And she clambered up on to my knee, and she was heavier than I'd remembered, actually, but it was so good to feel her there I couldn't have pushed her off. Not for all the world. Not for all the tea in China.

But I don't even like tea, that's the joke of it.

'All right,' I said softly. 'All right. What sort of story would you like?'

'A funny story,' she said. Of course.

'Funny,' I said. 'All right.' And so I told her of the girl she was going to be. And as I spoke to her in the darkness, as the words tumbled out, I could feel her growing colder and harder and more brittle, so brittle that I wondered why she didn't snap.

Tiny Deaths

1

There's no getting away from it – that Jesus Christ was smart, oh yes, he was smart, no question. But that doesn't mean he knew *everything*.

In matters of scripture he couldn't be beaten. He fairly zipped his way up and down and through those ancient texts, knowing them verse by impenetrable verse, to the delight of all his followers and the jealous fury of the rabbis. You could be having a perfectly ordinary conversation with Jesus, then throw him a curve ball – what did Elijah say to the angel, what did Elisha say to the bears – and he'd come back at you with the answer without even blinking. But on practical matters, forget about it! No point turning to Jesus if you wanted groceries buying – he'd stand there with his twenty shekel note trying to buy nothing more than a quart of milk, and would have no idea whether to expect change or not. As his parents had said, somewhat ruefully, there was a lad who knew the value of everything and the cost of nothing. And he was by no means blind to it; when the apostles teased him about it he'd roll his eyes in mock irritation, then break out into that lazy grin of his that had won him as many enemies as it had friends. He'd listen patiently as his disciples at the Last Supper tried to tot up the bill and work out how much everyone should put in – they should just split it thirteen ways Andrew had suggested, but Simon Peter pointed out that was all very well but he hadn't had a starter, and Thomas went on to say that he *had* had a starter but it had only been olives, that was the cheapest thing on the menu, that hardly counted, in some restaurants they'd be thrown in gratis, it was hardly his fault this one didn't. And Jesus would say nothing, just watch them indulgently, would wait until he was told what his contribution should be, and put in without further comment.

And, smart as he was, when they nailed him to the cross, and left him there to die, he couldn't possibly have known. That in two thousand years' time this very act of torturous execution would be adopted so easily into the culture. What would he have thought to have seen the cross necklaces hanging round the necks of ageing pop stars as they cavorted across the stage, lip synching to the thump thump thump of their latest hit single? To have realised that his death, and the very manner of his death, would be so remembered, would be so stripped down to the basics that they missed the *point* of what those basics could mean, would be packaged up and blanded down and *fetishised* in such a way. The cross turned into nothing more than a fashion accessory, something glittery to wear against your cleavage, something macho to tattoo into your skin. Really, what would he have thought? He wouldn't be flashing that lazy grin much, you can bet.

The cross wasn't planed smooth and flat, it wasn't designed for comfort. It was ugly and coarse and splintered. Its victim would be stripped naked, tied to a stake, and whipped. Then, once he was dressed again, he'd be made to pick up the cross and lug it to the place of execution. Crippled with pain already – but, oh, nothing to the pain he had to look forward to! – the victim could hardly help but drop it on the way, hardly surprising as it could weigh as much as one hundred and fifty pounds. And when he dropped it, of course, he'd be made to stoop and pick it up again, and beaten on, and all the time he'd be aware that he'd never not be in contact with this cross again, there would be no part of his life that was left uncrossed, and soon he'd be looking back on his association with this cross and seeing this as the *good* times of the relationship, that this would be the honeymoon period, the time to get nostalgic about.

Because once he'd reached execution point he'd be stripped once more. And made to lie down upon that cross, and be fastened to it with nails driven into place through the small bones of the wrists. Then they'd produce another nail, a *special* nail of extra length, and this would be hammered through both feet placed on top of the other. Binding the condemned man to the hard splintered wood until death. And then the cross would be raised upright, and there he'd sit, or lie if you prefer, or *hang* – often in the baking heat, often for days. The loss of blood could kill, of course – or the pain, the excruciating pain (after all, where does the word 'excruciating' come from?) – or the heat – but usually the real cause of death would be asphyxiation. With the weight of the whole body now supported by his stretched arms, the man would have great difficulty breathing, his lungs expanded to their full with no chance of relief. And, struggling for air, he'd try to haul himself up on to his arms, to his nail-skewered arms, hanging on, quite literally, for every scrap of life he could. Sometimes the soldiers might take pity and break the victim's legs – there'd be no way to fight the suffocation any longer. This was a death where you'd show pity by breaking a man's legs. And there he'd cook, still able to see the crowds at his feet drawing lots for his clothes, jeering him, spitting at him – the splinters in the wood now hardly a problem, the whipping no more than a flea bite, even the nails so savagely piercing his limbs no longer really worth getting excited about. All that's left is the drowning in mid-air, and the unending humiliation.

Jesus Christ knew all this. He was smart, oh yes, no question. He decided he wouldn't scream at the pain. But when they whipped him he just couldn't help it – the agony was so overwhelming and so *sudden*, he knew it would *hurt*, of course, but not that – one moment there'd been flesh on his back, and the next – there, gone! – something that had been growing and knitting there for years removed in an instant by a man with a stick. And why not scream? he asked himself. He was a martyr, where did it say that martyrdom had to be performed stoically; it was a bloody sacrifice, wasn't the pain the point? So Jesus screamed as he carried the cross, he screamed as they banged in the nails, screamed as he was raised up high.

'Oh, for God's sake,' croaked a man next to him. 'Can't you keep it down?'

'But the pain...' gasped Jesus.

'It's no worse for you than for me, I'll be bound. And yet I'm not screaming about it. Making someone's final hours that bit more unpleasant. Shut up, die in peace. And let me die in peace while you're at it.'

Jesus looked at the words above the man's head, saw that he was a thief. 'Sorry,' he mumbled.

'If you're so powerful,' said the thief, 'then why don't you save yourself? And save me whilst you're at it. Go on,' he coughed, and there was blood in that cough, Jesus saw that he wouldn't be bothered by his screaming for much longer, 'just flap your wings, make a wish, do whatever it is you do.'

'Leave him alone,' said a man to Jesus' right, and for a moment Jesus thought that he was taking the thief's side, telling him to let the thief be. 'He's done nothing to deserve this. But we have. Well, I know I have, anyway.' Jesus turned his head painfully and saw that he was a murderer.

'Thank you,' croaked Jesus. 'And I say this to you. Today you shall sit by my side in Paradise.' Even as he said the words they sounded so hollow, so *fake*, but he meant them. The murderer tried to smile, nodded. The thief raised his head, and Jesus thought he might be trying to spit at them both, but it was nothing but a final spasm before he died.

The murderer died soon afterwards. He didn't speak to Jesus again, but Jesus liked to pretend that he was a friend, that he was still alive, they were both hanging there side by side in companionable silence. It was a pity that the murderer's eyes were still open, rolled upwards into his skull – it made it harder to believe in it somehow.

'Oh God,' said Jesus, and even he didn't know whether he was praying or cursing. 'This isn't what I had in mind at *all*.'

And the skies seemed to darken, and everything froze, and the air grew still. Right, this is it, said Jesus, death, here I come. And he braced himself. Or braced himself as best he could, seeing that he was pinned against a bloody cross.

But it wasn't death. Not yet, anyway. 'I've been thinking it over,' said a voice in his head, and it wasn't just in his head, it was everywhere at once. 'And I'm not sure this was such a great idea.'

'What do you mean?' asked Jesus.

'No-one's saying you've not done a good job,' said the voice. 'Really. Splendid stuff. And well done, you know. On going through with it all. But, well.'

'But... what?' said Jesus, and it was hard not to let a little irritation show.

'We can stop this right now. I think you've done enough. Really, I do. I can heal your wounds. I can set you free. You can go on living, and we can wipe away this whole crucifixion part of the proceedings. Frankly, it's all very unpleasant, and I think we can just do without it.'

'Get thee behind me,' said Jesus.

'Oh, now, don't go all formal on me.'

And Jesus could no longer be sure whether the voice tempting him was his father or Satan or his own delusions – he could no longer even be sure, in all this pain, all this *weakness*, whether there even was a God or a Satan.

'One last chance – will you accept my offer?' he heard, and even though the voice was everywhere, it seemed dimmer now, to be fading away.

'No,' he said.

And then he died.

2

And after death, life.

Jesus didn't know why he was so surprised. It was what he'd been preaching all these years, after all. He supposed he'd expected it to be a lot less restricting. His hands couldn't move properly, and for a terrifying moment he wondered if this were a consequence of his crucifixion – but no, surely not, what sort of paradise would it be in which you carried the marks of your own death? And besides, the hands *were* moving, they just couldn't do very much, they were so puny. He looked around him, everything seemed so *big*, and there were people above him, far far above him, he couldn't reach them with those puny hands. And he noted, with calm astonishment, he seemed to be attached to some strange woman by an umbilical cord.

Now, what's this all about? Jesus asked himself, and realised that he could still think just the same as before – all the old memories, the sermons, the walking on water bit, that ending with the cross. He looked up at the face of his mother. 'You're not Mary,' he said. Who was this stranger, looking down at him so shyly but with such pride? 'Who the hell are all you people?' he cried out.

But even though he could remember language, he could remember *everything* – it seemed his vocal cords weren't yet developed enough to manage more than a wail. So no-one understood his questions, they looked down at him indulgently. He was given a slap on the bottom, and even though it had hardly hurt, not compared to all he'd just been through, Jesus wept.

Jesus was impatient to learn all he could about this new life he'd been born into, find out just what was going on. But it took him the best part of a year until he was able to croak out words, and another few until his little legs carried him to the sort of people who would be able to satisfy his curiosity.

In the mean time he learned that crying in the night was a Bad Thing and made his parents cross, that giggling and smiling was a Good Thing and made them giggle and smile in turn. And that his name wasn't Jesus at all, but something else. Unless he were really concentrating hard Jesus was inclined to forget what this new name was — he had, after all, thirty-three years of thinking himself Jesus of Nazareth, and it was hard to make the adjustment.

One day he toddled to the temple. 'What do you know of the teachings of Jesus Christ?' he asked the rabbi. The rabbi blinked at this funny little three year old, asking questions so imperiously. And told him he had no idea what he was talking about. Jesus tried to jog his memory, remind him of the incident with the loaves and fishes; he'd been quite sure that his exploits would have had *some* impact, that his life would have counted for something. But the rabbi grew impatient, and although he was really quite fond of little kids, had enough when Jesus began arguing interpretations of scripture with him.

His parents were furious when they found him. 'You can't go wandering off on your own.' 'Didn't you know,' said Jesus, 'that I would be in my Father's house?' 'It isn't your Dad's house,' said the mother who wasn't anything like Mary, not at all, 'it's a bloody temple. And that's straight to bed for you, young man, with no dinner.'

For a while Jesus felt dismayed that all that he felt he'd achieved had been for nothing. But he soon realised that this explained why he was born again — there was still work to be done. And now he had a mission. Little makes children happier than when they have a mission to fix their sights on, and Jesus vowed that this second time he'd get it *right*. Being a child was a handicap, of course; he knew full well that he would get little respect until he'd grown facial hair and his voice had dropped an octave. He'd start rubbing bits of gravel into his chin to make it look more rugged — a boy at school told him that was the quickest way to grow a beard, and Jesus was desperate enough to believe him. And he'd practise talking in as low a growl as possible until it made his throat sore and his parents would smack him for making silly voices.

At last he felt old enough to start spreading the good news. There were tufts of blonde hair growing out of the rock-ravaged crater that was his chin. And he could sustain his 'mature' voice for a good few sentences before it'd betray him with a squeak. He stood on street corners, told the world what he knew about death and life eternal, about a kingdom of love and light far removed from Roman rule. He discovered, to his embarrassment, that he had something of a lisp — it was only obvious to him when passers-by used to mock the impediment back at him. And his 'l' was weak, so key words like 'Lord' and 'love' and 'Leviticus' went for nothing. And when this was pointed out to him it made him so self-conscious that Jesus began to stammer. Once the stammer took hold, that was it. He'd stand there, bub-bub-bub-bubbing away like an idiot. The politer people used to ignore him. Most didn't.

'I really don't think you're suited to a career in the Church,' said the rabbi kindly. It was the same rabbi who had for years put up with Jesus' questions about the Messiah and Jewish orthodoxy, and in spite of himself he'd grown rather fond of the eccentric little boy. 'What you lack is *charisma*. You're not a handsome boy, your nose is too big, you walk funny. And your voice — stammer aside, your voice is *painful*. Sorry, but it's true. I'll wait half an hour for you to get your words out, then when you do, your voice is so dull I've forgotten what it is you're saying before you've even started.'

'But I know everything,' said Jesus at last, after he'd forced the words out. 'Surely that counts for something? I know how to save the world. It can't all just be in the packaging — the message must have *some* importance.'

The rabbi shrugged. He was fifty years old, and he still

looked good, and shrugging showed off his biceps most winningly. His congregation wondered whether he worked out. And when he replied to Jesus it was in the same low voice that sent guilty goose-pimply thrills down the women as they heard him quote the Torah. 'You must have other skills,' he said. 'Maybe there's something else you can put your mind to.'

Jesus hadn't thought much about carpentry in years. He'd only worked at it at all to keep Joseph and Mary happy, whilst he was biding time for his great mission in life. Now he went back to the tools and the wood, tried to remember how the one affected the other. He tried to make a table, but he realised that it was a little ambitious to start on something so big; no matter how he measured them one leg would always end up longer than another, and he'd whittle them down and whittle them further until there were barely legs left at all and he'd produced instead not a table but a dinner tray. But he dedicated himself to the work, with the same unsmiling concentration he'd once applied to his preaching, and he soon discovered the joy in creating something out of raw materials, in creating purpose out of chaos.

His parents would watch over him as he slept, having tired himself out making a high-backed rocking chair. In his hands he still clasped his hammer, hugging on to it as a child would a teddy bear. 'I think our son has found his calling at last,' the mother said.

'Thank God for that,' replied the father. 'I thought he was going to turn out to be a weirdo.'

His father died first, then his mother. He mourned them the best way he could. He knew that they'd loved him; but, from his point of view, they'd seemed at best fairly temporary. He knew they weren't his *important* parents. Jesus loved them, but loved them in the way, deep down, he still loved all mankind. He knew they'd felt his reserve, and that it had hurt them. But he couldn't help that.

He had a shop of his own. Customers would find him

skilled and reliable. They also found him surly — but then, they never came for the conversation. For his part, he emphasised the lisp, the stammer. If he were an ugly man, and he could see that he was, then let him be ugly. He would be a carpenter and nothing more. He poured his love into the wooden objects he beat and shaped and smoothed — and then, when they were done, he'd sell them without a second thought.

One day a woman came to see him. 'I want you to make something for my husband's birthday,' she said.

'What sort of something?' he asked.

'I don't know. Something wooden.' She flicked her hair and Jesus saw that it was long and black and beautiful, and that there was a lot for her to flick. 'I don't really care,' she said, 'I don't like him very much.' And she frowned at him, as if daring him to criticise her for that.

Jesus didn't know what to say. He was going to suggest he might make a box — a nice wooden box is usually appreciated, and has so many uses. But before he knew it she was against him, her lips were on his, she was running her hands all over his body. Her tongue was in his mouth, and she tasted rather sweet, and he wondered whether all kisses tasted like that or whether she'd simply had honey for breakfast. And then she stripped him, and he hadn't been stripped, not as an adult, not since they'd crucified his last body. And without a word she pulled him down on to the ground, and there they made love. For a few moments Jesus worried that he wouldn't know what to do, he had to put his penis into a hole, but what if he couldn't find the hole? — and he was, indeed, left jamming it up against her stomach pointlessly until she grasped it in her hand and directed it. And the first thing Jesus thought as he came was that *this* is what sex was like, then — how wonderful, how wondrous, how full of, well, wonder — and then, the second thing, that actually it was such a simple and such a clumsy thing, really.

He assumed that she was a prostitute. And after it was all over — and that was only a few minutes later, like the flaying of the skin from his back, his virginity could be taken away really so very quickly — he asked her how much he owed her. Money. Or maybe a chair. And she'd been offended. But not so offended that the next day she hadn't come back. And in the days afterward.

'I love you,' she told him.

'Why?' he asked her, genuinely perplexed. 'Where does that come from?'

'It doesn't matter,' she said.

'But I'm ugly. I'm charmless. I do nothing, not any more. I *am* nothing, now.'

'It doesn't matter,' she said again, put him back inside her.

'I can't tell you I love you,' he said afterwards, as they lay there amidst all the wood shavings. 'You're a married woman. I don't understand what it is we're doing. I wouldn't do it if I didn't care for you, I *couldn't*, you know that. I hope you realise,' he said, as she kissed him anyway, kissed him in spite of all these crass words, 'that even though I *might* love you, I could never say it.'

She was the only one he didn't stammer at. But he knew that he never much said anything worth saying. And she didn't seem to mind.

One afternoon, for fun, he taught her some carpentry. 'It's all I know,' he said. 'It's the only thing I can give you that's me.' And she nodded, eager to learn.

'This here is a mortise and tenon joint. This bit here's the tenon, see? And it slots into the mortise.'

'You speak as if it's from a text,' she said. 'We don't need to know the *words* for everything, you know. It's not holy scripture.' He wondered if this was why she never told him her name. 'Such things just aren't important,' she'd say and shrug.

One day a man came into his shop, bullish, angry. He told Jesus *his* name. 'You say that as if it should mean something to me.'

'I'm the husband of ____,' he said, and it was another name he didn't know. 'You bastard. You fucking bastard.' And he hit Jesus. And then he hit him again.

Jesus didn't even remember picking up the nail. His return punches were so feeble it just seemed the only thing that might give his silly little fist a bit of *power*. It stuck deep into the husband's throat. He croaked at Jesus disbelievingly, saw the blood dripping. He pulled out the nail, and that was a mistake – there was so much *more* blood after that, and the husband made a foolhardy attempt to put the nail *back*, he looked like an idiot, swaying there on his feet, a nail between his fingers he didn't know how to use. It seemed to Jesus as if offered it to him – you're the carpenter, what do you do with this? – before the man's strength gave way and he went to the ground.

Jesus waited with the husband whilst he died. He vaguely thought he should do something to ease the pain, even to comfort him a little. But, he supposed, he wasn't that nice a person. He wondered if she should run, but run where? All he had was his shop, that was a decision he'd made long ago. He supposed he could plead self-defence, but, thinking it through, this dying husband had been the one defending himself, defending his honour and the law.

He listened quietly at the trial. He was an adulterer and a murderer. There was nothing to disagree with. He was asked his name. 'Jesus Christ,' he said.

'No, it isn't,' they said angrily, and *told* him his name. Oh yes, that was it. He wondered why, if they already knew what it was, why they'd asked him in the first place.

When they told him he was to be crucified he threw up.

He screamed as they whipped him, he cried as he carried the cross. And could hardly help but give a shriek of agony as they drove the nails into his limbs. But as they raised the cross upright, he realised that through all the pain he could do what he'd learned throughout this second life, and keep quiet.

Unlike that poor feller they'd put next to him. Who couldn't stop shouting, begging for the pain to stop, saying it had all been a mistake.

The first time he'd been crucified it had, of course, been terrible. But even as he'd suffered, he'd known that that was the *point*. That this sacrifice would mean everything, that through this heroic death the world would be changed. What made this second crucifixion all the more bitter was that it was without meaning, his death just like his life, meaningless, and his name would be forgotten just as he himself had already forgotten it. Jesus Christ had been luckier than him. There was no heroism here.

'If you're so powerful,' said a voice on the wind, 'then why don't you just save yourself?' Jesus realised that the screaming from his neighbour had stopped, thought at first the words were coming from him. But no, from one cross further down. And then, of course, Jesus knew exactly who was being crucified beside him. That Jesus Christ, he was one smart feller.

He looked at himself, his former self. The *better* Jesus Christ. The blood, the crown of thorns. The words above his head, King of the Jews. He felt a wave of anger at him, this Jesus with a purpose. But then pity. This handsome man, this leader of men, who had been able to inspire people with the same truths that he couldn't.

'Leave him alone,' said the second Jesus. 'He's done nothing to deserve this. But we have. Well,' and he thought of the woman he loved, and of how shameful that had been, and the violence it had caused – and he thought that with all the greatness in his heart how little his life had meant, how he'd squandered everything – 'I know I have, anyway.'

Jesus looked at Jesus, and in that moment Jesus saw that he would have followed Jesus, right to the ends of the earth.

And Jesus thanked him, and said, 'Today you shall sit by my side in Paradise.'

Well, thought Jesus the murderer, as he closed his eyes and died. That would be nice. Here's hoping.

3

Oh, for God's sake, thought Jesus. You've got to be kidding me.

Again as a baby, another set of parents staring down at him. Already loving him, hoping he'll be their special one. He glared at them as they fussed around the umbilical cord. Where was the knife, oh dear, shall we cut it now? Give me the bloody knife, thought Jesus impatiently, I'll bloody do it myself. And he all but snatched it from them, and he'd have managed it too if his newly birthed body hadn't been so feeble, and all the adults looked at him and laughed, and the rabbi said that if he wasn't careful he'd be out of a job, and Jesus hated them, he fixed them all with a mature stare and hated them all completely.

The offer, he thought. The offer that was made to me on the cross. I made the wrong decision.

As a child he flirted with the idea of killing himself. He'd stand at the top of precipices, not sure whether today was the day he'd jump, hoping for some strong gust of wind that would take the choice out of his hands. But he knew really he was just too *angry* to die, he'd be *damned* if he'd let this ridiculous fucking world he was having to sit through for the third fucking time get the better of him. If he were going to die, he might as well do it enjoying himself. He began to drink. In all honesty, he didn't much like the taste of it, and he didn't like the inebriation – but there was a midway point where the taste didn't matter any more and he could still think straight that felt increasingly tolerable. His parents loved him, and worried for him – and he'd fly into a rage whenever that love and worry became too obvious. 'I didn't ask to be born,' he'd rail at them like an infant. They shyly hoped that he might find a job in the Church – that little anecdote with the rabbi which had been trotted out at every single fucking Hanukkah dinner had taken on an almost prophetic significance to them. But he wanted nothing to do with religion. He considered carpentry – looked at the wood, looked at the tools, contemplated the joy of creating purpose out of chaos, blah blah. And then he said, no, sod that, he'd rather be a thief instead. He practised thieving on his mother and father, and one day, when he decided he'd got the knack of it pretty much down pat, left the house and never saw them again.

The irony was that Jesus III had much of the charisma that Jesus II had so longed for. He'd hate people on sight; he'd judge them and detest them for the simplest of reasons – he didn't like their faces, their hair, the way they walked, the way they talked. But he was able to bury this hatred whenever it suited him. It almost became a game – he'd meet someone new, he'd charm them with an easy smile, and all the time he'd be thinking gleefully, *hate you, hate you, hate you*. Some days he would tire of the game and just growl at everybody he met. But he realised that in the matter of women he slept with – and he slept with a *lot*, there were so many to be had – it was important to get the order right: charm first, growl afterwards. For a while Jesus told himself that he was looking for the same woman he'd slept with when he'd been a shy carpenter. And then he told himself he was just looking for the same sensations she'd inspired. And then he gave up on that and just fucked them for the sheer hell of it.

He realised that somewhere out there were his previous selves. One day he went into the shop owned by Jesus II. He thought, in a moment of drunken hilarity, that it might be fun to go and rob himself. But when he stood in front of the little carpenter, and saw just how small and meaningless he had been, he felt a wave of nausea and left without saying a word. He didn't have the same scruples about Jesus I. Of course he knew exactly when and where to find him preaching, and he'd turn up early, always getting a good position at the front. Jesus would tell him his little sermons, and everyone who heard them would love them, and all the thief could hear was just how *little* this Messiah knew – whilst here *he* was, pissed on brandy, and he knew three times as much. 'Hey, Jesus,' he'd call out. 'When you're on the cross, when they nail you to that fucking cross. And they will, you bastard. You know it and I know it.' People would try to stop him shouting, but he'd have none of it, on he'd go – 'When the offer comes, when you hear the offer. Just say yes. The correct answer is definitely *yes*.'

He carried on stealing. He got very good at it. He discovered that it required a sleight of hand that was genuinely artistic. At times he felt as he had done when he'd been a carpenter, taking pride in creating something out of nothing, in the delight of a job well done. Then he'd laugh at himself bitterly and go and get drunk. Of course, they caught him in the end. He only wondered why it had taken them so long.

This time, he thought, I'm not going to scream. But scream he did. When the nails went in there was no way of stopping it. He looked across at Jesus I, screaming up there beside him. Couldn't resist a final dig. 'If you're so powerful, then why don't you save yourself? And save me whilst you're at it.' Jesus II tried to offer words of comfort to the Messiah, and Jesus III laughed in spite of the agony and thought, if you only knew what *I* knew. Once more Jesus came out with that lie, the worst lie he had ever told, 'Today you will sit by my side in Paradise', and it seemed to his thief self that this little glimmer of false hope was worse than any of the crimes *he* had ever committed.

He raised his head, and wasn't sure whether he was going to spit in disgust or make one last appeal – say yes! – and the effort made his heart burst. Good, said Jesus III to himself, and died.

4

I've got the measure of this now, said Jesus to himself. I bet next time I come back as a rapist. Or as an arsonist. Or as some bloke who hasn't paid their taxes. I get the idea.

But Jesus IV was a woman. You could have knocked her down with a feather.

She lived a quiet life in the Judea hills. She kept chickens. She married young, and had three children who honoured her and each day made her heart swell with pride. She kept waiting for her life to intersect with Jesus Christ's – but it never did. She never heard his name mentioned, would never even have known he was out there changing the world if she hadn't lived through it all already. Every once in a while she thought she should ask about him, find out what was going on. But the name always died in her throat. Best not to know. Better not to draw attention to herself.

All her life she waited to be crucified. She waited for some terrible tragedy to overtake her. Some ironic twist of fate that would set her on the road to Calvary, maybe, something that would propel her into a life of crime. (Because she knew she *would* kill, she would for her children, if she had to save them, if it did them the least good, she *would*.) But she died of the palsy, and it wasn't really painful as such. On her deathbed she babbled nonsense. 'Don't let them find me and bore nails through my flesh.' Her husband mourned her. She'd been a strange woman, all had said so – always with that hooded expression, always so fearful. But he'd loved her.

87

Jesus wondered how many times he could endure this merry-go-round before going mad. It wasn't the unending tedium of it all – now a baker, now a cobbler, a beggar here and there – though that was bad enough. No, it was the fact that every life he led, no matter how undistinguished, no matter how much you'd want to edit it down to a few salient points here and there and move on, stayed in his memories in all their minute details.

So many bodies he'd inhabited, with all their different sins, and all their deaths too, Jesus had died in so many varied ways. And the truth of it was that, for the most part, the deaths weren't interesting or lurid – they were just more chunks of dull inevitability. Rather than the experiences making Jesus wiser still, they seemed to dilute him rather – as if every fresh scrap of knowledge he inherited was pushing something more valuable out. There were so many conflicting thoughts bubbling away in Jesus' brain it was hard to discern which belonged to the current Jesus, which to the original, and which ones in between. How many people could he carry around in his head before something snapped?

The answer was simple. Eighty-six.

He didn't know what the original Jesus could do for him. But he was a purer Jesus, before he'd been tainted by all this adultery and robbery and murder and covetousness of his neighbour's ass. Before all this banality.

'Help me!' he cried to him. 'Jesus, you have to help me.'

'What is your name?' asked Jesus.

'I don't know any more!' he cried. 'Which name do you want? I can't remember them all. There's a whole legion of them inside me!'

And the old Jesus told him he was possessed by evil spirits. And the new Jesus began to protest that it wasn't quite as simple as that; nothing could be as *simple* as that, this new faith of his would never work if it divided people into the faithful and those possessed by spirits, how very convenient, how *fatuous*. But Jesus commanded the spirits to come forth, and he felt a tearing from within him, and his heart felt lighter and healthier and more singular than he'd known in many centuries. The other selves flew into a herd of swine, who panicked and ran off a nearby handy cliff.

Jesus the eighty-seventh — although he wasn't that now, what was left? He was Joshua, plain and simple Josh — got down on his knees and began to weep tears of gratitude. He asked if he could join the disciples, and delighted that for once he didn't know what answer Jesus might give him.

Jesus looked a bit puzzled, and the disciples exchanged glances. 'Erm, no, that's all right,' said Jesus. 'Why don't you just go home, eh?'

And Joshua went home, happier than he'd ever been.

Late that night the voices in his head came back.

'Evil spirits,' smirked Jesus XXIV, who had had a habit of smirking, it had irritated everybody. 'We're not evil spirits, we're *you*,' said Jesus XLIII.

'No,' he moaned softly. 'This was all over and done with.'

'If Jesus is there, he can banish us. But once he's gone, we'll just keep coming back.'

'But I *am* Jesus,' said Jesus. 'I thought that was the whole problem.'

And he banished the other selves out of his body once more. For a few hours he succeeded in banishing them into the curtains. But as soon as he'd done it, he wasn't Jesus any more, so he hadn't the power to keep them out. That's how he spent the night, banishing them back and forth. By dawn he'd banished them into the carpet, the chest of drawers, and the little cupboard under the stairs. All to no avail.

Self-exorcism really took it out of you. 'I'm exhausted,' said Jesus eventually.

'So are we,' admitted all the other Jesuses.

'I don't know how I can keep doing all this,' he said. 'All this remembering. I don't know how I can keep it all in.'

'So don't,' was the answer. 'Let go. Remember what you need to. Forget the rest.'

And that's what he did.

412

'You say you love me. And it's not that I don't believe you...'

'I *do* love you.'

'Yes. I said I believed you. Didn't you just hear me say that?'

'Yes. Sorry.'

'Well then.' Jesus licked his lips. He clearly wasn't enjoying this interview. He sighed, put a sympathetic hand on his apostle's shoulder. 'It's not easy to do this. But I just don't think you're pulling your weight.'

'You're going to sack me?' He couldn't believe his ears.

'The question you should be asking yourself is not so much 'Do I love Jesus?', to which the answer is obviously yes...'

'Yes,' he began, but Jesus held up his hand, shut him up. And continued.

'But more, really, 'Is that love I feel for Jesus doing Jesus any actual good?' All your love, James. Very nice, I'm sure. But do I have a use for it?'

It had taken the man well over four hundred goes before he'd got himself incarnated into somebody who was to live so close beside the original Jesus. But the apostle looked now into his predecessor's eyes and saw the contempt he had for him, and knew that deep down he felt it too. No, not contempt – that's too harsh. Pity, maybe. A world weary pity.

He'd felt so delighted to discover he'd been born as one of the twelve apostles. What a nuisance he'd come out as the rubbish one.

'If you get rid of me,' he said, 'it's because of my name, isn't it? Because you've already got a James.'

'No,' said Jesus irritably, 'it's not your name.'

He was James the Less. There was already a James, so they had to call him something different. To avoid confusion, they'd said. You know, so when they called them in for supper, they'd all know which one they were referring to. James the Less had suggested they simply call him Jim or Jimmy or Jimbo or other variants thereof, they would all be fine, he'd said – but somehow James the Less had stuck. They said it was because of his height, but he had his doubts.

And besides, he'd often think, they all ate supper together. So that excuse didn't make sense anyway.

It wasn't fair. His own brother Matthew was seen as a more trusted apostle, he got all the responsible jobs. But Matthew was only there in the first place because James had egged him on. 'We've got to join Jesus,' James had told him, all through their childhood. 'You don't know who he is yet, but he's going to be this prophet, and he's going to be *big*. Come on, it'll be great!' As a teenager Matthew would push his little brother over, laugh at him, yawn. 'Just don't see myself following some sort of preacher man,' he'd tell him. 'Now buzz off, pipsqueak.' When James had been to see Jesus, Matthew had only accompanied him ironically. And now look what had happened – they'd *both* been made apostles, and Matthew was the favoured.

'Look,' said Jesus kindly. 'If you're going to have twelve apostles, then someone's got to come twelfth. Stands to reason. There's no shame in it. But,' he went on, with that more-in-sorrow-than-in-anger shtick he usually reserved for the Pharisees and the moneylenders, 'you shouldn't be coming twelfth quite so *emphatically*. It's all right. Don't cry. Look. I'm giving you a last chance. All right? There's a very special job I need doing.'

'An important special job?' asked James, drying his eyes.

'Very important.'

'You're not just saying that? It's not cleaning out the latrine again?'

'No,' said Jesus. 'It's the most important job of all. I did have it earmarked for someone else...'

'No, no!' said James. 'I'll do it!'

'Okay. We can't talk about it now, it isn't safe. Meet me in the street tonight when all the other apostles are asleep. This is for your ears only.'

James thanked him, and Jesus said it was a great opportunity and that he hoped James wouldn't let him down, and James said he wouldn't, and Jesus nodded a little dubiously, and James thanked him again, and then they went in to eat. The rest of the gang were already seated, and some could hardly conceal their surprise that James was still there. 'I thought he was being fired for sure,' muttered Thomas to Bartholomew, and Bartholomew said something rude, and Jesus silenced both of them with a look. They all bowed their heads whilst Jesus said grace, then they attacked the bread like vultures. Typically, James the Less was left with the crust end. But for once he didn't mind. Jesus didn't look his way again all evening, he was too busy swapping jokes with the others, but that was okay, he didn't *need* to look, James knew they had a secret, just the two of them. He gnawed on his bread, absently tried to find some taste in it somewhere. A secret! he thought. What could it be?

He determined he wouldn't sleep that night. He'd just *pretend* to be asleep, so the others wouldn't suspect anything. He closed his eyes and thought how this could be the turning point for him. If he pulled off this job, then it went without saying that Jesus would be back for more. And they wouldn't be *secret* jobs, all the apostles could see what he was up to, they'd have to respect him then. And he'd be all the closer to Jesus, and that was important, because there was something he had to prevent, something only he knew about – and it kept sliding out of his head, he had so many peculiar thoughts in there and he sometimes forgot why, but he was sure it'd all come back to him when it was important. Yes, it'd be like that parable Jesus talked about, the one with the fatted calf being killed for the favoured son, this time the fatted calf would be killed for *him*.

And after a while James wasn't sure whether he was daydreaming about calves or *really* dreaming about calves, and it was only when the calves in question began speaking to him and inviting him to dance that he realised he must have fallen asleep after all and woke up with a start.

He picked his way past the sleeping bodies. Matthew stirred. 'Where are you off to, pipsqueak?'

'I don't know,' said James. 'I mean, I need the toilet.'

'You sure do need the toilet,' said Matthew, and he was so drowsy he probably thought it was a pretty good insult, because he chuckled himself back to sleep.

James stepped out into the cold of the night. The stars were out and lit up the street. He looked for Jesus, hoped he hadn't kept him waiting. When he saw him in the alleyway he almost cried out a hello – and then ducked back into the shadows when he saw he had company.

Jesus talked to Judas for a long while. They seemed to argue, and then Judas fell silent, nodded briefly, and went away.

Jesus was left on his own. Then he gave a shuddering sigh that made his whole body shiver. For a moment James thought Jesus was going to be sick – he bent down, hunched over, his hands clasped tight to his stomach, and gagged. But nothing came out.

James broke his cover. 'My lord,' he said. 'You're not well.'

Jesus straightened up. 'James the Less. You're late.'

'I overslept. I'm here for my mission.'

'No,' said Jesus. 'You're late.' And more kindly, 'Go back to bed.'

James made his way back past the sleeping apostles, doing his best not to disturb them. He cried, but made sure he did it very, very quietly. And when at last he dreamed, the fatted calves were not for him. They danced with Judas Iscariot, and wouldn't give him a second glance.

The next day Jesus told his disciples it was high time they all had a treat, and that they should go out to their favourite restaurant. That was fine and good, but no-one could agree on what their favourite restaurant actually *was* – but Jesus had the casting vote, and so they were soon all seated around a group table looking at menus. After they'd made a start on the main course, Jesus stood up and told them he had something to say.

James had hardly eaten for nerves. This is it, he thought. This is when he'll tell them I'm out of the gang. How embarrassing.

'One of you will betray me.' Steady on, thought James, I'm not *that* bad – and then he realised Jesus wasn't necessarily talking about him. There was consternation around the table, and James couldn't relax *quite* yet, after all, Jesus could throw in his dismissal as a sort of P.S. But as the recriminations and the desserts started, James felt relieved – he was off the hook. Indeed he got some of his appetite back, and as the others argued he felt able to tuck into the mixed meze.

Late that night Judas brought the soldiers to the garden of Gethsemane. Jesus was identified with a kiss, and the Romans arrested him. There was panic and confusion and all the apostles fled, James among them. He spent the next few hours hiding from passers-by who might turn him in to the militia – and eventually found he was hiding in the same place as Judas.

'You rotten shit,' said James, and even as he said it, he realised it didn't quite have the moral outrage he'd been hoping for. 'And after he gave you my mission too!'

Judas looked at James in honest bemusement. Worked

out what he meant. Then told him he was an idiot.

'You want a mission?' said Judas. 'Here's a mission. Fetch me some rope.'

'Where am I going to get rope from at this time of night?' But Judas gave him a bag of silver, and told him he'd find a way.

'We're closed,' said the owner of the hardware store.

'I need rope,' James called up to his bedroom window.

'Rope can wait until morning.'

'I have money,' James said. 'Look.' And the starlight picked out the silver coins.

There was a pause. 'I'll be right down, sir,' said the man.

James found Judas waiting in a field. Like Jesus had been the night before, he was doubled over. But Judas was retching far more successfully.

'Here's your change,' said James, and handed Judas the bag of silver pieces. Judas tossed it aside impatiently. 'Help me with the rope,' he said. 'Tie this end to the branch, make a noose with the other.'

'I'm not very good at knots,' said James. 'Sorry.'

'You're an idiot,' said Judas, but smiled a little fondly. 'You'll at least witness this for me. You can do that, can't you?'

So James watched as Judas killed himself. He watched the whole thing, because a part of him thought it was his fault somehow — if he'd only stayed awake everything would have been different. And in the same way James made himself watch Jesus' crucifixion. As the crowd jeered, James stood rock solid and silent in the midst of them all, refusing to take his eyes off him. He was the only apostle who had dared to come.

And James fancied that as Jesus died he saw him there. And that at last Jesus realised that he was James the Less, just as James now realised he was Jesus. But then again, James thought, he might well have imagined it. After all, Jesus had been rather busy at the time.

1026

Pontius Pilate was very excited to be meeting Jesus at last. Of course, he had to keep that excitement reined in, that was the point. Cold and detached, that was the way through this. That had been the way through everything. 'All right,' he told the guard, 'you can bring him in.'

Pilate's heart leaped when he saw Jesus in front of him, hands manacled behind, bleeding a little. He hadn't seen him in *so* long, not for centuries and centuries. He kept his face impassive. He dismissed the guard with as much languor as he could muster. Now they were alone together Pilate felt shy and flustered. 'Believe it or not,' he babbled, 'I've been dying to meet you.'

Jesus said nothing to this. Didn't even raise an eyebrow.

'They want me to kill you.'

'I know,' said Jesus.

'They want me to sentence you to death, I mean. Have you taken away and crucified.'

'I know,' said Jesus.

'I'm not going to let it happen,' said Pilate.

Jesus said nothing. But at least the eyebrow raised.

'The charges against you,' said Pilate, 'I'm dismissing them. They're not true, they're all lies. Or they *are* true, but I pardon you. Whatever you think is best. But you're free. You're free to go.'

Silence.

'All I ask is that you go somewhere else. Somewhere far away. From the threat of the cross, at least. Go somewhere where they'll execute you in a completely different way, if you want!' And he almost giggled.

'No,' said Jesus.

'What's that?'

'No.'

'Right,' said Pilate. 'Right. I see. Look,' he went on, 'I

wasn't going to say this. It's hard to explain. But you see, I *know*. I know everything that happens. To you. To *us*. Because I am you. Do you see? *I* am *you*.'

Jesus just looked at him.

'I'm not saying you're *me* or anything,' went on Pilate, 'that'd just be crazy. No, this is strictly one way round. Look, I can prove it. Look, I know what you're thinking right this second. Hang on, I have to work it out, yes, you're thinking I'm insane. You're thinking I'm possessed by evil spirits, ha ha, yes. See?'

'If,' said Jesus, 'you really *are* me, then you know that the crucifixion *has* to happen. You know that everything I have done on earth. The healing, the miracles, all my ministry, even – all of it's nothing to this one act of sacrifice and what it represents.'

'Right from birth,' said Pilate, 'I knew this day would come. I knew I had to get this right. I invented myself as someone cruel and brutal. Someone who would be put in a position to execute you – just so, when the time came, I could save you. All those people I've convicted already, I had them killed just so I could get to you. Do you see? They died so you might live.'

'You cannot save me,' said Jesus. 'That isn't what you're *for*.'

'And maybe I don't like the role I've been given in this stupid story!' said Pilate, losing his temper at last. And straight away he began to beg. 'Look, please,' he said. '*Please*. What do I have to do to convince you to carry on living? What can I give you? Wealth? Women? Anything!'

'Get thee behind me,' said Jesus softly.

And Pontius Pilate picked up the dagger, took Jesus by the hair, held the blade hard against his throat.

'And if I kill you now,' he said, breathing heavily, and he knew he was panicking, this wasn't what he'd planned. 'What then? I deny you your little stunt with the cross.'

'You won't kill me, Pilate,' said Jesus.

'You have no idea what I have been through. What *we* have been through. I'll do anything to stop it.'

'You won't kill me because you're a coward.'

And Pilate knew it was true. He had two sons, both of them scared him. The eldest boy was very nearly a man now, and Pilate didn't trust him at all. He ate too much and his mother spoiled him and Pilate suspected he tortured animals. The youngest would, at dinner, just look at Pilate without saying a word. Staring. Pilate would try to laugh it off, but he wanted to scream at him, what? What are you accusing me of? And he thought desperately, are you in there, Jesus, is that what this is? Is my son some future Jesus, some future me, come here to stare me down? Pilate's own wife would lie in bed, utterly passive as he rode her, she'd never make a sound as if deliberately withholding any sign of pleasure, and afterwards she'd just turn away from him and say, 'I don't know what it is, but something's missing.' She was probably a Jesus too, he was sure of it. And he hated her, he hated them all, but still he played the happy husband, the happy father, because he was scared of what they might tell him if he stopped.

Pilate let go of Jesus' hair. He'd been born into a coward's body.

'I'll stop you some time,' he said. 'Not this lifetime then. All right. But sooner or later I'll stop you.'

Jesus said nothing to that. And then *smiled*. Pilate stepped back, as if he'd been slapped. He ordered the guard back in. 'Take this man away,' he said. 'Let the Jews do what they want with him. I wash my hands of the whole thing.'

It was a Thursday, so that night his wife lay waiting for him, naked, bored. Ready to be entered with all the passion of a revolving door. 'Not tonight,' said Pilate. 'I have a headache.' It was the first time he'd surprised her in years.

The 1946th Jesus didn't live long. He was one of the first born that Herod had put to death at the nativity in his attempt to kill the Messiah. The irony wasn't lost on the child, but he didn't really mind. 'Thank Christ, at least this one didn't take long,' thought the baby, as the sword was driven through his little body.

He got close to the crucifixion many times. For a while he was Matthew, and as he watched his Jesus self he decided to chronicle the whole thing. As if only to make some sense of it. When, four hundred or so lives later, he was born as Mark, he decided to write the whole thing again, but this time from a different angle. By the time he was John he thought it might be rather fun to put another spin on it all, and deliberately changed the order the disciples were picked, and shuffled the events of the story around a bit. And as Luke he could barely conceal his yawns as he scribbled out yet another gospel. Watching the feeding of the five thousand yet *again,* having to hear the same old same old about camels passing through eyes of needles. 'Sorry, Luke,' said Jesus sarcastically, 'are we keeping you up? These miracles of mine not interesting enough?' 'No, no,' Luke would say, 'they're absolutely *riveting*, really,' and he'd draft out the latest triumph, and roll his eyes when he was sure Jesus wasn't looking.

But he didn't feel it was until he was born as Judas that he could really make a difference.

11,432

'I have a mission for you,' said Jesus. 'It is highly secret, and none of the other apostles must know of it. Everything rests upon its success. Do you understand me, Judas? Everything.'

'I understand,' said Judas.

'Don't be afraid.'

'No,' said Judas, 'I'm not afraid.'

'I need you to betray me,' said Jesus. 'I am going to be crucified, and I need someone to deliver me into the hands of the executioners. Without that sacrifice, man's sins cannot be purged. And through the spilling of my blood they may be given eternal life. Don't be afraid.'

'No, really,' said Judas, 'I'm not.'

'You should know what this will mean to you,' said Jesus. 'You will be the most hated of men. In this life, of course, but worse than that. Throughout all time. Poets will depict you suffering in the deepest circle of Hell, artists will paint you as the ultimate representation of evil. And your very name, Judas, will be forever more a byword for treason and apostasy. In a way, your sacrifice will be worse than mine. But it is necessary. Please, please don't be afraid.'

'I'm not,' said Judas patiently, 'afraid.'

'And worse still,' went on Jesus, and Judas sighed, 'because you have to know, don't you? You have to know. Your treachery will damn the Jews as well. You'll symbolise our entire race, and it will be persecuted forever more. Because of you there will be the pogroms, because of you the concentration camps. Are you afraid yet?'

'I think I might be afraid,' said Judas, 'if I knew what a concentration camp was. But, no, I'm not afraid.'

'Good.'

'But principally because I'm not going to do it.'

'What?' said Jesus. He looked genuinely flabbergasted. In all his many incarnations, Judas didn't think Jesus had ever looked so flabbergasted before.

'I'm not a coward,' said Judas. 'Do you hear me? You called me a coward once. But not this time.'

'I've never called you a coward.'

'Not as me. As Pontius Pilate.'

'I've never even met Pontius Pilate.'

Judas sighed. 'Well, you will, when you're betrayed to him.'

Jesus frowned in thought. 'I knew I should have waited for James the Less,' he said finally. 'Things would be going much more smoothly. You can't stop me, Judas,' he went on as he saw his old friend produce the knife. 'You could kill me, of course, right here and now. It'll change very little. I'll still have been the Messiah, and I'll still have been betrayed, and I'll still die saving the world. You'll go down in history as a traitor anyway, the sort of traitor who murders by stealth, in dark alleyways at night.'

Judas glared at him.

'You see,' Jesus said, 'at the end of the day. I am not afraid either.'

Judas hesitated. Then muttered, 'The hell with you then.' And he walked out of Jesus' life.

And so the story goes. Jesus then called his apostle James out of the shadows. The other James, the one we call James the Treacherous, James who was Satan's Own. And after Jesus was crucified, the very word James became forever more a byword for treason and apostasy.

371,194

And then, at long last. After so many lives had been lived and wasted and forgotten, he was born as her. The one he couldn't forget. The woman he had loved so clumsily on the floor of his carpentry shop.

It took Jesus a long time to realise he really was her. He expected so little from the bodies he inhabited now, he lived them as far as he could with his eyes closed. She wasn't, after all, an especially remarkable woman, she had no notable talents, no great beauty. And she was twenty-two and already married before Jesus looked in the mirror one day and saw that it was her, unarguably *her*. It may have been the way she'd started flicking that thick black hair of hers.

Straight away she set off to find her carpenter. She couldn't quite remember where he'd be. There were a lot of carpentry shops out there, and she hadn't visited his in a long time — several hundred thousand years or so. But she was patient. She scoured the whole town, poking her head around the doors, studying every face to see whether it was the man she'd loved. And when she'd exhausted the town, she began to search further afield. She had to be careful; her husband was a jealous man, and she rarely had time to check more than one or two shops before it was time to turn back home again.

But one day she found it. She recognised it immediately, how could she have forgotten it? And she rushed into the shop, her heart already bursting with passion. He was there, his manner surly and unwelcoming. She'd never realised before how ugly he was, having never seen his body through these eyes. But it didn't matter, all that mattered was that she had at last found her life's purpose.

She made up some excuse about wanting a present for her husband, but then remembered it was all such nonsense, she knew full well no such present would ever be made or delivered. So she kissed him, and made love to him. He didn't know how to do it, she had to show him exactly. But she knew he'd improve with practice.

'What's your name?' he'd ask her. And she wouldn't tell him. The truth is, when she was with him, she could no longer remember. At home with her husband, in the drudgery that was her *real* life, she knew her name, she knew her whole family history, she knew what she'd called their pet dog when she'd been a little girl. But with this other Jesus, she found the rush of all those memories and past lives confused her, and quite wiped out her identity. And that was good. She had a feeling she didn't much like herself anyway. And when they made love it was on a cloud of beautiful guiltless ignorance.

He taught her carpentry for fun. And she pretended she was learning from him, that she hadn't known for herself how to shape wood for countless centuries already. She liked the way it made him feel proud, that he believed in some way he was making an impression on her life.

And of course, he was. He was.

One day in the shop she idly made herself a wooden crucifix. It was only a little thing, no bigger than her palm.

'What on earth did you make that for?' he asked.

'I've no idea,' she replied, and hadn't.

But from that day on, she found that whenever she worked a piece of wood, it always ended up as a crucifix. Sometimes just a little one, to be threaded through a necklace chain. Sometimes just a miniature to be hung on the wall. Planed smooth and pretty. And, occasionally, if she were really daydreaming, she'd carve a little figure to the cross, with little knobs of wood for the nails.

The carpenter didn't want to criticise her, he loved her too much. But even so, he couldn't help but remark upon the peculiar choice of her handiwork. 'It's sick,' he told her bluntly.

She told him that she wouldn't do any more carpentry. She'd watch him instead — she'd like that. And they recovered their good humour: she'd laugh as she watched him labour so delicately over a chair or table, and then, when they both agreed he'd earned a reward, they'd make love. But whilst he dozed, she would get up. Go to the workshop. And start work upon the crosses once more. She couldn't help it, her hands would be itching, literally itching, for her to make them. Then she'd steal them home. She kept one wall decoration under her pillow, another under the mattress. The pendant hung layers beneath her clothes, and when she stripped for sex she'd take care to hide it before the carpenter or her husband could see.

One day she could stand it no longer. She was running out of places to hide all her crosses, it frightened her. She showed them to her husband, and told him about her adultery. 'I love him,' she said. 'But it can't go on. He makes me think of death.'

'Don't you love me?' he asked, and she was surprised how plaintive he sounded. 'Why did you marry me if you didn't love me?'

'I had my eyes closed,' she said simply. She then gave him the address of the carpenter, and he left in a fury. She knew how the story went, that she'd never see him again.

They executed her ugly little carpenter, of course. They put the word 'murderer' above his head as if that summed him up. All the people at Calvary were there to see the death of Jesus, King of the Jews. Except her. She hoped that her lover would see her as he died, would give her a look, anything – but he didn't. All that time she watched him on the cross she couldn't remember her name, and only when he died did it come back to her. It wasn't as pretty as she'd imagined.

Incalculable

And then, soon after that, after a very few million more lifetimes, Jesus was born as Jesus once more.

There were two specific things he recognised. The first was the face of Mary – after so many mothers, she was still the one he'd been waiting for. And the second was – everything else. All those past lives he'd been through, which he'd successfully buried away or deliberately misremembered. Each one came back to him in perfect clarity, every little detail, the ugliness and the beauty and the deep ocean of bland grey in between.

What a world, he thought to himself.

From that moment his life continued exactly as he knew it would. He'd already lived it, witnessed it from every conceivable angle, written four gospels about it. He sometimes felt he was acting out a dream, that it was just a question of remembering all his lines and he'd get through all right. On the road to Calvary a man stops to help him as he staggers under the cross, and that's him. A Roman soldier forces the man back into the crowd, and that's him too. They nail him to the cross, and he's those that hold him down, and the ones weeping to see his agony, the ones bent forward as if hypnotised by the gushing of all that blood. He is sick of the sight of himself.

And this time he does not scream.

He knows the men dying on the cross next to him, of course. He offers words of comfort to the murderer, and he knows they do him some little good. He'd offer them to the thief as well, but knows that the thief wouldn't want them. They all die one by one. The sky goes black. The wind stops.

'Here we are again,' says the voice.

'Here we are again,' agrees Jesus.

'Given any more thought to that offer I made? We can stop this right now, you know. You just need to say the word.'

He's waited a lifetime. He's waited everybody's lifetime. Just say yes. You know all the people you're sacrificing yourself for. Each and every bloody one of them. You know what they're worth. Just say yes.

'No,' he says again. Because, really, what else can he do? Because, really, who else is going to save them?

'Okay,' says the voice. And he dies. And it starts again.

Three days later the stone is wheeled away from Jesus' tomb. The body has gone, and the apostles are jubilant. The ultimate miracle has taken place. Jesus has risen from the dead, and will live forever.

Meanwhile, in a Small Room, a Small Boy...

...sat waiting.

Sometimes he stood waiting, never slouching, always as if to attention. Sometimes he lay down waiting, though he tended to confine those bits of waiting to his sleeping hours. But as a rule he sat waiting. He found it to be the most comfortable of the positions on offer.

Sometimes he was waiting for food – sometimes breakfast, sometimes lunch, sometimes a cooked evening meal. Sometimes he was waiting for the shadows to creep across the floor of his room, or the little patch of sunlight by the door to blacken and fade and then disappear altogether. (Sometimes he likes to watch the day go by like this, minute by minute, hour by long hour – sometimes he didn't like it at all, and would cry with frustration at its monotony.)

And sometimes he was just waiting to find out what mood he was in today – either the sort which likes to watch the sunlight fade, or the sort which cries out with frustration. Discovering which one was a genuine surprise, and he treasured it.

Whatever else he was waiting for, there was something else above it all, something that was always on his mind. But the small boy tried hard not to think of it directly. He suspected, with a thrill of superstitious fear, that if he ever waited for it too *obviously*, that if he drew too much attention to it, that it would never happen. That all the other waiting, the superficial waiting, the *practice* waiting, would be in vain. But he couldn't help think of it, once a day, no, be honest, several times a day, he tried hard but he couldn't stop himself. He got angry at the injustice of it all, and he bunched his hands into tight fists. He was just a little boy, it was too difficult, how could he *not*, just a little boy, how could he *not* think of her, they said he was a strong boy, they said he was a brave boy, they said he had to be strong *and* brave, his mother had said that, but it was sometimes too much, he couldn't help it, he was waiting, how could he *not*, he was always waiting, waiting for his mother. There, it was out. He was waiting for his mother. Where was she? Be strong, she'd said, be brave, she'd said, I'll see you soon, *I'll see you soon.*

In a small room, a small boy was waiting for his mother.

He realised that this was a day in which he cried with frustration, rather than be bothered with all that sunlight and shadow stuff. He secretly rather preferred the crying-with-frustration days, and was so pleased that he forgot for a whole minute how unhappy he was meant to be.

When he cried, he made no noise at all. And there was barely a tear to be seen in his eyes. But he knew he was crying, oh yes.

Outside his room there were two men. He had been told their names, but hadn't even tried to remember them. His brain was far too full already, waiting for things and not thinking about waiting for other things. They were friends of his mother, he knew that, they fed him and kept him well like his mother would, but he could never find any trace of her there in their faces or voices, and had long stopped looking for any. One of them always tried to chat to him, make jokes. He said he wanted to be his friend, but he did it so awkwardly it suggested to the boy that this tall man was really rather frightened of him. The other man never said much, did what he had to do, fed him, washed him, whatever, he would always leave as soon as possible. The boy preferred the second man. He was so much less effort.

One of them would bring his breakfast soon. There was

MEANWHILE, IN A SMALL ROOM, A SMALL BOY...

a gnawing in the boy's belly which told him so. And the shadows were creeping somewhere near the wardrobe too.

Since he was thinking about his mother anyway – and he was, there was no point denying it – he decided to play a game. He only played the game on special occasions, which was pretty much whenever he thought of it. He would count how long it took for one of the men to bring him in breakfast. He would count slowly, deliberately, that would be good. And he'd make a bet with himself. If the breakfast arrived before he reached a thousand, he'd see his mother today. He'd see his mother *this very day*.

He began to count. One, two, three. Slow. Deliberate.

Come on, he thought. Hurry up with my breakfast.

Two hundred and sixteen. Two hundred and seventeen.

He counted silently, watching the numbers in his head pass by, one by one. So many of them, but slipping past too quickly.

Five hundred and seven. Five hundred and eight.

Bring me my breakfast! (I want my mother.) I want my breakfast!

Seven hundred and eighty-four. Seven hundred and eighty-five.

Bring it, bring it, bring it, bring it, bring it.

Eight hundred and ninety-nine. Nine hundred. Oh dear.

He was tempted to slow down, stop the numbers marching on, give the men outside more time, give his mother more time. But he knew that would be cheating. And if he cheated, he lost by default.

Breakfast, breakfast, breakfast, oh, mother, mother, *mother*!

When he reached a thousand, he felt a pang of disappointment. So she wouldn't come today after all. She might have been on her way, she might have been outside the room at that very moment, about to turn the doorknob and come in, come in to hug him and take him away. But because of the gamble he'd made, she would now turn around and go back to where she came from. He'd carried on counting anyway. It seemed silly to stop now. On two thousand three hundred and eleven the door opened and the breakfast arrived. He saw it was the man who tried to be chatty, and his heart sunk that smidgen lower.

'Good morning, good morning, how are you today? Did you sleep well? I have your breakfast. Doesn't it look nice?'

It didn't particularly. The boy wondered why the man always used to bombard him with questions he had no intention of answering.

'What are you going to do today? Are you going to play with your toys?'

Something like a shrug.

'You know, old chap, I've been thinking.' The man's voice dipped almost an entire octave in concern. 'Well, not just me, we've both been thinking, ha ha, we both have!' Another joke, the boy didn't get it. 'It's not really healthy for you to spend so much time in this room. Why don't you come out to the rest of the house?' The boy saw spittle on the nervous man's lips. 'It's perfectly safe. So long as we don't go outside.' The spittle wobbled as it hung there. The boy waited for it to fall off. 'You should have more...' *Going...* '...than these four walls...' *Going...* '...to look at.' *Gone!* Hurrah!

But it was *his* room. It was his. And they couldn't take it away from him. They had taken so much else, but not this.

The man seemed unhappy. He was already backing out of the room, as if frightened the boy would chase after him and bite him. 'Well, it's up to you.' The boy watched him wring his hands. 'It's up to you, of course.' The boy wondered whether the two men had made bets with themselves too, playing for which one got stuck with bringing his breakfast. He wondered whether this frightened, door-backing, hand-wringing spittle-forming man had lost this morning. 'Up to you. You play with your toys instead.' And he was gone.

The boy had been smuggled away so hastily that there hadn't been time for him to select any toys. Instead his mother

MEANWHILE, IN A SMALL ROOM, A SMALL BOY...

had plonked into his arms a random assortment, kissed him on the cheek, and off he went. He wanted to tell her these weren't his favourite toys, not a single one of them – but she looked so close to tears already and he didn't want to make her even more unhappy. Now in his room, worlds away from her, he couldn't remember what his favourite toys actually were, but he held a certain resentment towards the second rate ones he'd been left to make do with.

There was the rubber ball, but it didn't bounce very high. The boy was young, but astute enough to realise that there was nothing in the world more useless than a ball without much bounce to it. Sometimes he'd roll it along the floor listlessly. Sometimes he'd roll it through his breakfast. But he'd never try to bounce it.

There was a board game, snakes and ladders. A wooden board marked with a hundred squares, complete with dice. In the early days the boy had played this quite a lot, sometimes even with the men outside the room. But they hadn't worked out what the game was – they had always tried to reach one hundred, whereas the boy knew if you kept sliding down the snakes you need never reach the end, you could go on and on forever. One day the boy realised that it didn't matter whether you were trying to reach one hundred or trying to avoid it, the dice would take you there eventually all the same. You had no choice about what happened to you. And in despair he hadn't touched the game since.

He had more important games to play now. Games with consequences. Games that would decide his destiny, and the destiny of his missing much-missed mother.

He looked at the porridge without enthusiasm. He had tried using it in the games once – his mother would come for him so long as he never ate again. This had greatly alarmed the men outside the room, and for a while after he lost that game he also lost his privacy, one or the other standing over him and he chewed and swallowed what they brought him. No, better he should eat it. It would give him the added strength needed for him to win the next game he'd play. He decided what it would be as the tasteless paste went down his throat. He'd hold his breath. If he could hold it until he reached a thousand, then his mother would come. Not today, that was already forfeit. But soon. This week. She'd come this week. He vaguely wondered whether not breathing for a count of a thousand would kill him, and decided he'd do it for nine hundred instead.

It was easy to begin with. He took a deep breath, and puffed out his cheeks with all the air he could find. He counted in his head as the mouth clamped tightly shut.

His lungs began to ache. Or perhaps he just imagined his lungs were aching. He wondered if he was turning red, and, if he were, whether he was brighter than the rubber ball. He began to feel sick, then, curiously, to feel nothing at all.

He wasn't at a hundred and fifty yet! He couldn't stop. Wouldn't stop.

Did stop, though. His mouth popped open, against all his firmest instructions, and he took in a whoosh of air, panting, coughing.

He'd failed again. He'd doomed himself to at least another seven days in this room, waiting for all the little somethings and the Big Something. In anger he kicked over his porridge bowl, then he kicked over his toys, then he kicked the bowl again, just for good measure. Outside the room the chatty man dithered whether to go inside or not, before deciding that discretion was the better part of valour. As boy kicked, the wooden dice spun across the room, hit the wall, and fell on to the floor.

The boy stopped dead. He looked at it, walked over to it. Then without thinking, he snatched it up into his hot, angry little fist.

Right, he thought. Right. One more game. Just one more. I shall try to throw a six. No, I shall try to throw three sixes, one after the other. And if I do, then my mother shall come for me, this cancels out all the other games, she'll be here

MEANWHILE, IN A SMALL ROOM, A SMALL BOY...

before I know it, she'll hold me in her arms and I'll be safe. And if I fail. If I fail. If the dice shows anything else. Even two sixes and a five... Then she's dead.

He felt numb. But continued.

Yes, she'll be dead. That's right. You'll never see her again. Not ever, no way. And she never loved you at all, or else why did she give you away to these men, one who smiles too much, one who doesn't smile at all, she put you in a world of finding patches of sunlight and tasteless porridge and balls that don't bounce. If you don't throw three sixes, *and throw them right now*, she's dead and nothing and she *hated* you. And the war that the men outside speak about in such hushed voices, they think you won't hear but you do, you *do*, the war will be lost and everything will be lost and you, you will be lost forever.

Oddly calm, in spite of what's at stake – perhaps because of it – the boy stands up. He doesn't slouch, he stands as if to attention. This is important. And he throws the dice.

It is a six.

He lets out a huge sigh. He's not sure whether it's relief or not. He'd thrown it defiantly, as if to show he didn't care, but he did care, didn't he? He must have done, because look at him now, the sigh winds him, and he has to get his breath back before he can pick up the dice again.

Second throw. Six, six, six. Come on. Six, six, six.

It leaves his hand. And as it does, the boy realises he should have given it one more shake. Another one for luck, for his mother's sake, for his own. He tries to catch it, take it back again, but it's too late. The dice hits the floor.

It is a six.

His head spins. He feels nauseous, and he realises that the porridge did have a taste after all, his mouth is full of it, and all the swallowing in the world won't change matters. He thinks for a moment he might black out, but he has no such luck, he *has* to bend down, he has to pick up the wooden cube, he *has* to straighten up.

He now knows without question it's not a game anymore. This throw of the dice will decide the lives of countless people. It's not just about himself any more.

And just for a moment, he hates his mother. It's just a brief flash of anger, but it happened, he can't undo it. He hates her for making this his responsibility. He hates her that she's made him grow up too fast, too soon. And although he wouldn't be able to find the words for it, he understands that he'll never quite trust her the same way again. If he sees her again – he will, he *will*, throw the dice and see! – he'll love her, of course he will. But never as unhesitatingly, there will always be that moment of hatred getting in the way. He bites his lip and tastes blood. He is crying, and this time the tears are wet, his cheeks are wet, it's all wet. He's changed irrevocably, become a different person. And his mother wasn't there to see it happen.

Hardly knowing what he's doing, his fingers let go of the dice. It makes no more noise as it clatters to the floor than it did before – indeed, it possibly makes less, because it's thrown with such little force. But at that very moment he catches his breath, and the sound of wooden dice striking floor is all he can hear.

Is she alive or dead? Did she ever really love him?

The dice has the answer. He backs away from it. He doesn't have to see. It's all decided now. It's either six or it isn't. Be he doesn't have to know what he's done. Whether he's saved her or killed her, he's only a little boy!

He sits on the floor, at a distance from it, and turns away. He dries his eyes, he dries his cheeks. At some point one of the men will come in. They'll clear up after him, as they always do. They'll put his toys away. And he'll never find out what the dice said. So long as he doesn't give in to temptation, and goes to look. So long as he sits here, nice and still, and doesn't move until it's safe.

He waits for someone to come in.

In a small room, a small boy sits, waiting.